MURDER IN THE
IRISH CHANNEL

Reviewers Love Greg Herren's Mysteries

"Herren, a loyal New Orleans resident, paints a brilliant portrait of the recovering city, including insights into its tight-knit gay community. This latest installment in a powerful series is sure to delight old fans and attract new ones."—*Publishers Weekly*

"Fast-moving and entertaining, evoking the Quarter and its gay scene in a sweet, funny, action-packed way."—*New Orleans Times-Picayune*

"Herren does a fine job of moving the story along, deftly juggling the murder investigation and the intricate relationships while maintaining several running subjects."—*Echo* Magazine

"An entertaining read."—*OutSmart* Magazine

"A pleasant addition to your beach bag."—*Bay Windows*

"Greg Herren gives readers a tantalizing glimpse of New Orleans." —*Midwest Book Review*

"Herren's characters, dialogue and setting make the book seem absolutely real."—*The Houston Voice*

"So much fun it should be thrown from Mardi Gras floats!"—*New Orleans Times-Picayune*

"Greg Herren just keeps getting better."—*Lambda Book Report*

Praise for *Sleeping Angel*

Sleeping Angel "will probably be put on the young adult (YA) shelf, but the fact is that it's a cracking good mystery that general readers will enjoy as well. It just happens to be about teens…A unique viewpoint, a solid mystery and good characterization all conspire to make *Sleeping Angel* a welcome addition to any shelf, no matter where the bookstores stock it."—Jerry Wheeler, Out in Print

"This fast-paced mystery is skillfully crafted. Red herrings abound and will keep readers on their toes until the very end. Before the accident, few readers would care about Eric, but his loss of memory gives him a chance to experience dramatic growth, and the end result is a sympathetic character embroiled in a dangerous quest for truth."—*VOYA*

By The Author

The Scotty Bradley Adventures

Bourbon Street Blues

Jackson Square Jazz

Mardi Gras Mambo

Vieux Carré Voodoo

Who Dat Whodunnit

The Chanse MacLeod Mysteries

Murder in the Rue Dauphine

Murder in the Rue St. Ann

Murder in the Rue Chartres

Murder in the Rue Ursulines

Murder in the Garden District

Murder in the Irish Channel

Sleeping Angel

Women of the Mean Streets
Men of the Mean Streets
(edited with J. M. Redmann)

Visit us at www.boldstrokesbooks.com

MURDER IN THE IRISH CHANNEL

by

Greg Herren

A Division of Bold Strokes Books

2011

MURDER IN THE IRISH CHANNEL
© 2011 BY GREG HERREN. ALL RIGHTS RESERVED.

ISBN 13: 978-1-60282-584-0

THIS TRADE PAPERBACK ORIGINAL IS PUBLISHED BY
BOLD STROKES BOOKS, INC.
P.O. BOX 249
VALLEY FALLS, NY 12185

FIRST EDITION: DECEMBER 2011

CREDITS
EDITOR: STACIA SEAMAN
PRODUCTION DESIGN: STACIA SEAMAN
COVER DESIGN BY SHERI (GRAPHICARTIST2020@HOTMAIL.COM)

Acknowledgments

Over the course of my life, I've been incredibly blessed to call the most extraordinary people my friends.

First of all, I would really like to thank everyone at Bold Strokes Books—Radclyffe, Sandy Lowe, Stacia Seaman, Shelley Thrasher, Connie Ward, Cindy Cresap, and I apologize to anyone I'm forgetting. What I like to call the league of extraordinary women welcomed me into the Bold Strokes family, and they have been an absolute joy to work with from the very first day. Bold Strokes has given me an opportunity to stretch and grow as a writer, and I cannot thank everyone there enough.

Here in New Orleans, I have yet another league of extraordinary women I can always depend upon for moral support, love, and laughter. Julie Smith, Patricia Brady, Susan Larson, J. M. Redmann, Gillian Rodger, Bev Marshall, Chris Wiltz, Nevada Barr, Laura Lippman, and Janet Dailey Duval are beyond exceptional, and I thank you from the bottom of my heart for always being there whenever I need any of you.

My coworkers at the Community Awareness Network office of the NO/AIDS Task Force are some pretty amazing people as well— their dedication to making the world a better place and working to improve the quality of people's lives blows me away on a daily basis: Josh Fegley, Martin Strickland, Mark Drake, Nick Parr, Brandon Benson, Matt Valletta, Robin Pearce, Allison Vertovec, Larry Stillings, and Sarah Ramteke.

I would also be remiss in not singling out my very dear friend Victoria A. Brownworth for recognition.

I finished writing this book at the Bold Strokes Writer's Retreat at Garnet Hill Lodge in the Adirondack mountains of upstate New York. I had the most amazing time there, and that is entirely all the fault of yet *another* group of extraordinary women: Carsen Taite, Nell Stark, Trinity Tam, Anne Laughlin, Linda Braasch, Ali Vali, Lisa Girolami, Lynda Sandoval, Rachel Spangler, Karis Walsh, and Ruth Sternglantz. Also worthy of mention is the delightful Niner Baxter—his sense of humor and gentle spirit was a joy to be around.

And of course, Paul Willis makes my life worth getting out of bed for every morning.

This book is for
LADY HERMIONE
"Come about!"

"I'm sure I don't have to tell a man as experienced as you that everything has its shadowy side?"

—Tennessee Williams, The Night of the Iguana

Chapter One

The house was a tired-looking single shotgun, badly in need of paint and slightly listing to one side. It was in the middle of a block on Constance Street in the Irish Channel, and the other houses on the block were just as sad and forlorn. The house next door had a For Sale sign planted in the front yard; still others had damaged cars parked in front of them on the street. This particular stretch of street was cracked and pitted with deep potholes, with gravel running between the asphalt and the drainage ditches. The lawns had scars of bare dirt exposed and many of them needed to be mown. The flowerbeds were choked with weeds. Massive live oak trees shaded the houses and yards, creating a green canopy over the street that blocked out the hot June sun. A black, white, and tan cat paused as it crossed the street to stare at me for a moment before continuing on its way.

Hoping I was wrong, I double-checked the address. The house I was looking for was indeed this sad wreck of a place.

I put my car into park and sat there for a moment, wondering why it hadn't been condemned. There was a rusted chain-link fence around the front yard, on the other side of the drainage ditch. In several places, it had pulled away from the posts. The shutters were closed on the front windows, and the front door was behind a black wrought iron security gate. There was no sign of life from the house. The patchy grass was choked with weeds. A statue of the Blessed Virgin Mary sat inside a sand-filled circle of stone to the left of the walk leading to the front gallery. The statue itself was chipped in places, and stained with dog urine. Her blue robes had faded in the sun, and some weeds were insolently poking up through the sand. The enormous live oak tree's roots had grown underneath the sidewalk from the other side, causing the cement to crack, buckle, and shift. Some flowering vine had completely covered the fence on the left side of the house, where a narrow path of dirt ran around to the back. I closed my eyes and resisted the urge to pound my head on the steering wheel.

In my line of work, it's never a good idea to make a decision when you're tired.

The guy I was seeing had asked me to come by and talk to Jonny O'Neill just as I was dropping off to sleep the night before. I'd been so tired I would have agreed to almost anything. Rory hadn't really told me anything about the kid's problem—well, he may have, but after agreeing I'd rolled over and gone into a deep sleep. Rory had gone home by the time I woke up this morning, and when I called his cell phone I'd gone straight to voicemail. Rory had thoughtfully left the kid's phone number propped up against the coffeemaker—and the coffee was ready to be brewed, according to the note he'd signed with a heart and a smiley face. I'd called after a couple of cups of strong coffee had swept the dust out of my mind, and made an appointment to come hear his tale of woe—which he didn't want to tell over the phone.

This Jonny O'Neill had sounded really young on the phone— almost like his voice had changed only recently.

That didn't bode well.

I hadn't promised I'd take the job—if there even *was* a job. Nine times out of ten people who think they need a private eye really don't, they just want someone to listen to whatever their problem is.

In fact, most of the time I wind up just saying either *sorry, there's nothing anyone can do* or *this is a job for the police.*

And besides, if this dump was the only place he could afford to live, he sure as hell couldn't afford my expenses, let alone my daily rate.

I shut off the engine and got out of the car. It was already over eighty degrees, and it wasn't even noon yet. Beads of sweat popped out on my forehead. It was the hottest June I could remember, and I'd lived through some pretty hellish Junes in New Orleans. If this was a sign of things to come, July and August would be even more unbearable than usual. It was unnaturally quiet—other than the sound of traffic on Louisiana Avenue, a few blocks away, there was nothing but stillness.

I sighed. This was going to be a colossal waste of my time.

Granted, it was Sunday. If I weren't here, I'd be sitting on my sofa in my underwear channel-surfing and complaining about paying a ridiculous amount of money for three hundred or so channels of nothing to watch.

I pushed the gate open. I winced as it gave off a loud, piercing squeak. It only opened about six inches before it caught on the buckled pavement of the walk and stopped moving. I stepped through, catching my jeans on the fence with a slight ripping sound. I swore under my breath and examined the tear. The hole was jagged and maybe about an inch long, right by my knee. I swore again. The jeans weren't new, but it was still annoying.

This was off to a *great* start.

A dog in the next yard starting barking, trying to stick his head through the fence. He was a terrier of some kind, with black and white markings. He was wagging his tail, so the bark was just for show. I whistled and he stopped barking, his ears perking up expectantly. There was a well-chewed tennis ball sitting in the dirt underneath the massive live oak, so I picked it up and tossed it over the dog's head. In one movement, he turned and took off after it.

The sidewalk in the shade of the live oak was covered with stinging caterpillars, which I kicked aside as I made my way to the front steps.

I fucking hate those things. Their sting hurts like a son of a bitch. The live oak in front of my house was covered with them—and so was my front porch.

The stairs leading up to the front porch were brick. The mortar was crumbling away—one of the bricks had fallen off and lay broken into pieces in what had been a flowerbed in years past. The once-blue paint on the front porch was cracked and peeling, exposing weathered gray wood. The shutters were also flaking, and I could see they'd been latched from the inside. The glass between the black iron bars on the gate outside the front door was grimy and covered in dust. A Post-it Note had been taped over the doorbell with the words *Doorbell Doesn't Work Please Knock* scrawled on it in grease pencil in a childlike hand.

Every board I stepped on while crossing to the door groaned and gave a little under my weight. The front door was weathered and warped-looking behind the gate. The lock and the knob both showed signs of rust. I debated with myself as I raised my hand to knock whether I should actually go through with it.

I hesitated.

It would be so easy to just turn around, walk back to the car, get in, and drive away from this derelict place and whatever problem the people who lived here needed help resolving.

The whole place reeked of decay.

Every instinct in my body was telling me to get the hell out of there.

But I'd promised Rory, so I ignored the little voice in my head and rapped my knuckles against the door frame.

And hoped I wouldn't regret it.

The girl who opened the door looked like she couldn't be much older than seventeen. Her light brown hair was greasy and pulled back into a severe ponytail. Her face was bare and pale. She was wearing a white cotton dress that exposed her bony, freckled shoulders. She wasn't wearing a bra, and there was a coffee stain on the front of her housedress between her heavy breasts. Dark smudges formed half-moons under her swollen, bloodshot eyes. Her face was bare of makeup, and her lips were dry and cracked. Her eyebrows had been drawn on with a pencil, and a cluster of pimples had formed in the center of her forehead. She was barefoot, and her feet were dirty.

She also looked to be about seven or eight months pregnant.

I couldn't believe how much boredom she managed to squeeze into the word "Yeah?"

"Hi, I'm Chanse MacLeod—"

"The detective guy, right." She let out a long-suffering sigh, her shoulders slumping. Her entire body seemed to shrink an inch or two. She rolled her eyes and stepped away from the door so I could go inside. "Come on in. Jonny's in the shower. Sorry about that—just have a seat and he'll be right out." She forced what was probably supposed to be a gracious smile onto her face. "He'll be late to his own damned funeral." She closed the door behind me and screamed, *"Hurry the fuck up, asshole! He's here!"* She slipped around me. "Wait here, okay?"

It was dark inside the house—all the shutters were closed on both sides of the house. It smelled musty and slightly sour. She didn't turn on any lights as she disappeared into the next room, leaving me in the dark. I took a deep breath and looked around, squinting through the gloom. I couldn't see if there was a place to sit down, which was just as well.

From the looks of things, I wouldn't be staying long.

"Sorry!" a young male voice said from the other side of the room, and the room suddenly filled with light, temporarily blinding me.

I was almost sorry I could see.

The overhead light came from a dusty chandelier with cobwebs hanging between the grimy globes. Three of the five lightbulbs were burned out. The room was sparsely furnished. There was a sagging sofa covered with piles of clothes and magazines. One leg was missing and several magazines had been shoved underneath that corner to prop it up. One of the cushions was significantly lower than the others, which meant the springs were ruined on that end. I could see footprints in the thick dust on the hardwood floor. A tired chair sat at about a seventy-five-degree angle to the couch, and there were damp-looking workout clothes piled on it: shorts, a tank top, a yellowed jockstrap. An open black and gold Saints duffel bag was perched on one of its arms, exposing more workout clothes. A coffee table was buried in food wrappers, empty plastic soda bottles, and crumpled chip bags. In the far corner, a new-looking flat screen television perched on top of several plastic boxes with *12:00* flashing in green numbers in the center.

The young man shoved the clothes in the chair onto the floor, exposing several more sour-looking jockstraps. He didn't look at me as he used his foot to push them behind the chair. He made a grand gesture at the now-empty chair. "Sit, please!" His eyes met mine, and he gave me a smile so dazzling I almost had to take a step back.

He was short—maybe about five-six, if he stretched a bit and stood up on tiptoe. His hair was wet and clinging to his head, but given how fair his skin was, I assumed it would dry to some shade of blond. He had a long nose and a bit of an overbite. He had blue eyes, but the right one was blackened and swollen half-shut. His bottom lip was cut and bruised. Another bruise extended from his chin about halfway down his throat. He was wearing a pair of navy blue nylon shorts with a white stripe down the legs, and a gray tank top with *Everlast* written across the front in black. His pale arms were scraped in places, red in others—but his biceps looked strong and well-defined. Blue veins crisscrossed his forearms. His shoulders were broad, his stomach appeared to be flat, and his exposed legs were dusted with blond hairs and also looked strong. There was a tattoo on his right bicep—a bleeding heart with several swords thrust through it. He was barefoot.

He wasn't handsome, or even cute—but there was something appealing about him—something fresh, wholesome, and likable. His grin was infectious and good-natured, lighting up his entire face. I couldn't help but smile back at him.

"Your face—" I started to say, but he cut me off.

"Oh." He laughed, clearing a space on the sofa. He smiled at me again as he sat down. "Yeah. That's right, Rory said he couldn't say anything about me to you. Confidentiality and all that kind of stuff." He bobbed his head back and forth, blushing a little.

Rory worked at the NO/AIDS Task Force, doing counseling and HIV testing. I nodded. "You went in yesterday to get tested." I'd assumed that was where Rory had met him, but it never hurts to get the facts.

He nodded. "I had a fight last night, and I gotta get cleared for HIV before they'll let me in the cage. It's not because I fuck around on my wife or nothing." He smiled again. "I won my fight, if you're wondering." His smile widened. "Still undefeated, you know." He bobbed his head up and down. "Eighteen and oh."

"In the cage?" I wasn't following him, and for a moment wondered if it was some weird kind of fight club.

"I'm an MMA fighter—mixed martial arts. We fight in a cage. You know—the octagon?" He punched the air with both fists and grinned again. "It's awesome, man. I love it. Such an adrenaline rush—nothing quite like it. I wrestled in high school and it was nothing like getting in the cage." The grin slowly faded as he remembered why I was there. He took a deep breath and changed the subject. "Dude, my mom's missing. Rory said you might be able to find her. Can you do that? I'm really worried, man."

I cursed Rory in my head. A missing person case was often a money pit for the client, and if the house was any indication, this kid didn't seem to have the cash flow necessary for even a day's worth of expenses. "Have you talked to the police, filed a missing persons report?"

"Yeah, I talked to those worthless motherfuckers." He spat the words out. "I haven't seen her since Wednesday, and ain't heard anything, either. That ain't like my ma, you know? I used to talk to her every day. The last time I talked to her was Thursday, you know? I didn't hear from her on Friday and I figured, you know, she got busy or whatever, and then I went over there, and she wasn't home, didn't look like she'd been home, and her car ain't there, and she ain't answering her cell phone, either—and that ain't like Ma, I'm telling you. And she didn't show up for my fight last night, either, and Ma ain't never missed one of my fights." He started rocking back and forth. "I told the cops that yesterday and I called the asshole who took my report about her not showing up to the fight last night, but I don't think he gives a damn, you know? He tells me she'll probably just turn up, and it don't mean nothing." His face twisted. "What the hell does he know? He don't know my ma."

"She ain't missing," the pregnant girl yelled from the next room. "She's off with some man, you just don't want to admit it, is all. You're wasting the guy's time, Jonny. You might as well just get the hell out of here, mister."

He gave me a look, shaking his head, and shouted back at her, "Heather, you know damned well Ma wouldn't do that—"

"She's a woman, ain't she?" Heather cut him off angrily. "She ain't so goddamned pure, ya know—just 'cause she's your ma doesn't mean she don't have needs like any other woman. You think you were a virgin birth? Where you think you came from?"

"I never said that! Why don't you get us some coffee, will ya, honey?" He gave me a forced and embarrassed "everything's cool" smile.

"Yeah, 'cuz I ain't got nothing better to do, right?" I heard her shuffling to the back of the house. "I'm just pregnant, you asshole."

"Sorry about that, Mr. MacLeod." He held up both hands and gave me a sheepish grin. "It's her hormones—I never know whether she's gonna start crying or screaming or both. She's due next month."

I nodded, fighting my instinct to get the hell out of the dirty little house.

"My mom wouldn't do that, Mr. MacLeod," he added quickly in a low voice. "I mean, I know she's a woman, and she's had plenty of boyfriends over the years, ya know, I ain't stupid no matter what some people think"—he glanced at the doorway—"but she's never just gone away without telling no one. That ain't like her. Like I said, she ain't answering her cell phone. She didn't come to the casino last night to see my fight." He shook his head. "That ain't like Ma. She ain't never missed one of my fights, Mr. MacLeod, never." He swallowed. "I'm worried. Something happened to her, I know it. My brother Robby and my sister Lorelle—they haven't heard from her either." He frowned. "Well, I haven't really talked to Robby since Thursday, I can't get a hold of him, but I talked to his wife yesterday, and she ain't heard from Ma, either." He folded his arms.

"Jonny, even if I take the case, I can't guarantee I'll find her," I heard myself saying before I could stop myself. "And it could get expensive—really expensive."

"I got money," he replied stubbornly, his lower lip sticking out.

"That money's supposed to be for the baby!" Heather screamed from the back of the house. I couldn't believe she heard him—I'd barely been able to hear him and I was only a few feet away.

I wanted to get out of there as fast as I could. "Look, I don't—"

"I got money," he insisted. "Not the baby money. Don't listen to her, man, you gotta find my ma. Please." He reached into the pocket of his shorts and passed a crumpled hundred-dollar bill over to me.

I held the bill in my hand.

I thought about telling him what my day rate was, and how that didn't include expenses—and it was usually the expenses that stabbed the client in the bank account. I thought about telling him one hundred dollars wasn't even close to the retainer I usually asked for.

I thought about explaining to him that when the majority of people disappeared, there were usually only two possibilities.

The majority of missing persons just walked away from their life. One day, they just woke up and took a long, hard look at their lives and didn't like what they saw. It could be a long process—with a sense of dissatisfaction and disappointment with life that just kept growing and growing until it finally reached the point where they couldn't go on anymore. Some people slit their wrists or took pills when they got there. Others said "fuck this" and ran away without a backward glance, just ran and kept running. They changed their names and started over again somewhere else. People who fell into this grouping did not, as a rule, want to be found. Some of them never came back, settling happily into their new lives. Some came back when they realized the change of scenery didn't solve the problem, or when they started missing and appreciating their old life.

But the ones who do come back don't until they are good and ready—and do not appreciate being found.

The other possibility was that something had happened to her—something bad. She might have been murdered in some random crime—a mugging or a carjacking or something—and the body just hadn't been found yet. Or some psychotic grabbed her off the street.

If someone had grabbed her, the odds were she wouldn't be found alive. She might not *ever* be found.

The right thing to do would be to say, "If she's alive, she probably doesn't want to be found. If she's dead, we may never find her body. In either case, letting the police handle it is your best option."

Sitting there, I knew I should be honest, give him his hundred-dollar bill back, and walk out the front door, forget that I'd ever been there.

But looking into his earnest, desperate young face, I just couldn't bring myself to say the words.

"You say she's been missing for about three days now?" I asked, getting my notepad out of my pants pocket and uncapping a pen.

The relief on his face embarrassed me, so I looked away. "I went over to her house on Friday morning and she wasn't there. I always have breakfast with Ma on Friday mornings." He swallowed. "Her car wasn't there, so I figured she'd run to the store or something. I sat down and waited, and after about an hour I called her. She didn't pick up—and Ma always picks up, no matter what, unless she's at Mass. That's when I started wondering if something was, you know, wrong. After about another hour, I went looking for her. I didn't see her nowhere, and I kept calling. Nothing. Heather had a doctor's appointment that afternoon and Ma didn't show up for that—and Ma don't never miss any of Heather's appointments."

"That's 'cuz she thinks I'm gonna harm the baby," Heather said as she walked into the living room, carrying two steaming mugs of coffee. She gave me what was probably supposed to be a smile. "She's always after me, like I'm some kind of idiot, you know. Like I don't know I'm not supposed to smoke or drink coffee when I'm pregnant." She sneered at me. "Like I'm gonna go out and do tequila shots or shoot up some heroin or something."

I took a tentative sip of the coffee. It was bad. I set it down on top of a newspaper on the coffee table. "And you checked with her friends? The rest of your family?"

He nodded. "I called my brother Robby right away Friday morning. I left a message for him but he never called me back." He made a face.

"Robby thinks he's better'n we are." Heather sneered. "He don't never take our calls or call us back."

"My sister Lorelle hadn't heard from her, either." He didn't acknowledge what Heather had said. "I'm the youngest"—he gave me the sheepish smile again—"the baby of the family. Robby and Lorelle are a lot older than me. They're in their thirties. I was what Ma called a change-of-life baby." He shrugged again.

"That's why he's so spoiled." Heather shoved a pile off the couch and sat down, folding her hands on her belly.

"I'm not spoiled—"

"The sun rises and shines out of your ass for Mona," she jeered at him, and looked at me. "Mona thinks I'm not good enough for him, you know. She's always dropping in here and making fun of the way I keep house, my cooking—she's *awful*."

I refrained from mentioning her housekeeping skills left a little to be desired. "So, her name is Mona?"

Jonny didn't look at Heather. "Mona Catherine Rowland O'Neill, yeah. Rowland's the maiden name."

I wrote it down. "Did she work?"

"Not since Katrina." Jonny frowned. "She used to work as a property manager for an apartment complex on the West Bank before the storm, but the place didn't reopen right away after Katrina—too much damage, and so Ma just retired."

"She always said she was too old to be looking for a new job, so she decided to stay home," Heather said. She made a face. "She had a nice little nest egg she was sitting on."

"My dad was killed when I was little," Jonny explained. "Mom got a big settlement from the insurance and the company he worked for—he was killed on the job. She didn't need to work, she just didn't like sitting around doing nothing—that's why she got the job in the first place, after I started school."

"So, how did she fill her days after the flood?" I asked.

"She did a lot of volunteer work—you know, helping people rebuild their houses and stuff—I mean, she didn't do construction work, but for a long time she drove around passing out supplies to people working on houses in the Ninth Ward," Jonny went on. "She also spent a lot of time volunteering at St. Anselm's, and you know, she got really involved in trying to save it."

That got my attention. "She was one of the protesters at St. Anselm's?"

St. Anselm's had been in the local news for months. One of the side effects from the depopulation of the city after Katrina and the levee failure was a corresponding drop in attendance—and donations—to the Catholic Church. As revenues fell, the archdiocese decided it needed to tighten its belt, and part of that tightening included the closing of two churches in the city. Archbishop Pugh was stunned when the parishioners flatly refused to let their churches be closed, and St. Anselm's had become the focal point of the battle—because of its location in Uptown New Orleans. St. Anselm's was technically in the Irish Channel, but it was only a few blocks on the river side of the Garden District on Louisiana Avenue. Our Lady of Prompt Succor on the West Bank wasn't as beautiful or historic, so the news coverage had focused primarily on the war over St. Anselm's. The parishioners were fighting the archbishop with everything they could muster. Archbishop Pugh was not from New Orleans originally—which was pointed out fairly regularly by the rebellious parishioners. He also didn't appreciate the disobedience of loyal Catholics, and imperiously refused to budge or compromise. As the struggle dragged on, it was becoming increasingly acrimonious.

The St. Anselm's parishioners had taken to holding twenty-four-hour-a-day candlelight vigils inside the church, and the archbishop had demanded the police evict them earlier the previous week. Every news program in the city had camera crews there that day, it seemed, and public opinion had not taken kindly to the sight of good Catholics being dragged out of their church in handcuffs by the police. An ambitious local politician denounced the police raid as a violation of the separation of church and state. The switchboard at the archdiocese—and at City Hall—had lit up.

Archbishop Pugh quickly dropped the charges, but the damage was already done.

Jonny nodded. "Yeah, she was doing vigils over there all the time—"

"She was there all night every night—she was one of the ringleaders," Heather chimed in. "She wasn't happy she wasn't one of the ones that got hauled off to jail, let me tell you what. She tried getting me—*me*—over there." She sniffed. "Tells me because I'm pregnant, the police wouldn't dare do anything to me." She shifted in her seat. "I'm not risking my baby for your stupid church, I told her. Can you imagine the nerve?" She narrowed her eyes, and in a snotty voice, added, "She says she was spending the night there praying." She snorted. "No telling what she got up to in the church all night with strange men." She pushed herself up to her feet and padded off into the back of the house.

"Don't pay her no mind," Jonny said, his face sad. "Her and Ma don't get along too well, as you probably figured out already."

"Was your mother doing a vigil the night before she disappeared?"

"I don't know." He looked sheepish again. "I mean, that's

what I thought—she was pretty much there every night, but I don't know none of those people…I haven't been to church in years." He hung his head. "Ma was good about it—I mean, I know she was disappointed I didn't go anymore, but she never pushed me on it. Ever since I dropped out of de la Salle, I just didn't see no point in going to church anymore, you know? I mean, it just don't make no sense to me, never did. And I figured the cops would talk to them anyway, so I didn't have to, you know? You know how those people are. Why don't you come to church no more, Jonny?" He shuddered. "I mean, why deal with that if I don't have to?"

I nodded. "Why don't your mother and Heather get along?"

"It isn't as bad as Heather makes it out to be, you know." He lowered his voice. "Yeah, Ma thought Heather got pregnant on purpose, so I'd have to marry her. She didn't think me marrying her was a good idea—she thought we were too young to get married." He scratched his head. "The rubber broke, ya know? How did Heather do that on purpose? But Ma wouldn't listen. She never liked Heather from the first."

"She wouldn't like any girl you married," Heather shouted from the other room. "Nobody was good enough for her *baby*. I could have been the Queen of fucking Sheba and she wouldn't have cared."

"She bought us this house, didn't she?" Jonny shouted back, his face turning red. "Which is more than your ma ever did for us!"

"My parents never made you feel like white trash!"

"Why you want to say stuff like that?" He got up and gave me an apologetic look. "Give me a minute, okay?" He disappeared through the doorway, and I could hear them murmuring to each other. After about a minute or two, he came walking back in. "Sorry." He plopped back down on the sofa. "Hormones, like I said. I sure will be glad when the baby comes."

Yes, because things will be so much easier with a screaming baby in the house, I thought. "Where does your mother live? Close by?" I could feel a headache coming on. I was starting to regret this already.

"Just up the street—the next block over."

"Do you mind taking me over there so I can take a look around her place?" I stood up and stretched. I also wanted to get out of the house.

"Not at all." He got up and stretched. "Let me get the keys and I'll walk you over there." He wandered back out of the room.

I walked over to the front door and prayed I would never have to set foot in the depressing little shotgun house ever again.

CHAPTER TWO

Once I was out of the claustrophobic atmosphere of the house Jonny shared with his wife, I felt like I could breathe again.

It had gotten hotter while I'd been inside—going back out into it felt like I had stuck my head inside an oven on its highest setting. I started sweating as soon as I stepped out onto the porch. The glare of the midday sun was blinding, so I slipped on my sunglasses. A gray cat that had been cleaning itself on the porch took off like a bolt of lightning, vaulting over the fence into the next yard. I mopped at my forehead as I headed for the front gate, and waited for Jonny on the other side of it.

"It's just on the next block—not too far," Jonny said, fighting with the gate. He freed it from where it had lodged against the walk and slammed it closed behind him. "Damn, it's hotter than a motherfucker out here."

He kept up a running patter of talk as we walked down Constance Street, away from the sounds of the cars a block or so away over on Louisiana Avenue. There was no sign of human life anywhere on Constance—the houses were all closed up. It was eerie—if not for the traffic sounds in the distance, we could have been in a post-apocalypse movie. We crossed Harmony Street, and just like in any number of neighborhoods in the city, crossing the street was like stepping into another world. The houses on Jonny's block were in disrepair, but this block was decidedly more upscale. There were still shotgun houses and Creole cottages, but they were much better kept. The lawns were lush, green, and carefully manicured. Flowerbeds erupted in riotous colors. The scent of sweet olive hung in the air. The houses were pristine, and the cars parked in driveways or alongside the street looked newer and more expensive.

Almost every house had a security company sign planted where it could be plainly seen in the flowerbeds.

Jonny never stopped talking, not even to take a long breath or to give me a chance to respond with anything other than a monosyllabic grunt. He clearly was one of those people not comfortable with silence. But there wasn't any way I could think of to ask him to be quiet without sounding rude—and I have found it's never a good idea to be rude to a client.

Even if said client couldn't afford to pay my standard rate, he was *still* my client and deserved to be treated with respect.

And there was, of course, the possibility that his nonstop chatter might have simply been a symptom of being worried about his mother, and if rambling on and on made him feel better somehow, who was I to deny him this small comfort?

Oddly enough, he was talking about everything under the sun *except* his mother.

I found my mind wandering a bit as he went on about his training regimen, his diet, his unbeaten ring record, cage fighting strategies, and how MMA was different from boxing and wrestling even though it was a combination of the two disciplines. His voice rose and fell as he became more excited about his topic, and every once in a while he would demonstrate a striking technique for me. It was a little hard for me to take him seriously, since I was almost a foot taller and almost certainly a hundred pounds heavier.

Still, I was well aware that a skilled and well-trained fighter always has the ability to inflict some serious damage on a far larger opponent—and he obviously took his sport very seriously.

So I managed to politely nod or make appropriate noises whenever it seemed to be called for—which fortunately didn't seem to be very often. I began wondering if he was just trying to impress me, or if he didn't have anyone else he felt comfortable talking to about his fighting.

Then again, his wife seemed to be the kind of woman who wouldn't want her husband to keep his friends—especially since she was pregnant.

You're being judgmental and misogynist, I scolded myself. *You don't know her well enough to make those kinds of judgments, and she may be completely different when she's not pregnant. How would you feel if you were eight months pregnant in this heat, living in a dump, and your hormones were raging out of control? You'd be kind of abrupt and bitchy, too, at the very least.*

We had almost reached the end of the block when Jonny stopped and said, "Here we are."

Mona O'Neill's house was on the same side of the street as Jonny's, but was so completely different it could have been on the moon. It was a beautiful double camelback-style shotgun house painted a rich, dark purple with black trim. Unlike her son's house, hers appeared to be in perfect repair. Her front porch didn't sag, and the house looked level and solid. There was a porch swing on the opposite end of the porch from the front door. The shutters were latched open, and the curtains were also open. The windows looked clean. There was a paved driveway to the right, behind an electric gate. The black wrought iron fence was in perfect repair. Red, white, and pink roses bloomed in the flowerbeds that ran along the front of the porch, and a few bees were buzzing around the open faces. The lawn was a dark emerald green, perfectly manicured but getting close to needing to be mowed. Her statue of the Blessed Virgin Mary was in perfect repair, and looked brand-new. It stood on top of smoothed-out white sand, in the center of a circle of polished stones. The entire front yard was shaded by the massive live oak next door, its long, heavy branches protecting Mona's place from direct sunlight.

Where Jonny and Heather's house was uninviting and looked to be in danger of being declared blighted at any moment, Mona's was warm, friendly, looked cared for and lived in. It was easy to imagine family gatherings and holidays being held there, children laughing and playing in the front yard.

"It used to be a double, but when Ma and Dad bought it they turned it into a single," Jonny said as he opened the wrought iron gate, which didn't catch on the sidewalk and swung all the way open. He smiled at me and started up the walk. "They did most of the work themselves. My dad was really good at that kind of stuff." He hesitated for a moment. "Looks like I need to mow the grass." He gave me a self-deprecating look. "Heather says I'm a mama's boy, but I don't mind mowing Ma's lawn for her. She's getting too old to be pushing a mower around in this heat."

You should think more about your own lawn than your mother's, I thought rather cynically as I pulled the gate closed behind me.

"What kind of car does your mother drive?" I asked, climbing up the steps onto the porch behind him.

Jonny bent over and picked up a couple of newspapers, tucking them under his arm. "She just got a new green Mercury Marquis last year," he replied as he unlocked the gate in front of the door. "One of those luxury cars. It's like riding in a couch." He winked at me. "Ma always had medium cars, said she always wanted one of them big expensive ones."

I walked down to the end of the porch and looked at the driveway. "You said you talked to her on Thursday. What time was that?"

Jonny frowned. "It was about nine o'clock, maybe? She was getting ready to head down to the church, for the vigil."

"When was the last time you actually saw her?"

"She stopped by on Wednesday morning on her way home from church." He remembered. "Heather had called and asked her to pick up a gallon of milk for us on her way home, for my cereal. I'd just gotten up when she came by."

"How did she seem?"

He shrugged. "Normal, I guess. No different than usual."

I walked back to the front door. The roof of the front porch was painted sky blue, and two ceiling fans spun lazily. There were several wicker chairs spray-painted white placed at various intervals along the porch. Jonny unlocked the front door and went inside. I stepped over the threshold just as he punched code numbers into the alarm system. I closed the door behind me. I could see why Mona kept her curtains open. The room was filled with natural sunlight, and the windows themselves were spotless. It was very cool inside—borderline cold. He flipped on a light switch, and a pair of chandeliers filled the double parlor with an almost blinding white light. The ceiling fans also began turning.

Jonny made a noise and turned the dimmer switch until the light wasn't quite so obnoxious. "That's weird," he commented. "Ma never has the lights turned up so bright. And it's pretty cold in here." He walked across the room to a thermostat mounted on the wall and whistled. "It's set on sixty degrees—that's not like Ma, either." He slid a lever to the right, and the air-conditioning system turned off. He frowned at me. "Ma's big on not wasting energy—she gets mad about the power bill all the time. I can't believe she'd walk out of the house and leave the a/c turned down so low." He shook his head. "I can't believe she'd ever have it that low to begin with. She's always yelling at me for running my air so much." He gave me a look. "Heather likes it cold, and you know, she's pregnant…"

I didn't answer him at first. I glanced around the big room. A huge emerald green Oriental rug with gold accents covered most of the hardwood floor. An entertainment center filled with an enormous flat screen television, a DVD player, a stereo, and stacks of DVD boxes took up almost an entire wall. A sofa and two reclining chairs faced the entertainment center. On either end of the sofa sat an end table with matching lamps centered on each. Three remote controls were lined up perfectly on the coffee table, which had a light coating of dust dulling its sheen. There was a stack of magazines neatly staggered so their names were exposed next to the remotes— *Entertainment Weekly*, *Vanity Fair*, *Cosmopolitan*, and *Crescent City*.

"Does anything look out of place to you?" I asked, impressed with how organized and orderly the living room looked. Mona O'Neill certainly ran a tight ship.

"No." Jonny glanced around again. "This is how it always looks. Nothing's ever out of place." He grinned at me. "Ma always said everything has its place and that's where it goes—if you always put it where it goes you'll always be able to find it." He grinned. "Heather and me—we're a little different."

A little, I thought.

To the left, the double parlor opened through pocket doors into a dining room with an enormous table surrounded by chairs, set up underneath yet another chandelier. There was a stack of mail on one end of the table, next to some rolled-up newspapers still rubber-banded closed. The outside wall had two large windows with heavy green velvet curtains pulled closed on each. The wall between the windows was covered with photographs in cheap-looking frames. I walked into the dining room and looked at the pictures.

"Is this your mother?" I asked, pointing to a photograph of an older woman standing with her arm around a beaming Jonny. The resemblance between them was remarkable. The shape of their faces, noses, mouths, and eyes—there was no question they were related in some way. She didn't look nearly as happy as he did—her smile looked phony, and didn't quite reach her narrowed eyes. He was wearing a three-piece navy blue suit over a pale yellow shirt. She was also dressed nicely, in a matching red jacket and long skirt over a white silk blouse. An enormous gardenia was pinned to her left lapel. Her hair was dyed that unnatural shade of black older women sometimes use to cover gray, and she was also wearing a pair of tortoiseshell glasses. She looked to be in her late fifties, a little thick in the waist and the hip, and the forced smile didn't extend to the rest of her face.

"Yeah, that's from my wedding," Jonny replied.

I scanned the other pictures quickly, but Heather's face was conspicuously absent. There wasn't even a photograph of the bride and groom together.

Apparently, the only picture Mona O'Neill could abide hanging on her dining room wall from her son's wedding didn't include his wife.

"This is my brother, Robby," Jonny said, pointing to an old, fading graduation picture just below the wedding shot.

Robby looked like Jonny in some ways—the overbite, the blue eyes, the long nose were the same—but the sparkle in Jonny's eyes was missing from his brother's. The photography studio had tried to airbrush out some acne scars but hadn't quite succeeded. Robby's hair was the same color as Jonny's, but the style in the picture at least twenty years out of date.

"And this is my sister, Lorelle." Jonny pointed to another senior picture, hung to the left of his brother's.

Lorelle had the same nose and eyes as her brothers, but her face was softer and rounder. She was smiling in her senior picture, braces glinting on her teeth. She had enormous hair, teased and feathered and shellacked to the point where it almost completely filled the picture. She had the same sparkle in her big brown eyes that Jonny had in his. She looked like she was the kind of person who enjoyed life—while Robby looked a little sour.

"Like I said, I was a change-of-life baby," Jonny said, in answer to my questioning glance. "Robby and Lorelle are a lot older than me—they were in high school when I was born." He flashed his smile at me again. "The doctors thought I might be a tumor at first." He shrugged. "Robby always says they were right—I am a tumor. He's kind of an asshole." His face darkened. "I mean, Ma doesn't like Heather, but she makes an effort. Robby—" He stopped himself.

"Have you talked to your sister about your mother's disappearance?" I asked, changing the subject. I turned away from the wall and began idly sifting through the stack of mail. It was all bills and junk, nothing personal.

No one writes letters anymore.

Jonny's face flushed and his eyes narrowed. "She thinks I'm making a mountain out of a molehill," he replied angrily. "And Robby can't even be bothered to call me back, you know? They never take me serious. Never. They're worse than Ma about treating me like a baby. Lorelle's not so bad—I mean, she doesn't treat me like I'm stupid, but I know she thinks I'm overreacting and it's all nothing. Robby's an asshole, like I said." A vein bulged in his forehead. "Robby can go fuck himself. Ma would never just take off without saying nothing to me, 'specially not with Heather so close to her time and all. They might not get along, but Ma's excited about the baby." He pulled out a chair and sat down, hanging his head a bit. "She just wouldn't do it," he insisted. "I don't care what anyone says. She wouldn't do that."

"So, what happened to your father? You said he died when you were young?" I walked over to a door off the dining room. I flicked on a light switch. The small room was a small office. An aging computer and printer sat on top of a cheap-looking desk that was bowing slightly under their weight. There were several bookcases against the far wall, filled with worn paperbacks neatly stacked on the shelves. There was a thin layer of dust on everything. The wall next to the door was covered with three framed MMA promotional posters mounted under glass. I stepped closer and took a look at them. Each featured a photo of Jonny to the right, with his name in big red letters beneath. All the fights were held at the Chateau Barras Casino, just over the state line in Biloxi. Jonny wasn't smiling in the pictures—rather, he was scowling at the camera, his expression clearly stating *I am going to fuck you up*. He held up his fists in a fighter's stance. His torso was lean, the muscles deeply defined, and his forearms were crisscrossed with bulging blue veins.

He looked menacing. I'd had some trouble seeing him as a brutal fighter, but these pictures convinced me.

"He died when I was a baby—I was maybe a year old, I think." Jonny got up from the table. "He worked down on the docks, got killed in some kind of work-related accident. Ma got a nice settlement from the company he worked for and the union—the money put both Robby and Lorelle through college, and there was some for me, too—trusts, the company set up trusts for all of us, with

Ma in charge of 'em. That's where the money for my house came from—when Heather and me got married, Ma picked out the house for us and paid for it with my trust." He leaned on the door frame, giving me the lazy grin again. "I mean, college was just gonna be a big waste of time and money for me, right? I flunked out of high school—well, I didn't really flunk out, they just wanted me to repeat my senior year, but that just seemed like a big waste of time to me, you know? And what's the point of going to college? I'm not smart enough for that."

"Do you make enough fighting to live on?" I asked, walking over to the desk.

"I do okay," Jonny replied. "The promoter thinks I have a big future, you know, I could be a champion, and champions do pretty well." He gave me the grin again. "Ma's kind of my business manager—I let her deal with the contracts and all that, manage my money, you know? She's not sure the promoter's offer is good enough, you know?"

I was about to ask what he was going to do when he was through fighting, but decided against it. It had nothing to do with the investigation. I liked the kid, but needed to keep a professional distance.

The desk had a narrow drawer over the opening for the chair, and two more down the right side. I opened the top drawer—all it contained was neatly organized paper clips, rubber bands, envelopes, rolls of stamps, and several boxes of pens. The bigger drawer below it contained file folders, neatly labeled with red ink: *Bank Statements, Car Insurance, Entergy, Bell South, Taxes*. I slid the drawer shut and sat down in the rolling chair. I opened the narrow drawer in the center. The only things in it were a box of checks and a blue checkbook. I shut the drawer but heard the sound of crunching paper. I pulled it open and slid it shut again—hearing the strange noise again. I knew that sound—I'd heard it myself plenty of times while sitting at my own desk.

Something was behind the drawer.

I pulled it out again, lifted, and the drawer came loose. A piece of paper fluttered down on top of the file folders in the drawer below.

I picked it up and let out a low whistle.

It was a check made out to Mona O'Neill for fifty thousand dollars.

The payer was the New Orleans Property Development Corporation. The name was familiar—and then I noticed the signature: In a flowing scrawl, it read *Morgan Barras*.

"What's that you got there?" Jonny asked from the doorway.

I looked at him. "Why would your mother have a check for fifty thousand dollars from Morgan Barras?" I asked. "That's kind of strange, don't you think?"

Morgan Barras was almost universally reviled in New Orleans—I'd never heard anyone say anything positive about him. A real estate mogul who liked getting his picture in the tabloids almost as much as he liked making money, he'd swooped down on the Gulf Coast after Katrina like a vulture, buying up property for a fraction of its actual worth from heartbroken owners who were sick of fighting with FEMA and their insurance companies. Almost every issue of the *Times-Picayune* included a column, an editorial, or a letter to the editor roundly denouncing him as an opportunistic monster and begging New Orleanians not to sell to him. He'd built a massive condo complex in the Central Business District called Poydras Tower that almost everyone in the city considered an eyesore.

There were a lot of rumors about Barras bribing people at City Hall, and it was also rumored the former mayor who'd welcomed him and his money with open arms was in his hip pocket.

The nicest thing anyone had to say about him was to call him a "carpetbagger."

Jonny stared at the check, and shrugged. "Mr. Barras owns the casino where I fight, and I know he's a partner in the promotion I fight for," he replied. "Like I said, they think I have a big future in MMA, and I know Mr. Barras wants me to sign a contract with him—you know, pay for my training and my living expenses for a piece of my take from my fights, you know? I don't have a manager, so I just had Ma deal with Mr. Barras. Maybe she made a deal with him she didn't have time to tell me about yet—before, you know." His eyebrows came together. "You think maybe this has something to do with what happened to her?"

"It might. It might not." I took the check back from him. "You mind if I make a copy of this?"

"Yeah, sure, okay." He frowned. "Maybe you should take it with you, you know, for safekeeping?"

"You think that's a good idea?" I checked the printer attached to the computer. It was also a copier, so I placed the check face-down on the glass and put the lid back down, pressing the Copy button.

"I don't have no place to keep it safe at my place, and I don't like the idea of it just sitting here waiting for someone to steal it."

The printer spat out a copy of the check. I folded the copy and slipped it into my wallet. I put the check in with it and wrote out a quick receipt for him. "I have a safe in my apartment, I'll keep it there until your mom turns up." I stood up. "Show me the rest of the house."

The rest of the house was no different from the front rooms—neat and tidy, everything covered in a thin layer of dust. There were three bedrooms downstairs, and a huge kitchen. Mona O'Neill's design ethic wasn't exactly what I would have chosen, but it was simple and neat. There were plaster saints placed here and there, and the occasional religious painting, but it wasn't overdone and in-your-face the way some working-class Catholic homes were. There was a slightly stale feel to the air, like no one had been in the house in a while.

It didn't feel lived in anymore.

A staircase led up to the camelback, which had been converted into one massive bedroom suite. Nothing seemed to be missing from the walk-in closet, or from the chests, but Jonny couldn't swear to it. Her luggage set, though, was still resting on the closet floor. The bed was made, and everything in the big bathroom seemed to be in place. A large pink towel was draped over the shower rod. I felt it—it was stiff. The bathroom smelled slightly of bleach.

I went back down the stairs into the kitchen, Jonny at my heels. I walked out the back door into the backyard in time to see a black-and-white cat vanish over the fence into the neighbor's yard. The backyard was just like the front—neat and tidy. A massive live oak in the back corner cast shade over most of it. There was a brick barbecue pit close to the house and a wooden picnic table in the shade. A wooden slat fence about six feet high closed it in on three sides. I walked down the back steps and could imagine Mona's family gathered, grandchildren laughing and playing while white smoke rose from the barbecue pit, hamburgers and hot dogs sizzling over the coals.

"Hey, Jonny!"

The voice was female and came from the house on the right. I looked up and saw a rather pretty young woman in a white bikini and sunglasses, her skin glistening with suntan lotion, waving from the sagging back balcony of the huge house. An enormous floppy hat shaded her face.

"Oh, hey, Lois, how are you?" Jonny shaded his eyes.

"You mind if I come over? I want to ask you about something."

"Sure."

"Give me a second." She pulled on a robe and slipped her feet into some flip-flops before disappearing inside her house through a pair of French doors. A few minutes later, I heard a door open and slam on the other side of the fence.

"Lois Armstrong," Jonny said to me in a low voice before crossing the yard and unlocking the back gate. "She's been living next door to Ma for about three years now. She's really nice."

I sat down at the picnic table as Lois Armstrong came through the back gate. She pulled the big floppy hat off and shook her thick curly hair loose. The blue terry-cloth robe she had on wouldn't stay closed, and she kept trying to retie it as she made her way over to the picnic table. Jonny shut the gate behind her and joined us at the table.

"Lois Armstrong," she said to me, sticking out her small hand. Her nails were neat and trimmed, with just clear polish. She wasn't wearing any makeup, but she didn't need any. She had long eyelashes fluttering over enormous green eyes. Her lips were full and red, her skin olive, and her teeth were even and white. She was older than I'd originally thought, maybe in her mid-thirties rather than mid-twenties.

"Chanse MacLeod." I took her warm hand and shook it. Hers was so small it seemed to be swallowed up in mine.

"Pleased to meet you, I'm sure." She fussed with the robe some more before sitting down. "Jonny, I'm worried about your mom. I haven't seen her for a few days, and that's just not normal. Have you talked to her? Is she mad at me about something?"

"I haven't talked to Ma since Thursday." Jonny gave me a significant look. *See?* "That's why Mr. MacLeod's here, Lois. I've hired him to look for Ma, find out where she is."

"Oh." She flashed a smile at me before turning back to Jonny. She swallowed. "So, it's serious." She folded her hands together on the picnic table. "I thought I might have done something—you know, made her mad and she was avoiding me or something."

"So it's not normal for you to not see Mrs. O'Neill for a few days, Ms. Armstrong?" I asked. "Is there another reason you might be concerned about her?"

She looked at me, tilting her head to one side and narrowing her eyes a little. "Like I said, I haven't seen her in three days, and she never goes away without telling me." Her eyebrows went up and she turned to me. "We feed this stray black-and-white cat that hangs around in our yards. If she's not going to be around, she makes sure I know, so I know to feed him. And every afternoon when I get home from work I always come by for a glass of wine—around four thirty. Mona is wonderful to talk to, you know—it's a way I can unwind after dealing with the kids all day—it's nice to have an adult that's not another teacher to talk to, you know? And every Saturday morning when she gets home from her vigil at the church, she comes over and we have coffee." She gave a little shrug. "If she's not going to be home, she calls me and lets me know. Friday she wasn't here—and neither was her car, and she didn't call me. She didn't come by yesterday morning for coffee, and I haven't seen her car at all." She turned back to Jonny. "I was going to call you today, but I knew you had a fight last night…" Her voice trailed off as she focused her big eyes on me again. "So, you think something's happened to her?" Her hand went to her throat gracefully, like she'd practiced the gesture.

"That's what I'm trying to find out, ma'am," I replied. "Do you know if Mrs. O'Neill was seeing anyone?"

"I already told you she wasn't," Jonny said, his tone low and angry. His hands clenched into fists, and veins bulged in his forearms. "Heather was talking out her ass, I told you."

Lois placed a hand on his wrist. "Jonny, your mother is seeing someone. She just didn't told you—well, because you don't always take it well." She gave him a faint smile. "She's worried you wouldn't like it."

Your ma ain't so pure, I heard Heather's nasal voice echo in my head. "Who was he, Ms. Armstrong?"

"Call me Lois, please." She ran her hands through her thick curls. Her ringlets sprang back as soon as her hands passed through. She shook her head. "I only met him once, but she talks about him all the time." Jonny made a noise, and she put her hand back on his arm. "Jonny, your mother has been a widow for a long time. Don't you think she has a right to be happy?" When he didn't answer, she turned back to me with a gentle smile, as though saying *boys don't like to think their mothers have needs, do they?* "His name is Barney Hogan…"

"Mr. Hogan?" The words burst out of Jonny in an explosion, and his face darkened.

"You know him?" I asked.

Jonny scowled. "Yeah, he's been around as long as I remember.

He was a friend of my dad's." He rubbed his eyes. "He's been married a few times, but his last wife died a few years back, and he owns a bar down on Tchoupitoulas Street. He goes to St. Anselm's, too, and I know he was involved in the Save Our Churches thing."

"They often keep vigil together. I thought it was, you know, sweet." She sighed. "They mostly just hold hands and talk, is what Mona told me. I think they're both more lonely than anything else, you know?"

"So, you don't think she could be staying with him?"

"No, that's not like Mona, not at all. Mona would never just go off and stay over somewhere and not let any of us know. She isn't like that at all. Besides, I stopped by the bar last night, just to see if Barney'd heard from her—he said he hadn't."

"And you think he was telling the truth? She's not staying with him?"

"I can't imagine why he'd lie. Besides, like I said, Mona'd never do that without telling someone—if not me, than she certainly would have told Jonny. She isn't impulsive—she's very responsible." She shook her head, the ringlets flying. "I've called her cell a few times and it goes straight to voicemail. And she'd definitely not want Jonny to worry—especially with Heather so close to her time, you know." Her lips tightened into a narrow line. "She's really excited about the baby."

"Can you tell me the name of Barney's bar?"

Her eyes rolled up as she thought about it for a moment. "The Wharf, I think. I don't know—it's something like that. It's down there on Tchoupitoulas, near the Rouse's and Tipitina's at Napoleon. You can't really miss it, you know." She raised her shoulders again in a little shrug. "I'm not really a bar person, that's the only time I've been down there…bars aren't really my scene. But they aren't Mona's, either. She only goes in there to see Barney."

I made a note of the bar's name and location. "I'll check it out."

Lois gave me a sad smile. "There was something bothering her last week—she seemed really worried about something, but I don't know what it was…I figured she'd tell me when she was ready." She sighed. "I suppose I should have pushed her to confide in me, but I figured it wasn't really my place…I didn't know, you know—" She shook her head. "You just never know when something's going to turn out to be important later, you know? You just never know…"

CHAPTER THREE

I wish," Police Detective Venus Casanova said, sitting down across the table from me, "that I could arrest people for being assholes."

I smothered a grin as she scowled at a young woman in her early twenties who was still messing around at the condiment bar. Completely oblivious to the dirty looks she was getting from one of New Orleans' finest, she kept yakking loudly on her cell phone while adding more things to her coffee. She'd already added both vanilla and cinnamon flavoring powder. Still talking loudly and gesticulating with one hand, she added cream and a packet of sweetener and started stirring it all with a spoon, completely disregarding the sign requesting patrons use the wooden stir sticks provided rather than the silverware. Finally finished turning her coffee into some bizarre hybrid of clashing flavors, she carried the cup past us to a table at the opposite side of the coffee shop, the phone still apparently surgically attached to the side of her face.

"If we could do that, we'd never have time to investigate serious crime," said her partner, Blaine Tujague, with a slight laugh. He winked at me. "There're just too many assholes around these days."

I'd asked them to meet me at Mojo's, my favorite coffee shop. It sat on the corner of Magazine and Race streets, a mere couple of blocks from my apartment. The place was empty, other than the young woman who'd annoyed Venus, and a group of gutter-punk-looking kids in their early twenties. Wearing filthy clothes, their faces covered with tattoos and piercings, they were clustered around a table a few yards away from us. Every so often they would burst into raucous laughter. The young woman with multicolored hair working behind the counter was now reading *Gambit Weekly*, the city's local alternative newspaper.

Blaine and I had been rookie cops together on the NOPD before I got tired of the politics and the rest of the bullshit that went along with being a cop and quit to start my own investigation agency. Venus and I had butted heads a few times over the years—she didn't appreciate a private eye sticking his nose into her investigations. She'd even threatened to arrest me once. Once Blaine became her partner, we started getting along better, moving from dislike to grudging respect and finally, after the levee failure, to friends.

Venus was a tall woman, an inch or so over six feet without shoes—and she always wore heels to add a few more inches to her impressive height. She was lean and muscular, with long legs— she'd put herself through college on a basketball scholarship and had kept herself in shape with regular workouts at the gym in the years since she'd gotten her degree. Her skin was smooth and she kept her hair cropped close to her scalp. I had no idea how old she was—I knew she had two married daughters in their twenties, so she had to be at the very least in her mid-forties, but she was one of those women who simply seemed ageless. She'd been divorced for years—her husband was long gone by the time I joined the force. A lot of the men on the force thought she was a lesbian—I'd wondered myself—but that was just typical straight male misogynist bullshit.

She was also one of the best cops on the force. In the weeks after the flood, Venus had thought about taking an early retirement and moving up to Memphis near her daughters. Her home in New Orleans East was completely destroyed, and the entire New Orleans Police Department had taken a beating in the national press. She'd eventually decided to stay and work, to help rebuild not only the city but the department as well—which was a good thing. New Orleans couldn't afford to lose someone like Venus. She'd lived in the carriage house behind Blaine and his partner's house for a couple of years before finally buying her own home in Uptown New Orleans, on General Pershing Street. She kept saying she was going to have everyone in our little group of friends over for dinner, but it hadn't happened yet. She kept saying she was waiting until she had the house fixed up just the way she wanted it.

I knew better than to press the subject.

Blaine was my age, give or take a year or so, and the youngest son of a prominent old New Orleans society family. He was about five-nine, and obviously spent a lot of time in the gym. He liked to wear his shirts tight with the sleeves rolled up to his elbows. When he was off duty, he favored tight sleeveless T-shirts (when he bothered to wear one) and loose-fitting pleated madras shorts. He had beautiful dark blue eyes, olive skin that tanned easily, and curly black hair with a bluish sheen to it. He shaved every morning, but by midafternoon he always had a blue-black shadow on his cheeks and chin and under his nose. He used to like to go out dancing in the Quarter gay bars every weekend, but over the last few years had tapered that off quite a bit. He had a wicked sense of humor, was a merciless tease, and never seemed to let anything bother him for long. He lived on the opposite side of Coliseum Square from me with his partner, Todd Laborde, in a gorgeous mansion they'd renovated. Todd was about fifteen years older than Blaine and owned a number of successful businesses around the city. They'd been together since Blaine was in his early twenties, and they had an open relationship. Blaine and I had been fuck buddies for a short period of time. That was ancient history, though—now we were just close friends.

"I don't know why people can't just drink regular coffee anymore." Venus shook her head, apparently not finished with her tirade. Her big gold hoop earrings started swinging. "I mean, seriously. Why does everyone have to have some kind of goddamned thing no one ever heard of ten years ago? What the fuck is a goddamned triple mocha skinny latte with a shot of this or that or whatever? Who even thought about putting that shit in their coffee in the first place? When you're done putting all that crap into it, it doesn't even taste like coffee anymore." She closed her eyes and took a deep breath. "Coffee is fucking coffee, for God's sake."

I glanced down at my iced mocha and tried not to let her see me smile. "Next you'll be yelling at kids to get off your lawn."

"Yeah, well, if you had your own lawn you wouldn't want kids running all over it and tearing it up, either." Venus threw her head back and barked out a loud laugh. "And you're not getting any younger yourself, there, buddy." Venus trained her big round brown eyes on me, a smile playing at the corner of her lips. "And it's generally not a good idea to be rude and insulting to someone you need help from." She nudged Blaine with her elbow. "Right, partner?"

It wasn't strictly kosher, but sometimes Venus and Blaine would slip me some information I shouldn't have access to, or would do some checking for me—as long as it was never traced back to them. Cops have a *lot* more access to information than private eyes—and private eyes have access to a lot more information than your average Joe Citizen. In return, I've been known to help them out with some of their cases from time to time—whenever they needed something done that might not necessarily hold up in a court of law.

It's a nice little arrangement that some of their higher-ups might not look kindly upon, but it worked for us.

"Yeah, well, be that as it may, you know as well as I do if Chanse doesn't find this woman, she'll never be found. You know who caught the case, Chanse?" Blaine took a sip from his coffee and wouldn't look me in the eye. "Delvecchio."

My heart sank. "Fuck."

There really wasn't much else to say. If Venus was one of the better cops on the NOPD, Albert Delvecchio was the epitome of why the department had such a bad reputation. Lazy, racist, homophobic, *and* sexist, he'd been assigned to Missing Persons primarily because it was a place where he could do the least amount of damage. The general consensus around the department was Delvecchio had something on someone—it was the only explanation anyone could come up with for why he hadn't been fired with extreme prejudice years ago. His virulent homophobia meant Blaine would get nowhere with him—the racism and sexism ruled Venus out as a confidant. Delvecchio hadn't seen the inside of a gym since high school—if he had then. He was balding but tried masking it by combing his graying hair over the baldness. He had an ever-expanding beer belly and the disposition of a warthog—an angry warthog, at that. He was a lousy cop—the kind who talked smack about the higher-ups when they weren't around but would shove his head as far up their asses as possible when they were. He was insulting and crude to his fellow officers, and I'd come close to slugging him any number of times during my brief tenure in uniform. I still regretted not loosening a few of his teeth for him. He was also a lazy son of a bitch who always tried to pass his work off to anyone available, and wasn't especially smart either.

If it were left solely up to him, Mona O'Neill would never be found.

"Well, in that case I'm not going to owe either one of you a favor," I observed, taking a drink of my iced mocha. "Because if it's Delvecchio's case, he maybe did a half-assed interview with Jonny and didn't bother with anyone else—so undoubtedly I know a hell of a lot more than he does."

"Yeah, well, I can't argue that point with you. But he did put out the APB, at least—I checked on that." Venus blew on her coffee before taking a drink. "But you're right, that's about all he did. He's probably forgotten all about her already."

"Unless he's changed, he forgot about her two minutes after he finished talking to Jonny," I replied.

"If you got her credit cards, I can run them." She rolled her eyes. "I don't think he even did that."

I slid the list I'd made before leaving Mona O'Neill's house across the table. Venus didn't look at it. She just folded it and slipped it into her purse. "Thanks."

She shrugged. "She's one of those church protesters, isn't she?"

I stared at her. "How did you know that?"

"Are you confusing me with Delvecchio's sorry ass?" She looked at Blaine. "He apparently thinks I'm too stupid to run her name."

Blaine grinned back at her. "You'd think he'd be nicer to cops risking their jobs to do his work for him, wouldn't you?"

"You'd think." She turned her head back to me, her face without expression. "You heard about the archdiocese deciding to try to stop the vigils by having the protesters arrested for trespassing. The cops had to kick in the damned doors—can you believe that? Police officers kicking down the doors of a church. In New Orleans." Her eyes glinted. "The bastards at the archdiocese dropped the charges, of course, once the message boards online lit up." She shook her head. "Idiots. Even if public opinion wasn't on the protesters' side, it sure was after that. Nobody wants to see the cops kicking in the doors of a church on the news." She sighed. "But that's what happens when you have an archbishop who doesn't have a fucking clue about the city he serves. I don't know why they can't give us an archbishop from New Orleans. Anyway, she was the one giving interviews to the press after the arrests. She was all over the news." She shook her head. "You should watch the local news more often."

"But do you really think having a local as archbishop would make a difference?" I asked. I'd heard this argument made, but it had always struck me as another example of New Orleans' particular xenophobia against anyone and anything Not From Here. "I mean, an archbishop who was a local would be facing the same money problems Archbishop Pugh is facing. Wouldn't he want to close churches, too?"

"I always forget you aren't from here," Blaine replied as Venus just glared at me. "The major reason everyone's complaining about Archbishop Pugh is because he doesn't understand the importance of the individual churches. For him it's all about money—and neither one of those churches is really costing the archdiocese money to stay open. Both parishes are self-supporting. That's why the parishioners are so pissed off. There are other parishes in the city that aren't self-supporting. If it was really about losing money, why these particular churches instead of the ones that *are* losing money?"

I debated with myself for just a moment, but plunged ahead anyway. "Well, there's something I don't understand. I mean, who cares if your church closes? What difference does it make what church you attend services at? Catholic is Catholic, isn't it? Isn't it all about communing with God?"

"Chanse—" Venus reached across the table and grabbed my right hand with both of hers, squeezing. "Maybe it's different in other places, I don't know, I don't live somewhere else. All I can tell you is what it's like here. In New Orleans." She let go of my hands and looked out the window as a Coca-Cola delivery truck went by. She took a deep breath. "St. Anselm has been serving its parish for over a hundred years, and so has Our Lady of Prompt Succor. People who were baptized there, confirmed, married, had their kids baptized and confirmed and married there—the place itself matters to people—it matters." She shrugged. "And it's hard to let go, Chanse—it's like having your heart ripped out." She swallowed. "I've been going to St. Anselm myself since the flood. My old parish in the East isn't there anymore." She closed her eyes. "I was baptized and confirmed at Mary Queen of the Universe. I was married there. My kids were baptized, confirmed, married there. It kills me that Mary Queen of the Universe isn't there anymore, Chanse. And now I go to St. Anselm—and soon if the archbishop has his way, it's not going to be there anymore, either. And that's just wrong." She finished her coffee and pushed her chair back. "Haven't we lost enough here already? Do we have to lose our churches, too?" She took her cup back to the counter for a refill.

"Have you talked to Paige at all?" Blaine asked as she sat back down.

"Paige? Why?" I asked, startled.

Blaine laughed. "Some friend you are!"

Venus tried not to smile, but gave up and grinned broadly at me. "Seriously." She got out of her chair and walked over to the counter, picked up a magazine, and walked back. She slapped it down on the table in front of me and started laughing.

It was the latest issue of *Crescent City*, and the cover photograph showed a group of people standing in front of a church with their arms linked. The headline said simply, FIGHTING FOR RELIGIOUS HERITAGE. Beneath that, it said in a smaller font: *An in-depth look at the church closing controversy by Paige Tourneur.*

Paige was my best friend, the editor of *Crescent City*, and had been dating Blaine's older brother Ryan for about four years.

"Paige has been covering this story since the archdiocese announced they were closing the churches," Blaine went on as I flipped to the article. "You mean she's never mentioned it to you? And you don't read her articles?" They exchanged glances.

"Can't wait to rat your ass out to her," Venus said with a grin. "You're gonna have some serious 'splainin' to do, Mr. Man."

I looked at her. "Okay, I admit, I never read the newspaper and rarely watch the news. And she's used to it. She used to get mad at me when she worked at the paper, but it doesn't bother her anymore. But can you explain something to me? If it's two churches, why does St. Anselm's get all the coverage and no one ever talks about Our Lady of Prompt Succor—which is a ridiculous name for a church, I have to say."

"Because it's over on the West Bank," Venus replied. "And that best-selling novelist is a parishioner at St. Anselm—so he gets them a lot more coverage, people listen to him when he talks. But the archbishop is trying to close *two* churches." She pushed her chair back and stood up. "It's a pity, too. St. Anselm is a beautiful old church, and the parishioners are really great people. They really made me feel at home there." She picked up her purse and stalked out of the coffee shop.

Blaine leaned back in his chair. "Don't mind her. This whole church thing has got her riled. I can't say as I blame her—she already lost one church to Katrina, and now she's about to lose another? And I think her younger daughter's having marital trouble, but you know how she is. She won't say a damned thing until she's ready—and in the meantime I got to put up with her damned moods." He winked at me. "Speaking of, how are things going with Rory?"

"Okay." I shrugged. "Taking things as they go, really. I don't want to rush anything, and neither does he."

"I'm just glad to see you—"

My iPhone started ringing, and I gave Blaine an apologetic smile as I ran my finger over the screen to accept the call. "Hello, Abby," I said into the phone, "can you wait a sec?"

Blaine pushed his chair back and stood up. "I got to go, anyway. I'll call you later, man."

I nodded, giving him a fist bump before he walked out of the coffee shop. "Sorry about that, Abby."

"No worries." Abby Grosjean was my business partner. She'd originally started as my assistant, but I'd made her a partner a few years back. She had amazing instincts and took to investigative work like an old pro. "So, your message said we have a new client?"

"Yeah." I hesitated. "Doesn't have a lot of money, though—so I'm kind of giving him a break."

She sighed. "Taking in another lost puppy, are we?"

"You don't have to—"

"I know I don't have to help out." She cut me off. "What can I say? I'm a sucker for lost puppies, too. What's the story?"

I filled her in, and I could hear her typing as I talked. One of the things that absolutely amazed me about her (and made her completely invaluable) was how quickly she could type. She always took extensive notes of every business-related conversation she had—although she also had a phenomenal memory—which had come in handy more times than I cared to remember. She was also a whiz with gadgets—she was the one who'd convinced me I needed an iPhone, which I'd resisted for years. The iPhone and its ability to shoot video had more than paid for its cost since I'd broken down and bought one. She often called me a Luddite. She'd graduated from the University of New Orleans with a degree in pre-law (she paid her way through working as a stripper at the Catbox on Bourbon Street before she started working with me), but was trying to save up the money to pay for law school at either Loyola or Tulane.

When I finished, she said, "Okay, I think the best thing for me to do is try to find a connection between Morgan Barras and Mona—besides Jonny's MMA thing. I'll get Jephtha to do some checking, too." Jephtha, her live-in boyfriend, was probably the most talented computer nerd in New Orleans. There wasn't, he boasted, a system he couldn't hack into. He'd spent a few years in the juvenile detention system for changing grades when he was in high school, and we had a strictly don't ask, don't tell policy on how he found the information I needed. What he really wanted to do was be a computer game designer, and he'd come up with several prototypes so far that I thought looked like winners. He hadn't gotten anywhere with them yet—which was good news for me, since he needed the work I tossed his way.

He was so good I kept him on a retainer, and I dreaded the day he made it as a game designer.

"Okay, great," I replied. "I'll head over to St. Anselm's, see if any of the protesters are willing to talk to me, see if they know anything."

"All right. I'll check in later." She disconnected the call.

I rolled up the copy of *Crescent City* Venus had given me and walked out to my car.

St. Anselm's was on Louisiana Avenue between Tchoupitoulas and Magazine. It was a beautiful building, made of yellow brick with a massive bell tower at one end. Like most Catholic churches, it was laid out in a giant cross. I parked underneath a live oak tree and looked around. I didn't see a green Mercury Marquis parked anywhere on Louisiana, so I checked the side streets as well. It wasn't parked anywhere nearby. I walked through the wrought iron gate and climbed the cement steps to the double doors. They were scarred from being kicked in, and I pushed slightly on them. They swung open without a problem, and I walked into the darkened church.

I'd never really set foot in a Catholic church besides St. Louis Cathedral before—I hadn't set foot in a church of any kind since I'd left Cottonwood Wells, the little town in east Texas I grew up in, for LSU when I was eighteen. St. Anselm's wasn't as majestic as St. Louis; but then I doubted any church in New Orleans could compete with St. Louis. St. Louis was so magnificent it hardly registered in my mind as a church—particularly when compared to the Church of Christ I'd endured growing up.

There was a weird sense of peace and serenity inside St. Anselm's, and as my eyes grew accustomed to the gloom I noticed at the far end of the church there were candles burning on the altar and there were several people seated in the front pews.

I walked up the aisle toward the altar, trying to process the calm. On the occasions when I'd been inside the Church of Christ when there was no service going on, it just seemed like a big empty room. It didn't feel holy—not that it ever felt particularly holy to me during services, when the preacher was screaming about sin and fire and brimstone. Everything was a sin—makeup, skirts above the knee, being naked in front of another human you weren't married to, mixed swimming, television—it seemed like every Sunday the preacher in our church condemned another function of modern life as a sin in the eyes of an angry God. It wasn't until I was a teenager that I began to really notice the hypocrisy. There was no way, for example, I could play football without being naked in front of another human being I wasn't married to—but football trumped sin. My parents didn't forbid my sister from wearing makeup, her cheerleading uniform certainly didn't reach below her knees, and some of the moves she was required to do as a cheerleader certainly incited lust in teenaged boys—and in some adult men who shouldn't have been looking.

Once I left Cottonwood Wells for LSU, I never set foot in another Church of Christ.

But then, the Church of Christ didn't have enormous stained-glass windows on both sides of the building depicting incredibly gory and violent deaths of saints. The bright sunlight streaming through the windows and spilling over the pews was colored brilliant hues of yellow, green, blue, and red. And of course no Church of Christ had an organ, and certainly there would be no enormous cross with a bloodied and suffering Jesus on it behind the altar. The Church of Christ didn't go in for such nonsense; while they did adorn their bare chapels with a cross, it was always a big metal one—and there was never a leanly muscled man in a loincloth with a crown of thorns on his head hanging from it.

That was idolatry, specifically prohibited in the Old Testament.

Funny how you never really get away from religion, I thought as I walked up the aisle.

Between the windows were marble statues of what I assumed must be saints, with their heads bowed over hands clasped together in prayer.

How do people find comfort from such a horrible sight? I wondered as I drew closer to the front and could see how exquisitely detailed Christ's passion was depicted. The eyes were so incredibly mournful, pained, and sad as they looked up to heaven. The muscles stood out in agonized relief. The sword wound in his side dripped blood.

My God, my God, why have you forsaken me?

"May I help you?" a female voice asked quietly from the gloom to my right.

I turned; I'd reached the steps of the altar without realizing it. The woman who'd spoken was smiling at me. She was very short, maybe five foot tall or so. She looked to be in her late fifties, with graying hair that hung to the shoulders of her purple LSU sweatshirt. She was round, with a moon face and very kind eyes. Her hands were folded in front of her, and she exuded an aura of peace and calm that was hard to resist.

I cleared my throat, which sounded ridiculously loud in the quiet church. "I was wondering if I could ask you and your friend a few questions?"

"Why?" This came from a man sitting in the front pew. He made no move to get up. He just sat there and glared at me with suspicious eyes. "Who are you? Did Archbishop P. U. send you?"

"My name's Chanse MacLeod, I'm a private investigator, and I've been hired to find Mona O'Neill by her son Jonny. I just have a few questions—"

"Go ask the Archdemon," the man interrupted me angrily. "That's who's behind it, you can bet your bottom dollar. That son of a bitch needs to be tarred and feathered and run out of town before he finishes destroying the faith in this city."

"Ed, hush. Don't be disrespectful. That's not going to get us anywhere, and you know it." The woman waved her hand at him. "Pay him no mind, Mr. MacLeod. We might not agree with His Eminence, but we don't wish him any ill will. He's not a bad man, he's just a little misguided, that's all. We all pray that he sees the light and changes his mind. We must have faith, right, Ed?" She held out her right hand, which I shook. "I'm Belle Browning, and the disrespectful lout over there in the pew is my husband, Ed." She smiled, taking the sting out of her words. "We'll be glad to help you in any way we can. Mona is a wonderful person. Her family must be so worried."

"You can defend that prick all you want, Belle, but I'm not so forgiving," Ed snapped. "He's sold his soul—"

"Language!" She gave him a nasty look. "Not in the church, Ed."

"So, did you two know Mrs. O'Neill well?" I asked, figuring the best course was to ignore the bickering and move forward.

"We've known Mona for years, since before Danny was killed." Belle gestured to the pew where Ed was sitting. "Shall we sit? My feet are killing me."

I sat down next to Ed, and Belle sat down on my other side.

"That was a tragedy—Danny O'Neill was a hell of a man." Ed Browning shook his head. "Poor Mona—at least the two older kids were old enough to help her out with the baby."

"We all rallied around Mona," Belle said. "I knew her before that only slightly, but it was after Danny was killed that we really became friends. Mona always said that if it weren't for this church she wouldn't have made it." She patted me on the leg. "That's why St. Anselm's meant so much to her. It shames me to admit that were it not for her, this church would have been closed already. But she rallied us all, got us organized—"

"And now she's missing," Ed snarled. "And you know that bastard Pugh is behind it."

"We don't know any such thing!"

"Mona always said Pugh wants to sell the land." Ed went on like she hadn't said anything. "How much is this land worth, do you think, Mr. MacLeod? We might be down in the Irish Channel, but this is still pretty damned close to the Garden District—and what are the property values down here? Even before Katrina they were pretty high. And now? They tear this church down, put up some condos—how much do condos go for in New Orleans since the flood? This land is worth a lot of money—and that carpetbagger of an archbishop damned well knows it." He shook his head. "And the Archdemon is hand in glove with that devil Morgan Barras."

I thought about the check from Morgan Barras I'd found. "Do you know if any developers were looking at buying the land?"

Ed shook his head. "No, can't say that I do. But it wouldn't surprise me."

Belle smiled at me. "Pay him no mind. He doesn't believe Lee Harvey Oswald acted alone."

I couldn't help but smile back at her. "When was the last time you saw Mona?"

"Mona always took the overnight shift here. We always keep vigil in pairs, you know. Sometimes there are more than two—usually in the evening, when people get off work—but overnight sometimes it was just Mona. She was here every night, no matter what."

"Since she disappeared, we've had trouble getting people here overnight," Ed added.

"Ed and I usually get here around seven, to relieve Mona and whoever was keeping vigil with her," Belle went on, frowning at Ed. "But Friday morning when we got here, there was no one here. I know she'd had to sit by herself on Thursday night, but we didn't think anything about it, did we, Ed?"

"So you didn't see her Friday morning?"

"No, she was here Thursday morning when we arrived—and everything seemed fine—she seemed her usual self. We just figured Friday morning she'd left early—she did that sometimes, you know, but not usually unless she had someone here with her." Mona scratched her head. "She didn't come that night, either. We didn't really start worrying until we got here Saturday morning and there wasn't anyone here. That wasn't like Mona, you see. If she couldn't make it she always got someone to fill in for her. She didn't ever want the church to be left empty, and you know she was in charge. So I called her boy, Jonny. He hadn't seen her since Thursday night himself, and he called the police." She snorted. "Fat lot of good that did, though. Do you know not a single policemen has come by to talk to us?"

Ed laughed nastily. "Like the cops aren't owned lock, stock, and barrel by the archdiocese." He snorted. "You saw them acting like storm troopers on Wednesday! Kicking in the doors of a *church*! Arresting us like we were some kind of criminals—how many crimes were committed in the city that day while the damned cops were wasting their time here doing the Archdemon's bidding?"

Something occurred to me. "Didn't the raid take place in the middle of the afternoon?"

"Yes, in broad daylight!"

"But Mona was here for the raid, right? I thought she always took the overnight shift?"

They exchanged a look, and Belle bit her lower lip. "Mona had a source inside the archdiocese," Belle whispered. "We knew the raid was coming, and so we got as many people here as we could. She let the newspapers and the TV stations know, too."

"Do you know who her source was?"

Belle shook her head. "No, she thought the fewer people who knew, the better."

I asked them a few more questions, but they didn't know anything helpful.

I excused myself and made my way out of the church.

CHAPTER FOUR

To have a bad meal in New Orleans, you really have to work at it. The general rule of thumb for locals is to avoid places that cater to tourists—and be willing to take a chance every once in a while.

The Please You Café certainly doesn't look like much from the outside—just another hole-in-the-wall greasy-spoon dive with a faded linoleum floor, bad overhead lighting, and water served in thick, red plastic cups. It was sandwiched between a dive bar and a Sherwin-Williams paint store on the block of St. Charles Avenue just before the light at Felicity Street. There's also a quick oil change place and a ridiculously overpriced chain restaurant on that same block. The Please You was a throwback to the days when there wasn't a fast food place on pretty much every corner; when customers preferred to sit in a booth and be waited on by a gum-chewing waitress with a carefully coiffed bouffant and an apron, and an order pad in her hand. The place was immaculately clean on the inside, even though the big front windows were kind of grimy. There was always a dry-erase board in one of the windows with the day's specials in barely legible handwriting scrawled on it, sandwiched in between some Jazz Fest posters from the early 1990s. The inside walls were covered with old Saints schedules and Mardi Gras posters thumbtacked haphazardly here and there. The faux wood paneling had probably been the height of style in the 1970s, but now it just looked dated and tacky. There was a counter with old-fashioned swivel-top stools amd an ancient cash register, and the menu probably hadn't changed since the Eisenhower administration.

It looked like the kind of place you should avoid at all costs if ptomaine poisoning wasn't in your plans, but in this instance, looks were definitely deceiving. The Please You was one of my favorite places to eat. And not only was the food better than pretty much anywhere else in the neighborhood, but it was also ridiculously cheap. The waitresses were friendly and always called customers "hon," and remembered what good service was supposed to be. They acted like they actually enjoyed working there, were glad you'd come in, and wanted you to enjoy your experience.

I'd been hungry when I walked out of St. Anselm's, so when Abby called me to tell me she had some information she thought might be important, I suggested she meet me at the Please You. Abby prefers to meet in restaurants, and I was in the mood for a shrimp po'boy.

After all, I'd been doing a good job of eating healthy lately and was entitled to a treat—and the Please You's shrimp po'boy and onion rings definitely qualified as a reward.

I parked at my apartment and walked—it wasn't far from my place. It was still hot, but the temperature was starting to cool a bit. Some dark clouds were on the horizon, and the wind had picked up some. The wind was cool and felt damp, and my sinuses were starting to bother me—which definitely meant rain was on the way.

Abby was already there when I walked in the Please You front door, waiting for me at the first booth. A red plastic glass of ice water was sweating in front of her on the table. She grinned at me and gave me a mock salute with her left hand. Her hair was different than the last time I'd seen her—but she rarely kept her hair the same way for more than a few days at a time. Her years dancing at the Catbox Club on Bourbon Street (which she still did from time to time, to "keep her hand in," was how she explained it) had turned her into a self-styled master of disguise. "You have to keep it fresh for the spenders," she told me once, "or they get bored with you and move on to some other dancer. Changing my hair, my makeup, and my costumes from week to week always kept them coming back for more—and I don't want no stinking dollar bills, thank you very much. I want twenties." Her stage moves had been perfected during her years on her high school cheerleading squad—the Catbox Club didn't have stripper poles, which, in Abby's words, "would cheapen the place. We're strippers, not whores."

She had an entire room devoted to her wigs and costumes in the shotgun house she shared with Jephtha. She had racks and racks of clothes, acquired at the secondhand shops that proliferated all over town. Her ability to effortlessly lose herself in a role was a skill most movie stars would kill for. She could do any accent, sometimes added facial tics, and had even taken several classes in stage makeup. Her ability to transform herself completely into another person was remarkable—there were times when I didn't recognize her, would even speak to her without knowing I was talking to Abby. I sometimes wondered that she didn't try to get work with all the movie and television productions in town, but never suggested it. She was too valuable to me—the last thing I wanted was for her to decide she didn't want to be a private eye anymore. She was just too damned good at her job. I worried sometimes that I was becoming a little too dependent on her. She was, after all, going to go to law school one day once she saved up enough money—and then what the hell was I going to do?

She was wearing a red wig cut in a pageboy style, and tinted contact lenses had changed her eyes from their natural gray to green. She was wearing a pink Polo pullover that stretched tightly over her full breasts, and a pair of khaki shorts, with sandals on her feet. Her toenails were painted the same shade of pink as her shirt.

"Let me guess—you're going for sorority princess?" I asked as I slid into the booth across from her.

She made a face and a gagging noise. "Spoiled Uptown princess, thank you very much—destined to make five future ex-husbands very unhappy. I drove over here in my white Lexus convertible, stopped and got a latte on the way, and was texting the whole time!

So I ran a few red lights and didn't notice those pesky stop signs and didn't bother to use my turn signal. I'm an Uptown girl!" she replied, giving me a vapid smile and widening her eyes.

As always, she was incredibly convincing.

The waitress put a glass of water down in front of me along with a menu. Abby smiled at her. "We're both going to have shrimp po'boys with onion rings, and I'll have sweet tea. What do you want to drink, boss?"

"Sweet tea for me, too." I smiled at the waitress as she scribbled on her pad, picked up the menus, and walked away. "So, what did you dig up that was so important that it's costing me lunch?"

"Well, I don't think it's that important—I was hungry and Jephtha's spending the day with his mom up in Baton Rouge." She smiled at me. "But I'll tell you what—that fuckwad Barras sure has got his fingers in a lot of pies in New Orleans." The smile faded into a frown. "I had no idea how bad it was."

"What do you mean?"

She waved a hand. "I mean, I knew about the Poydras Tower—who doesn't, you can't miss that monstrosity—and that he was trying to buy up land from people around town and all, but man oh man." She shook her head. "But I think…" She sighed. "I really didn't find any definite *connection* between Barras and Mona O'Neill, outside of Jonny's fight career—but there's some things that look really suspicious, if you have a twisted and devious mind like me."

My stomach growled. "What did you find?"

"Like I said, I don't have anything concrete." The waitress placed our glasses of iced tea in front of us, and Abby squeezed a slice of lemon in hers. "But like I said, I do have some suspicions—weird stuff." She fiddled with her straw wrapper for a moment. She hesitated. Abby had a rather creative mind, but she never liked to play "what if"—she only liked to report facts to me. Her hunches and wild guesses had paid off enough times in the past for me to respect anything she might say, no matter how far-fetched it might sound. But she never liked to theorize in front of me.

"Abby—"

She lowered her voice and leaned across the table. She checked to see where our waitress was before she continued. "There's talk that Barras wants to buy the St. Anselm's property, but not to develop it into condos or anything like that. You know he lives in the penthouse of Poydras Tower, right? Well, supposedly he wants a house in Uptown—and he wants to turn the church into a house."

"Where did you hear that?"

She rolled her eyes. "On a message board about the church closings." She immediately held up her hand before I could say anything. "I know you think those are just places for bored crazy people with Cheetos-stained fingers who live with their moms to gossip and say crazy shit, but you'd be surprised at what you can find out on there." She shook her head.

"But that doesn't make a lot of sense, Ab. Why would he want a church, of all places? I would think that would cost a mint to convert into a home. And it's not like there aren't any properties for sale in Uptown—or in the Garden District, for that matter. And he's got the kind of money where he could just knock on someone's door and make an offer they couldn't refuse."

"He's notoriously cheap, Chanse. If he can get a nice piece of property like that for next to nothing from the archdiocese, why wouldn't he? And St. Anselm's is a beautiful structure, and sound architecturally." She gave me a look over the top of her glass.

"I don't know, Abby," I replied dubiously. "It sounds like one of those Internet rumors people like to start and spread."

"Well, we can always just ask him."

I laughed. "Yeah, because it's just that easy to get in to see him. I don't think so."

She gave me a sly look. "Apparently, whenever he's in town he likes to frequent the Catbox Club. And he tips with ones and fives." She scowled. "I told you he was a cheap bastard."

"Seriously?"

She nodded. "Yeah—I mean, he's never come in when I've been working, but I haven't pulled a shift in a couple of months. I had lunch with my friend Dixie yesterday—he gave her three whole dollars on Friday night—and tried to monopolize her for most of the night. Three bucks. What a douche—he's lucky she didn't slug him." She shook her head. "But my source inside the archdiocese—who won't talk on the record, which goes without saying, right—says Barras definitely is interested in the St. Anselm property. And the person running Save Our Churches just happens to have a check from him for fifty grand in her desk?"

"It could just be a coincidence—Mona also had a source inside the archdiocese, I wonder if it's the same one you have?" Now it was my turn to play with my straw wrapper. "But—" I swallowed. I didn't like the direction my mind was taking. "Suppose Barras and Mona came into contact because of Jonny and the fighting—and he decides he wants to buy St. Anselm's—and the protests are just a cover to drive the price down?"

She looked down into her glass. "I think the easiest thing to do would be to just ask Barras why he gave her that check." She smiled at me. "He drops into the Catbox Club with some regularity—and I saw on one of those gossip sites that his wife left for Paris to do some shopping this morning...I can pick up a couple of shifts."

"And you think you can get him to talk?"

She looked at me. "It'll be a lot easier than you think." She took another drink of the tea. "All of his ex-wives are blondes who look like they're from Eastern Europe—so is my friend Dixie. All I have to do is transform myself into his type—and I've certainly got the boobs for it." She winked at me. "I have plenty of blond wigs." She started speaking in what could easily pass as an Eastern European accent. "And the day I can't convince a man I am from Eastern Europe, I will eat my wigs, dah-link." She smiled. "*And* it'll give me a chance to use my new recording device." She grinned. "It fits inside a pasty."

"As in a nipple cover?" I stared at her. "Can you get a pasty camera, too?" I shook my head. She was really into gadgets. "Don't tell me, I don't think I want to know."

"Great, I'm so on it." She smiled at me. "Someone who's such a shitty tipper deserves to get screwed over, and then some." She held up a hand to stop me as I started to say something. "Maybe the money *was* a payoff, or an attempt at one. But there's something else really weird about it." She pulled her phone out and touched the screen several times. "Okay, here's the copy of the check you sent me." She turned the phone toward me. I squinted at it.

"Yeah, okay."

She used her fingers to make the picture bigger and adjusted it so that I could see the date. "That check was made out two weeks ago, Chanse. Why would anyone hold on to a check of that size for that long? Does that make sense to you? Wouldn't someone like Mona O'Neill have run straight to the bank with that kind of money?" She scowled. "I think Mona was hanging on to it for a reason—maybe as evidence."

"Evidence?" I nodded. "Yeah, that makes sense. Suppose she *wasn't* trying to drive the price down for Barras—but wanted to prove the whole deal was crooked." The more I thought about it, the more I liked it. "That's the kind of scandal that could make the archbishop back down for sure."

"Which would mean St. Anselm's would get to stay open." She smiled and nodded. "And she gets to be the big hero who saved the church. I like it, boss, I like it a lot. Who wouldn't want to be a hero in front of the whole congregation?"

"And that's a really good reason for both Barras and the archdiocese to want her to just disappear," I mused. "But why pay her off in the first place?" I shrugged. "That's the piece that really doesn't fit. Wouldn't it make more sense to threaten to keep Jonny from fighting?"

The waitress placed our food on the table and refilled our glasses.

I took a bite of my po'boy and almost moaned in pleasure. The Please You's homemade onion rings were far and away the best in New Orleans. I made a puddle of ketchup on my plate and dragged an onion ring through it. "The only person who can explain why she didn't cash it, though, is Mona."

"You don't really think she's still alive, do you?"

I shook my head. "She's been missing for three days, Abby. There's no reason I can think of why anyone would kidnap her. It's not like she's got money for a ransom, or her family. And kidnapping her didn't stop the protests at St. Anselm's, either—if anything, it would mean more negative publicity for the church." I chewed another bite of my po'boy.

Abby nodded. "Leader of church protest disappears."

"And Ed Browning—he's one of the protesters I just met with at the church—he's convinced the archbishop is behind it." I went on, "And I'm sure a lot of people would believe it."

"He's not exactly a popular man in town. And it's not like Archbishop Pugh hasn't been involved in a massive cover-up before."

I stared at her for a moment and closed my eyes. "Let me guess—kids molested by priests?"

"It's almost a cliché, isn't it?" She shook her head, muffling a burp behind her hand. "But yes. Archbishop Pugh was heavily involved in one of those scandals when he was in Baltimore. Two of the priests he covered for were eventually arrested years later, that's why Pugh was moved out of Baltimore and brought here…Pugh paid out a lot of money covering up for those bastards in Baltimore, and they molested God only knows how many other kids after they were reassigned from there." She scowled. "I just don't understand that mentality. Why would the Church cover up for child molesters? I mean, it's disgusting."

"Well, I'm sure they thought they were protecting the Church, and that's the most important thing to them." I frowned. "It's good to know the archbishop has no problem with circumventing the law," I said. "But kidnapping someone?"

Abby shrugged. "It's all a matter of degrees, isn't it? Once you've covered up the crime of child abuse, what's a little kidnapping? Or murder? Or bribery?"

"On the other hand, it could have been just some kind of random crime…but her car wasn't at the church and isn't at her house. And she wasn't there Friday morning when the Brownings showed up to take over the vigil. But she definitely showed up on Thursday night."

"And the police haven't found her car anywhere?" Abby squirted ketchup on a stray piece of fried shrimp before popping it into her mouth.

"Not yet." I kept thinking as I finished my po'boy. I leaned back against the back of the booth, stuffed and feeling dangerously close to exploding. I covered my mouth and belched. "Then again, Delvecchio's not exactly known for his work ethic, so he may not have even filed the plate number." I rubbed my forehead. "So, whoever took her also possibly took her car—and it must have happened while she was at the church." I pulled my notebook out of my pocket and flipped it open. "I need to talk to the guy she was seeing. And I want to talk to her other kids, too—maybe canvass some of the neighbors around the church."

"I'll talk to the neighborhood people." Abby ate the last of her onion rings and washed them down with iced tea. "I'll also work the Barras angle some more, see if I can't dig up some more stuff connecting the two of them. I'll check with the fight promoter at the casino over in Biloxi." She made a face. "I might have to drive over there." Abby's car was a twenty-year-old Oldsmobile that had belonged to her grandmother. It ran like it was new, but when it was parked it looked abandoned. The paint job was leprous, the windshield was cracked, and the driver's side mirror barely hung on to the side.

"Set it up and we can take my car," I replied.

"Excellent. All right, I'm going to get on it." She grabbed her purse and got up, kissed me on the top of my head, and dashed out the door.

She *always* stuck me with the check.

I paid the bill and left a generous tip.

The wind had picked up some, and it was even damper and cooler than it had been on my way to the Please You. The dark clouds were getting closer, and it looked like it was raining over on the West Bank. I walked hurriedly down Polymnia Street and looked for Paige's Toyota. It was a Sunday, and she'd be home if she wasn't over at Ryan's. I didn't see her car, so I kept walking. It had been a while since I'd talked to her, I realized as I crossed Prytania Street and headed for Coliseum Square. She'd gotten serious with Ryan right around the same time she left the paper to be editor-in-chief of *Crescent City* magazine. I missed her—but was glad she'd finally found someone who made her happy.

As I crossed Coliseum Square, I saw Rory's red Mustang parked in front of my apartment building.

I'd met Rory during the course of a previous case. He'd asked me out when the case was over, and despite my initial misgivings, I had said yes. It was going pretty well between us, actually, which had come as a surprise to me. We were very different. Rory came from a very prominent political family—his father had been mayor years ago, and the Delesderniers were still active in city and state politics. Rory frequently worked on political campaigns and often went up to Baton Rouge to lobby state legislators. He was in his mid-twenties and idealistic—he still believed that hard work, elbow grease, and dedication could change the world.

I was a little more cynical than that.

He worked at the NO/AIDS Task Force, out of their satellite office in the Marigny. He was an HIV counselor and ran a program focusing on building a social network outside of the bars for young men between the ages of eighteen and thirty-five. He loved his job—more of that idealism—and was working on getting his master's degree in public health from Tulane University.

Rory and I were comfortable with the way things were—he had his place in the Bywater and I had mine. Every once in a while I wondered if we were going to take our relationship to the next level—which meant moving in together. On paper, it made sense—my rent was ridiculously cheap, and my place was a lot closer to the university campus than his. But we both liked to have our privacy, and the one time it had come up, Rory had said the only thing that made sense was for us to find a two-bedroom place that would be new to both of us.

We agreed to table the discussion, and it hadn't come up again.

I unlocked the front door and grinned. He was sitting on my sofa, the big screen TV turned onto a *Real Housewives of Somewhere* marathon. "Hey, baby." He grinned at me. He wasn't wearing a shirt, and he patted the sofa cushion next to him. "Did you meet with that fighter guy?"

I tossed my keys into a dish on my desk and sat down next to him. "Yeah." Jonny had gone into Rory's office for an HIV test the day before and had unloaded on Rory his worries about his mom. In turn, Rory had given him one of my cards. "I'm on the case." I glanced at the television. Two women Botoxed within an inch of their lives were screaming at each other in a restaurant.

"Sorry, I wish I could just hang out, but I've still got some work to do." I gave him a sad smile. "It shouldn't take too long—if you don't mind hanging out for a few more hours?"

"No worries." He gave me a big grin. "I'll just hang out here—I've got class in the morning." Rory always stayed over on Sunday nights. "You up for Chinese for dinner?"

I kissed his cheek and nodded. "Sounds great."

A few moments later I was heading out the driveway in my dark blue Subaru. According to my notes, Jonny's brother lived in Broadmoor, just before the big curve where Napoleon Avenue turned into Broad Street. I took Martin Luther King to Claiborne and turned left, heading uptown. I turned right again when I got to Napoleon. The house was a few blocks down, just past the corner at Rocheblave. It was a big two-story plantation-style house, with a pair of massive live oaks between the curb and the sidewalk. I parked underneath the first one and shut off the engine. There was a big black Chevy Tahoe with a GEAUX SAINTS bumper sticker parked in the double driveway, in front of a garage. It looked dirty and needed to be washed. The house itself was raised about three feet off the ground, with covered galleries running around the house on both floors. It was painted white, with dark green shutters standing open at every set of windows. The area under the house was fenced in with wooden lattice work, painted green to match the shutters.

I got out of the car and walked up to the front steps. A few drops of rain hit me, and more started coming down as the sun disappeared behind some dark clouds. There was a crack of thunder, and I dashed up to the gallery as a downpour started. Other than cars driving extremely slowly on Napoleon, and the rain, it was weirdly silent. As lightning lit up the sudden gloom, a black cat made a quick getaway down the gallery, darting off a chair and around a corner of the gallery. A loud crack of thunder set off some car alarms in an annoying cacophony.

There were two newspapers on the porch just in front of the screen door, and there was some mail crammed in the black metal box next to the front door. I rang the bell and listened. There was no sound from the inside. I pressed the buzzer again a few times for good measure, but there was still no sound from the inside.

Curious, I pressed my face to the window to the right of the front door and peered through the gloom. No one, apparently, was home—perhaps they were out doing errands. But I didn't want to dash back to the car in the downpour, so I figured what the hell and walked along the gallery, looking in each window as I went. I went around the corner and along the side gallery toward the back. I looked down at the SUV, listening to the steady downpour drumming on its roof. I reached the back corner of the gallery and looked into the backyard. There was a rusty swing set and a sandbox. Multicolored balls of all shapes and sizes were scattered throughout the grass, which was also scarred in places. I walked around the back and noticed the back door was open.

There was another flash of lightning that was so close the hair on my arms stood up, and thunder followed within seconds. More car alarms went off.

I felt a knot form in my stomach. "Hello?" I called inside, reaching for my phone and unlocking it with a swipe of my finger. I debated getting my gun out of the car—but decided there wasn't a need. The house was too quiet—whatever was wrong here, there wasn't anyone around that I needed to worry about.

Besides, I'd get soaked to the skin.

I walked over to the back door and nudged it with my toe. The door swung open, and I stepped over the threshold and found myself in a hallway. The door to my immediate right looked to be a utility room—washer, dryer, and a deep utility sink. There was a huge hot water heater in the far corner. To the left was a door to the kitchen. I stepped into the kitchen, calling "Hello" again as I went.

The kitchen had probably been rather nice at one point, but it was so filthy it was hard to tell. There was an island with a butcher block top in the center of the room, and it was covered with food wrappers, empty plastic bottles, and dirty dishes. Pots and pans hung from a chain suspended from the ceiling above it, and the double sink was also filled with dirty dishes. The coffeepot was half-full, and some bananas had turned black on the counter. There was a small pot on the stove with a couple of hot dogs floating in greasy water.

I took a deep breath and debated going back outside and just calling the police.

Something was definitely off here.

Instead, I walked back into the hallway. Rather than going out the back door, I headed toward the front of the house. The door on my right opened into a large bathroom with a walk-in shower and one of those fancy sinks that cost a ridiculous amount of money. The next door on the left looked like a den of some sort. There was a desk facing the door with a computer on it, and bookshelves had been built into the back wall. I could see flies buzzing around in the air, and I could smell death.

I could see a pair of loafers sticking out from behind the right side of the desk.

I took a deep breath and took a few cautious steps into the room. I got about halfway into the room and peered over the top of the desk.

The man lying there had apparently been shot twice in the

chest. The desk chair was lying beside him. He'd been sitting down when he'd been shot. His shirt was soaked in blood, and he was lying in a sticky puddle of dark red. I felt my gorge rising and fought it back down.

I forced myself to look at the face.

He was older—and apparently hadn't exactly aged well, but I recognized Jonny's older brother from the senior picture on his mother's living room wall.

He'd been dead for a while.

I walked back outside to the gallery, took a few deep breaths, and called Venus.

Chapter Five

Y ou got in late last night."

I yawned and poured myself a cup of coffee. "Sorry," I said, trying not to yawn a second time. I shook my head to try to get some blood flowing into my brain.

It was just after nine in the morning, and I hadn't slept particularly well, which was my normal reaction to finding a dead body. I'd decided long ago that the day when finding one didn't unsettle me on some level was the day I would find another line of work. It had been around two in the morning when I finally made it home, and I'd smoked a joint to relax and help me sleep. It was just after three when I finally fell into bed.

I stifled another yawn. "Yeah, I just figured it was easier to go down to the police station and give my statement last night so I wouldn't have to do it today." I added creamer and sweetener to my coffee and took a long drink. "I didn't want to wake you when I got home—you were in a deep sleep." I flashed a tired smile at him.

Rory had already showered and his bluish black hair was still damp. He was dressed for work in a tight olive green AIDS Walk T-shirt and a pair of jean shorts. He spread peanut butter on an English muffin and looked at me out of the corner of his eyes. "You okay?" he asked in a careful tone.

I took another swig of the coffee. "All things considered, yeah. I'm just really tired, I didn't sleep all that great." I gave him my best effort at a smile. "Besides, it's not like it was my first time finding a dead body."

He visibly winced before he carried his coffee and English muffin into the living room. He sat down on the couch, taking a bite from the muffin. "I know it's not, but you know if you need to talk about it..." He let his voice trail off.

I followed him in, sitting down at my desk and turning on my computer. "Really, I'm fine," I insisted. I swiveled around in my desk chair as the computer sprang to life and gave him a real smile this time. "But I appreciate it. Really."

One of the biggest issues we'd faced since we started dating was his job. He was a trained HIV counselor, and his undergraduate degree was in social work. I didn't believe in "processing my feelings"—it all just seemed a little silly to me. I hadn't been raised to sit and stare at my navel while getting in touch with myself. The few times we'd had arguments was when I felt like he wasn't treating me like his boyfriend, but rather like one of his counseling clients. I found myself biting my tongue a lot because I didn't want to hurt his feelings, or escalate a situation to DEFCON 5.

The constant reassurances that he was "available" for me if I ever needed to "process" my feelings or just needed a shoulder to cry on got on my nerves, frankly.

It's not that I didn't appreciate it—I just didn't think it was necessary for him to remind me all the time.

As I'd yelled at him once during an argument, "If I need you to shrink my goddamned head, *I'll fucking tell you!*"

He started to say something, but finished eating the muffin instead and smiled at me. He stood up, brushing the crumbs off his jean shorts. "Okay, well, I'm off to the office." He leaned over and kissed the top of my head. "I've got that work party tonight, remember—you're more than welcome to come if you want."

"Thanks, but I'll probably be working."

"If you change your mind, we're all meeting at the Bridge Lounge at seven. It would be great if you could make it—everyone would love to see you." Unspoken were the words *since you didn't go to my supervisor's birthday celebration two weeks ago.*

I turned back to my computer. "Bridge Lounge at seven. Got it."

I heard the front door shut behind him. I sighed and stretched in my chair. I finished drinking the coffee and went back into the kitchen for a refill. *He does make good coffee,* I thought, taking another sip. It wouldn't kill me, I reflected, to stop by the Bridge Lounge for a drink or two with his coworkers. I'd already met most of them, and they all seemed like pretty decent people. They certainly did good work for low pay.

Unless something comes up, I'll do it.

Congratulating myself for being such a good boyfriend, I sat back down at my computer. My mind was still foggy, so I paid my bills while I waited for the caffeine to push the cobwebs aside and jump-start my mind. Once I was finished with that, I checked my e-mail—nothing new or interesting there.

I opened my notepad and opened a new document, and copied all the notes I'd taken so far into it, hoping that doing this mindless task might trigger something in my mind. I saved it under the file name O'NEILL and reread it all one more time.

Nothing jumped to mind, so I got another cup of coffee and sat down on the sofa.

Okay, Chanse, think.

Robby O'Neill had been dead for at least forty-eight hours, give or take, when I'd found him. So he'd been killed sometime on Friday, maybe late Thursday night. The last time anyone had seen his mother was late Thursday night. There was no doubt in my mind that if Mona O'Neill was still alive, she'd disappeared on purpose. But why would she disappear, with her daughter-in-law so close to giving birth? If Mona had voluntarily gone into hiding, the reason had to be pretty extreme—she had to be afraid either for her own life or that of someone who was really important to her. Maybe she'd seen who killed her son?

Maybe she'd killed Robby and gone on the run.

It was possible, but I discarded that option. Mothers don't, as a rule, kill their adult children.

One thing was for sure—I was pretty sure none of this had anything to do with the archdiocese, other than peripherally. This wasn't the Middle Ages—I seriously doubted the Catholic Church was killing people because they were opposed to closing a couple of churches down.

No, I was pretty sure the O'Neill situations were one and the same. It was the only thing that made sense.

One of the reasons I'd decided to head down to the police station and give my statement last night was because I'd given Venus Jonny's number. She'd called and arranged to have Jonny come down to the morgue and identify the body, and I'd wanted to talk to him myself.

Jonny was clearly shaken up. His eyes were red, his face pale, and his hands were shaking when he came out of the morgue. "Come on, let's head down to the Carousel Bar for a drink," I'd suggested, even though I knew he wasn't yet old enough to drink. "You don't look like you're ready to head home yet anyway."

"I got a fake ID," he replied in a monotone as I led him out of the police station and turned left on Royal Street.

"I'll pretend I didn't hear that," I replied with a smile. He hadn't said another word until we walked up the steps into the Monteleone Hotel and sat down in a dark booth in the Carousel Bar.

The cocktail waitress barely glanced at his fake ID, and I figured it wasn't my problem. We both ordered beers, and Jonny started talking in a low voice.

He didn't really tell me a whole lot. He and Robby hadn't been close—they barely spoke or saw each other outside of family get-togethers and holidays, "and Robby didn't really come to those if he could help it. Ma says since he married Celia he thinks he's too good for the rest of us. She was a Queen of Rex or something." Jonny had shrugged. "Whatever."

Jonny did know that his brother's wife and kids were at a

beach house in Sandestin, Florida, which belonged to her sister. "Ma wasn't real happy about that, because the kids were gone for the summer, and of course Robby would never invite any of us over to the beach—he never does." Robby had been in the habit of driving over to Florida Fridays after work, and driving back to New Orleans late on Sunday nights. Jonny had called his sister Lorelle before coming to the police station and asked her to get a hold of his sister-in-law. "I don't have her cell or nothing." Lorelle had called him back and told him Robby had called his wife on Thursday morning and told her that he wasn't able to make it over this particular weekend, that something business-related had come up, "but he would definitely drive over on Monday and stay the week. Lorelle said Celia said it sounded like it was something important, and he was all excited about it. Celia said she was going to let the kids sleep and head back over here tomorrow. I told Lorelle to tell her if she wanted to stay at Ma's it was fine with me." Jonny had shrugged and finished his beer. "Lorelle asked if you could come out and talk to her tomorrow. She said she really wants to talk to you about all this. She's pretty upset."

I'd said sure, and he'd given me her address and phone number.

That was all he knew, but he was still upset, and not really in the mood to head back home yet. I hung out with him and kept him company over another beer before putting him in a cab and sending him home.

I hadn't come up with anything, and finally had come home around one in the morning to find Rory sound asleep.

I glanced at my watch. Sandestin was about a four- or five-hour drive—and it was just now ten o'clock. I doubted she'd gotten up early with the kids—Jonny said they'd had three and the youngest was around four—and packed everything up to head back to New Orleans. I decided to check around noon to see if they'd arrived back in town.

I printed out the notes from the computer and reread them several times, but still nothing really jumped out at me.

It *was* possible that the whole thing was simply a coincidence, but I wasn't a big believer in coincidence.

Mona O'Neill was last seen on Thursday night around ten o'clock; her eldest son was shot to death either that night or the next day.

No—I shook my head—there had to be a connection.

I walked into the kitchen and turned off the coffeemaker. I wasn't getting anywhere, so maybe a visit to Lorelle O'Neill Nesbitt was in order.

I took a shower and got dressed.

The sister, Lorelle, lived just over the parish line in Old Metairie, just off Metairie Road. I took I-10 out there and exited at City Park/Metairie Road, turning left and driving under the highway. Old Metairie was the only part of Jefferson Parish where New Orleans snobs would consider living, and it was easy to see why. With the massive trees, graceful houses, and lush green lawns, it looked as though Uptown had somehow been magically transported over the parish line. I found the street the Nesbitts lived on and turned left. Their big house was about halfway down the block—a graceful two-story plantation style house built out of red brick with large white columns. The large lawn was immaculate, almost completely shaded by the massive trees. There was a beige Volvo parked in the driveway. I parked at the curb, walked up the driveway, and rang the doorbell.

Lorelle O'Neill Nesbitt had, unlike her late brother, aged rather gracefully. There were some lines around her eyes and the corners of her mouth, but her chestnut brown hair was free of gray and was cut short in a pageboy style that framed her round face, giving it depth. She was wearing a pair of purple LSU sweatpants and a white T-shirt. Her eyes were red from crying or lack of sleep (or maybe both) and she was wearing very little makeup. She looked a little harried. "Yes?" She gave me a weak smile. "May I help you?"

"I'm sorry for not calling first, Mrs. Nesbitt, but my name is Chanse MacLeod—"

"You're the detective Jonny hired," she cut me off, nodding. She stepped aside and gestured with her left hand. "Do come in, I'm having some coffee in the kitchen, and you're certainly more than welcome to join me if you like."

The living room the front door opened into was tastefully furnished and enormous. A huge television set dominated one side of the room—two boys were lying in front of it playing some kind of video game that apparently required shooting people and blowing things up. There were large lamps, a long couch, and several reclining chairs scattered about the room with end tables arranged around them. The walls were devoid of any kind of artwork or even family photographs. The boys didn't look up as I followed her through the room into a large, well-lit chef's kitchen Rory would have cheerfully killed for. She poured me a cup of coffee and directed me to sit at the island. I sat on a large bar stool and sipped the coffee. It was really good. "I'm really sorry to bother you at a time like this," I said, putting the coffee down. "Do you mind answering some questions?"

She made a small, defeated gesture. "Now's as good a time as any," she said. "My mother's disappeared and my brother's been murdered—when would be a good time to talk about it?" She gave me an ironic smile, slightly amused, and I liked her better for it. "Besides, my husband's at his office. I kept the boys home—they were supposed to go over to a friend's for the day, but as you can see"—she gestured back toward the living room—"it's not like they're taking their uncle's death particularly hard." She glanced over at the clock. "And one of the other moms is taking them to baseball practice later on. I wasn't going to let them go—but what's the point? I might as well get them out of here and let them have some exercise—at least that's something." She looked at me. "It's not like they were close to their uncle or anything. Hell, he was my brother and we weren't particularly close, for that matter. We've barely spoken in years." She rubbed her eyes. "I guess I'll have to get used to talking about him in the past tense." She looked at me.

"We were close when we were kids, but we drifted apart after Dad died." She shrugged. "I guess it's normal—we had our own lives to lead, but I wish we could have stayed close, you know?"

"What exactly happened to your father? Jonny mentioned he was killed on the job, but didn't really go into a lot of detail about it." I took out my notepad and uncapped a pen.

"Well, he was barely a year old when it happened, so he never really knew much about it. It wasn't something Mom liked to talk about, understandably." She stared into her coffee cup. "Dad worked at the docks, for Verlaine Shipping. He was a longshoreman—he'd worked there since he was a teenager. He was helping load some really heavy machinery when one of the cables broke and he was crushed to death. It was a closed casket funeral." She looked out the window. "I was in my junior year at Sacred Heart. Mom pulled me out of class that day. I'll never forget it. She was crushed, just crushed. But the Verlaines were very good to us."

I was all too familiar with the Verlaine family of Verlaine Shipping. I'd done some work for them around the time of Hurricane Katrina, and it wasn't a fond memory for me. They had believed their money put them above the law—and for the most part, they'd been right. Percy Verlaine, the family patriarch, had been rotten through and through—and while I'd never been able to prove it, I believed he'd had his own son-in-law murdered. He'd certainly had his niece locked away in a mental hospital for over thirty years. But he'd died—heart failure—and the only surviving Verlaine was his youngest son, Darrin. I'd heard somewhere he'd sold the company and left New Orleans.

Good riddance.

"It was like the whole world had turned upside down," she went on. "There was life insurance, of course, and there was some other kind of insurance—I don't know what all, but the company also gave Mom an awful lot of money. I don't know how much it all came out to, but I know she paid off the house, set up college accounts for all of us—we might not have been able to go to college if not for Percy Verlaine. Well, we would have, but it would have been a lot harder. I would have had to work my way through, and thanks to them, I could just focus on my schoolwork." She got up and refilled our cups. "Jonny didn't go to college, of course. He flunked out of de la Salle, and Mom gave him the money to buy that terrible little house for him and that awful girl he married."

I hadn't exactly been a big fan of Heather myself, but I was getting a little tired of everyone running her down. "What exactly is the problem with her? Jonny mentioned that your mother had an issue with her, too."

"Jonny's not exactly the sharpest knife in the drawer, Mr. MacLeod. He's a very sweet boy, but he's really not terribly smart. He thinks he is, of course, but some of the scrapes he's gotten himself into—Mom had the patience of a saint. I don't know what I'd do if one of my boys turned out like him, but I wouldn't be as forgiving as Mom, I can tell you that." She sat back down, stirring sugar into her coffee. "Mom spoiled him, maybe babied him a bit much, who knows? But he was her baby, and there was a big age difference between him and me and Robby, you know, and then Dad died, and so Mom had to raise him on her own…and Robby and I were both out of the house in a couple of years, so it was just the two of them. He was never much of a student, was always on the edge of flunking out. Then he got into this fighting thing." She shook her head. "I went once, you know—it was horrible. I didn't want to, but Mom said I needed to support Jonny." She closed her eyes. "I'll never go again—and I don't care how much money Jonny can make doing it, or if he becomes a world champion or whatever. I won't go, and I won't watch it on television. It was so—animalistic and brutal." She shivered, wrapping her arms around herself. "Why would anyone want to do that? Get paid to be violent? I don't understand it—it was like something out of ancient Rome. The crowd was screaming for blood, it was horrible." She said the last in a whisper.

"What does that have to do with Heather? He was fighting before he met her, wasn't he?"

"Yes, well, you know he only married her because she was pregnant." She made a face. "Yeah, Mom told me she was just some groupie who had a thing for fighters, she used to go with another one of them, and she hooked up with Jonny when the other guy wouldn't marry her. She's just trash, and she got pregnant and he married her and Mom bought that house with his college fund. I tried to talk him out of it, tried to talk Mom out of buying that house—that horrible little house, have you seen it? But Jonny won't listen to anyone. Try to tell him he's wrong—he's so damned stubborn and used to getting his own way." She sighed. "Jonny, I guess, has a lot of potential. The promoters think he can be a world champion or something, I don't know, but he supposedly can go far, make a lot of money doing it. I didn't want to know anything about it, like I said, it was just too barbaric for me, you know? Mom talked about it a lot, but I'll be honest, I didn't listen. When she would tell me about it, all I could think about was my baby brother getting all of his teeth knocked out or his brain scrambled. Mom was supportive of it all."

"What about your brother? You said you two weren't close anymore. Was he supportive of Jonny's fighting?"

"They always say you're not supposed to speak ill of the dead." She got up and refilled my coffee cup. "Well, I've always thought that was stupid, you know? Like dying changes the fact that Robby was an asshole while he was alive? And that wife of his." She wrapped her arms around herself. "Robby and Celia both thought—I don't know, maybe I shouldn't say." She started drumming her fingernails on the table. "Look, it's not like I didn't do my research into all of this, you know. When Jonny started fighting, I looked into it all. I'm not stupid." She ran a hand through her hair. "It's not like boxing, you know, where someone can make millions. These guys—the top guys might make six figures, but the majority of them don't make shit. They risk their bodies, risk brain injury, and for what? I don't get it. But Robby—Robby thought Jonny could be a star, a champion, one of the big-money fighters. That asshole Morgan Barras sold Mom and Robby and Jonny all a line of bull."

"Morgan Barras? The billionaire?"

She made a face. "Yeah. I don't know, I didn't want anything to do with it, you know? Maybe they didn't care if Jonny's brains got scrambled, but I did."

I pulled out my copy of the cashier's check from Morgan Barras. "So, could this check have been a down payment of sorts?"

She raised her eyebrows. "Maybe."

"Why do you think your mother has disappeared?"

"You know, I thought Jonny was overreacting when he called me on Friday morning. I just figured it had something to do with the church. She just couldn't let St. Anselm's go. I don't understand it, never could—I'm lapsed Catholic myself—I send the boys to Country Day." She made another face. "Mom wasn't too happy about that, but what good did Sacred Heart do for me? I mean, really. Country Day is a better school, and they don't try to brainwash the kids there like the Catholic schools do."

"Did your mother seem worried, or concerned, the last time you talked to her?"

"I talked to her last Thursday morning. She was supposed to come over that morning when she was finished with her stupid vigil, but she called and canceled. She was really pissed about the church, and the arrests the day before." She got up and started another pot of coffee. "But if you want to know what I believed, I thought she was focusing on the church because she was really stressed about the lawsuit."

"What lawsuit?" I stared at her. "I haven't heard anything about a lawsuit."

She sat back down, with a sigh. "Jonny didn't say anything to you about it?" She rolled her eyes. "After Dad was killed, Mom stayed home with Jonny until he started school. Once he was in school, she took a job with Marino Properties. She was a property manager for an apartment complex they owned on the West Bank somewhere. Cypress Gardens, or something like that."

"I thought property managers had to live on the premises."

She shook her head. "No, she had an office there, and was on call. There was a maintenance guy who lived on the property. The place was pretty much uninhabitable after Katrina."

"But the West Bank didn't flood."

"Wind damage, is what Marino Properties was claiming. Roof damage, windows blown out, that kind of thing. The insurance company claims there was only about fifty grand or so that was caused by the hurricane—that Marino Properties is trying to collect millions fraudulently. Mom was going to be a star witness for Marino Properties. She didn't evacuate, and as soon as she was able, she got over there and looked the place over. Went through every unit, took pictures and everything. The trial is going to start in about a month or so, I think."

I stared at her. "Seriously? An insurance company is going to actually allow a Katrina claim dispute to go to court in Orleans Parish?"

That was so astoundingly stupid I couldn't believe it. There were very few things New Orleanians agreed on: the Saints, and a hatred for insurance companies and everyone who worked for them.

"Yeah, Mom thought the insurance company was trying to ruin Marino Properties—that eventually they'd run out of money or something and would have to drop the suit. You know how insurance companies are complete and total scum of the earth." She laughed. "But the firm representing them was willing to do it for a percentage of the final settlement."

"What firm?"

"McKeithen, Fontenot, and Drake."

I kept my face expressionless. I had dealt with Loren McKeithen before; he was an excellent lawyer whose devotion to his clients meant people who weren't his clients couldn't trust him. He was also gay, and worked hard for gay rights in Louisiana—which was pretty much a lost cause. "Do you think your mother's disappearance might have had something to do with this lawsuit?"

She shrugged. "I don't see how—insurance companies are scum of the earth, but I doubt even they would go that far. And I can't believe they'd go so far as to kill."

"How much money are we talking about?"

"I think twenty million, is what Mom said."

I whistled. Twenty million dollars was an awful lot of money. "Who was the insurance carrier?"

"Some local brokerage put the package together—but the main carrier was Global, I think." She gave me a rueful smile. "I really didn't pay a lot of attention when Mom talked about it—and she didn't really talk about it that much. But I know she wasn't looking forward to going to court, and having to testify, and all that. But she did think Global was trying to cheat Mr. Marino."

"Did your brother have any enemies?"

"Like I told you, we haven't been close in years."

I got out one of my business cards and handed it to her. "If you can think of anything else, give me a call."

She walked me to the front door. "Do you think there's a chance she might still be alive?"

"There's always a chance," I admitted. "But I don't hold out a lot of hope, to be honest."

She nodded. "That's what I figured." She wiped at her eyes and closed the door.

I got in my car and called Abby. "See what you can find out about a lawsuit—Marino Properties v. Global Insurance." I filled her in on everything Lorelle had told me.

Abby whistled. "Insurance companies are bottom-feeding bastards," she commented. "They won't pay out unless you put a gun to their fucking heads. I'll bet you they took her to keep her from testifying."

"Abby, there wouldn't be any point. I'm sure she's given depositions. If she disappears or is killed or whatever, I'm sure they could have the depositions read into the court records."

"I'm getting a law degree, remember?" I could almost see the look on her face. "And a statement doesn't carry nearly as much weight with jurors as someone testifying in front of them—that's Basic Courtroom 101, Chanse. Having that deposition read into the record? They don't listen. Making them read it themselves? That won't fly." She sighed. "Jurors like to watch the person testify, see them be cross-examined, make up their own minds if the witness is lying or not. A deposition—especially if it's from a key witness—well, the opposing lawyers can have a field day with that, you know, and can pretty much put enough doubt on the veracity of the deposition to make the jury disregard it almost entirely—and it's just the kind of thing an insurance company would do."

I chose not to argue with her. Abby's hatred of insurance companies bordered on the pathological. I couldn't blame her—no one with a heart could. Her family home down in Plaquemines Parish had been destroyed by the Katrina storm surge. The hurricane insurance policy refused to pay out because it was flood damage. The flood insurance company refused to pay out because the flood was caused by the hurricane. The battle had gone on for years—was still going on, in fact.

To Abby, the only good insurance company was a dead one.

I also strongly suspected the reason she wanted to become a lawyer was partly based in her family's experience—and wanting to destroy every insurance company she could.

"Just find out the particulars of the case," I said. "Have you turned up anything on Robby O'Neill yet?"

"Jephtha's not quite done yet, but I can tell you one thing—Mr. Robby and his family were living pretty damned high on the hog," she replied. "I mean, he worked as an investments counselor—but from everything I'm seeing so far, I don't see how he could have possibly afforded the high life he was living. The mortgage on the house alone was ridiculously high—and there was a second mortgage, too."

"Well, e-mail it all to me when it's ready, and get on the lawsuit, see what you can dig up," I told her, disconnecting the call.

I started the car and put it into gear.

Chapter Six

"Thanks for agreeing to see me," Loren McKeithen said, sitting down on my sofa and placing his black leather briefcase on my coffee table, "especially on such short notice." He beamed at me, exposing his perfectly straight, bleached teeth. "It's good to see you, Chanse—it's really been a while, hasn't it? I trust all is well with you?"

I didn't say anything. I simply nodded and sat down in my desk chair, swiveling it around so that I was facing him. I leaned back, folded my arms, and waited to hear what he wanted.

He'd called my cell phone on my way back into the city from Lorelle's, asking if he could meet with me as soon as it was convenient for me, but emphasizing *soon.* And much as I wanted to go question Mona's boyfriend, I decided to put that off and agreed to meet with him at my apartment.

He never called unless he wanted something—and I was curious to find out what it was.

Loren McKeithen was one of the top attorneys in New Orleans, according to *Crescent City* magazine, and much as I was loath to admit it, would be the man I would hire if I ever needed a lawyer. He was a partner in McKeithen, Fontenot, and Drake, one of the most successful and well-known firms in New Orleans, with a gorgeous suite of offices in One Shell Square in the Central Business District. He was a gay man of mixed race, with toffee-colored skin, a shaved head that looked polished, and golden brown eyes behind gold-framed glasses. He was short, maybe five-four or five-five on a good day, and over the course of the years I'd known him, had become rather corpulent with an ever-expanding waistline.

I'd first met him at a gay rights fund-raiser many years ago—Loren had been an activist while in law school at Tulane, and as soon as he passed the bar he amped up his work for gay equality. He was an active member of the Louisiana Stonewall Democrats and was also heavily involved in the state party. He always generously opened his checkbook whenever he was asked, served on the boards of several gay organizations in the city, and was politically well connected. He frequently drove up to Baton Rouge to lobby for legislation designed to drag Louisiana out of the Middle Ages, which was often, he would say with a sad shake of his head, a fool's errand. He was also a damned good lawyer. His first priority was whatever was best for his clients—and anyone who got in the way could, and did, get screwed. Loren and I had a precarious relationship—it's hard to be friends or work with someone you can't trust. He used to throw some work my way whenever he could, but after a case where he'd cheerfully thrown me under the bus because it was in his client's best interest, we were finished. Since then, I kept my distance and never accepted any of his referrals or offers of employment.

My first instinct when he'd called was to tell him to go to hell and hang up. But he'd been so insistent he'd piqued my curiosity, so I figured what the hell.

I crossed my legs and watched him through narrowed eyes, not saying a word as he removed a bottle of rather expensive vodka from his briefcase. I resisted the urge to grin and kept my face impassive as he opened the bottle.

Back before he fucked me over, this had been a regular routine of ours. Loren was a big vodka drinker, but always complained I only had "rotgut" in my place. So he always would bring over an expensive bottle of vodka in his briefcase, and we'd have a drink or two while we talked over the particulars of a case. He never took the bottle with him when he left—yet always brought a fresh bottle the next time he came over. Vodka wasn't my drink of choice, so I'd accumulated quite a few of the large bottles.

He removed the cap and looked at me, raising his eyebrows. I resisted the urge to roll my eyes. Instead, I got up and walked into the kitchen, filled a glass with ice, and placed it down in front of him on the coffee table.

"You're not going to join me?" he asked, his voice sounding small and more than a little hurt.

"I'm on a case, Loren," I replied. "Unlike you, I can't function properly after having a drink or two—and I have to drive Uptown and interview a witness when we're finished here—a witness I should be interviewing right now, actually. So, tell me—what's so damned important it couldn't wait another day?"

He shook his head sadly as he opened the bottle and poured a couple of fingers of vodka over the ice. "You're sure this isn't sour grapes over—"

I cut him off. "The past is the past. Get to the point, Loren."

He looked at me again, his eyes narrowing to slits. He clutched both of his pudgy hands to his heart. "You wound me to my very soul, Chanse." He picked up his glass, toasted me, and took a sip, letting out a sigh of satisfaction. "There's absolutely nothing like a good Russian vodka over ice, is there?" He set the glass back down and reached into his briefcase again. He pulled out a file folder and opened it. He handed me a check, drawn on the firm's account.

It was for twenty thousand dollars. On the memo line was printed: *Marino Case.*

I kept my face impassive and set it back down on the coffee table. "That's a big check, Loren. What exactly do you want that you're willing to pay so much money for? What's the Marino case?"

"Now, now, we actually are both after the same thing this time, Chanse." He leaned back on the sofa, watching me carefully. He was still smiling, his tone was light and pleasant, but his eyes were hard, glittering like dark marbles. "And you can't tell me Jonny O'Neill can afford your day rate—and if he can, he should be saving the money for when the baby comes—which can be any day now, am I right?" The corners of his mouth twitched a little.

My heart started racing, but I denied him the pleasure of a startled reaction. "Are you telling me that you're looking for Mona O'Neill, too?" Now I allowed myself to smile. "Isn't that interesting? Hmmm. Now, why on earth would a lawyer in a three-thousand-dollar suit be interested in Mona O'Neill?" I tapped my index finger against my forehead. "And be willing to pay me a whole lot of money to find her?"

His smile broadened. "Chance, I know you're one of the best damned private eyes in New Orleans, or I wouldn't be here wasting my time or my money." He shrugged. "You know me—I've always believed that the best are worth any price."

"I'm flattered," I deadpanned, crossing my arms over my chest again. "I can't tell you how much that means to me."

This time, he threw his head back and laughed. "Damn." He wiped at his eyes and reached for his vodka. He finished it and refilled the glass. "I really have missed working with you."

"Wish I could say the same."

"I don't blame you for not trusting me—you shouldn't." He took another sip of the vodka. "Never trust a lawyer who isn't working for *you*."

"I'll keep that in mind."

"There's a lot going on you don't know." He spread his arms in a magnanimous gesture. "I'm here to save you some time—no sense in letting you go barking up the wrong tree, is there? And it's in my client's best interest that you find Mona O'Neill, and fast." His eyes glinted.

"What is your interest—rather, your client's interest—in a retired Irish Channel widow? Are you working for the archdiocese?"

He erupted in laughter. I waited until he got hold of himself, and repeated the question.

"No, Chance, I'm not working for the archbishop. I could give a shit about St. Anselm's. No one's paying me to give a shit." He took another swig of the vodka. "But you've only been on this case for a day at most. I know you're the one who found Robby O'Neill's body last night, and I know you were just out in old Metairie talking to Mona's daughter, Lorelle."

"Got someone watching their houses, Loren?" I kept my face impassive and my tone jocular. "Did your guy see who killed Robby O'Neill, by any chance? That would make Venus and Blaine's lives a lot easier, you know."

"No, I don't know anything about who killed Robby O'Neill." Loren sighed and finished the vodka. He picked up the bottle to refill the glass again, but thought better of it and put the bottle back down again, putting the cap back on. "Mona O'Neill, on the other hand, is a damned important witness to a case my firm is pursuing. Maybe even the most important witness, and so whatever goes on with anyone in her immediate family is of interest to us." Loren leaned forward. "Since I've worked with you before, the lead attorney on the case—my partner, Jim Drake, I think you may have met him— thought it was best if I met with you to discuss you coming on board and working for us."

"Seriously?" I laughed—it really was funny. "Your partners actually think that you and I have a great working relationship? What kind of bullshit do you tell your partners, Loren?" I shook my head. "All due respect, Loren, but I'd be a hell of lot more likely to trust a complete stranger than you."

"You are still holding a grudge. After all these years?" Loren shook his head, running a hand over his shining bald head. "You really wound me, Chanse. You know that wasn't personal, don't you? It was business. I had to do what was best—"

"I know, I know." I rolled my eyes. "You always have to do what's best for your client, even if it means fucking over a friend."

"That's my job! If you will recall, Chanse, I warned you to get your own lawyer, didn't I? I could have not said a damned word, you know. I did what I could for you. It wouldn't have been ethical for me to do anything more than that."

"It was ethical for you to take the heat off your client by pinning a murder rap on me?" I felt myself starting to get angry all over again, and forced myself to stay calm. "Is that what they teach you at Tulane Law, Loren?"

"I always do what is best for my client, Chanse. If that makes me a bad person, so be it. I can live with it." He leaned back on the couch. "But for what it's worth, I am sorry."

"Yeah, well, I appreciate that." I narrowed my own eyes. "But what makes you think I'd be willing to go to work for you again?"

"The devil you know."

In spite of myself, I laughed.

Loren smiled. "Look, that's a twenty-thousand-dollar check on the coffee table. Don't you want to know why I'm here? At least hear me out." He held up his hands. "If you listen to what I have to say and you're still not interested, then I will grab my check and walk out of here—and leave this fine, expensive bottle of vodka behind, for your time and trouble. Fair enough?"

"Fair enough."

"You know anything about the Cypress Garden complex?"

"Lorelle told me that's where her mother worked before Katrina." I shrugged. "Before that, I never heard of the place, and all I know is the place was damaged in the storm and Mona didn't go back to work afterward."

"Ah, there's so much more to it than that." He steepled his fingers together in front of his chest and gave me a satisfied smile. "Then sit back, relax, and I will tell you a sordid tale of corporate greed." He peered at me over the top of his glasses. "You played football at LSU, didn't you?"

"Yup, full scholarship, lettered three years, started as a senior." I nodded. It had been my ticket out of Cottonwood Wells, Texas— and the trailer park where I'd grown up. I'd never looked back once I drove east on I-10.

"So you know the name Luke Marino?"

"Luke Marino?" I started laughing. "Seriously, Loren, I'm not deaf, dumb, and blind. Who in Louisiana hasn't heard of Luke Marino?"

Luke Marino was a senior when I was a freshman and had been

elected one of the team captains. A graduate of Jesuit High School in New Orleans, he'd been starting since he was a sophomore. His senior year we won the Southeastern Conference, primarily behind his running, and had gone to the Sugar Bowl where we kicked the crap out of Penn State. When we needed short yardage, he was our go-to guy. Luke Marino had been King of LSU that year. His picture was all over the state newspapers, he was always being interviewed on the news, and replicas of his jersey had been the biggest selling LSU jersey that year.

Hell, even I'd bought one of them.

I didn't really know him all that well—freshman tight ends and senior running backs didn't really mix all that much. But he always seemed like a good guy, always had a smile on his face, and always had something nice to say to anyone. We'd probably never exchanged more than three sentences together the entire time we'd both been on the team together. But he'd been good-looking, had an amazing body, and I'd always had a bit of crush on him. His girlfriend had been one of the Golden Girls—the girls who performed with the band in little more than a gold-sequined bodysuit and long white gloves. I couldn't remember her name, but she'd been blond and one of the most beautiful girls I'd ever seen. Luke and his girlfriend really were the epitome of the stereotype of the Big Man on Campus and his Homecoming Queen.

He'd been drafted by San Diego after his senior year, but had only lasted two years in the pros before an injury ended his career. He'd come back to New Orleans. His family lived Uptown and owned a couple of restaurants around the city. Marino's on Magazine Street was probably the best known of them. I'd eaten there once—they had killer lasagna.

"Luke invested most of the money he made as a pro player in an apartment complex on the West Bank called Cypress Gardens when he came back to New Orleans in the late nineties." Loren went on. "It wasn't *all* his money, of course—he took out some bank loans he was able to get based on his last name, and I think his parents loaned him some as well, but he paid them back fairly quickly once the place was open. It was a pretty nice place, Chanse—nice big apartments for middle- to low-income families. Cypress Garden wasn't his only investment, of course, but it was his primary, where most of his income came from. He was a pretty good businessman, turned out. Within a few years of opening the place, he'd paid off his loans and owned the place free and clear. There was some Section 8 housing, so he had some city and state contracts, but for the most part it was nice, clean affordable housing for working-class people. About ten years ago, he hired Mona O'Neill to run the place for him as property manager. Mona worked hard, and Luke trusted her. She was like a member of the family to Luke and his wife—she even watched their kids sometimes."

"So?" I shrugged. "Does this heartwarming story have a point?"

"So, a few years back a one-eyed bitch named Katrina came to town." Loren's eyes glittered. "And Cypress Gardens sustained some pretty heavy damage—to the point where the majority of the apartments weren't livable."

"The West Bank didn't flood—so it was wind damage?"

"Wind damage, yes—but just because there was no flooding didn't mean there wasn't any water damage, either." Loren took his glasses off and rubbed his eyes. "Several roofs came off the complex—a lot of windows were blown out and there was a lot of rainwater damage. You remember what it was like, right? No power over there, windows blown out, water got in, with all the heat and humidity of late summer. The mold got everywhere—in the a/c and heating vents and ducts, the walls, ceilings, and floors were all covered with it in almost every unit. The place wasn't truly habitable after Katrina. Luke, of course, immediately put in a claim with his insurance company—Global Insurance—and he was insured to the teeth for everything—wind damage, water damage, loss of revenue—Luke was really smart when it came to buying coverage. And so the insurance company sent some inspectors out."

I had a feeling I knew where this was going.

"The claims investigators didn't check out anything. They

didn't go up on any roofs of any of the buildings—there were ten buildings total—and they only checked out a few apartments, all on the first floor, you know, where they could get access because they didn't try to get a hold of anyone to meet them and show them around, anyone with keys. The Marinos—Luke and his family, his parents, siblings, the entire family—they all evacuated to Houston, so they weren't here. Mona, however, didn't evacuate. She stayed in New Orleans and rode out the storm and the aftermath here."

"But she couldn't get over to the West Bank, could she? Didn't the cops have the bridge blocked off to keep people from leaving New Orleans?" I closed my eyes. I'd heard lots of horror stories about people trying to evacuate over the bridge, only to be turned back by armed cops on the other side.

"Oh, she was over there, all right. She was over there before the insurance inspectors were." Loren refilled his glass with vodka. The ice was melted, but when I started to get up he waved me to sit back down. "Needless to say, when the inspectors turned in their report, they claimed only thirty-five thousand dollars' worth of hurricane related damage had occurred." Loren slipped his glasses back on. "Now, with over twelve hundred units, and at least five roofs coming off completely—you tell me how the hell a property of that size only sustained thirty-five thou worth of hurricane damage? Luke was furious. He'd been paying a small fortune in insurance premiums for years, only to have the insurance company try to screw him."

"Yeah," I replied with a shrug. "That sucks." But it was a story told so often in post-Katrina New Orleans it had almost become a cliché. Everyone had been fucked over by their insurance companies—to the point where the word *insurance* had become an epithet almost on the same level as FEMA. "So, I guess it's safe to assume Marino is suing? And has hired your firm."

"Wouldn't you?"

"You said Mona got over there to check out the property before the insurance inspectors. I assume her story is a bit different from the insurance inspectors'?"

"Mona O'Neill." Loren smiled at me. "Mona O'Neill is the

key to our case, Chanse. You see, Mona took her responsibilities as a property manager seriously." He poured more vodka into his glass. "Mona sent her son Jonny out of town with her daughter Lorelle and her family, and *actually rode the storm out at Cypress Gardens.*" He smiled. "While I'm grateful she did, because of our case, I also can't believe she did it, you know? But after the storm was over, Mona used her passkeys and checked out every apartment in every building. Her original intent wasn't to check for the damage—she was checking for residents who hadn't evacuated, to make sure they were okay. But what she saw—the extent of the damage—she went back and got her digital camera, and took pictures of everything she saw. Those pictures, mind you, were time and date stamped." He made a face. "She didn't do this because she thought the insurance company was going to try to screw Luke—she did it because she knew they'd want pictures to go with the claim. She was just doing her job, being responsible. She stayed at Cypress Gardens for over a week, and documented everything. The growing mold problem, the way the water damage continued to wreck things as more time passed. She literally took thousands of pictures. And as soon as she could, she drove over to Houston and turned them all over to Luke to file with the claim."

"Then I don't understand why this lawsuit is even necessary." I stared at him. "First off, why would an insurance company allow a case like this to even go to trial in New Orleans? Do they really think an impartial jury can be found here? And with the pictures... and an eyewitness—" It was insane. "That just doesn't make any sense, Loren."

"Global Insurance is a corporation, and they are driven, like all corporations, by greed and profit." Loren's eyes glinted. "Last quarter, for example, they showed a two-billion-dollar profit. *Two billion dollars*, Chanse. Paying out a twenty-million-dollar claim isn't even a drop in the bucket to them. It's not even their goddamned monthly payroll for their worldwide operation. It's practically goddamned petty cash." He picked up his glass and stared at the oily vodka. "I thought, from the very beginning, that they were willing to settle and pay out, but wanted to drag their feet and take as long as they possibly could before writing a check. After all, there was always a chance Luke would either run out of money or get tired of fighting them. And that's how insurance companies operate."

Like so many people in New Orleans had found out the hard way after Katrina. "Bastards," I said before I could stop myself.

"Yes, well, Luke hasn't run out of money or desire to make them honor their policy, and we are finally going to have our day in court in three weeks. But we have a new problem, one that just surfaced last week." He took another drink of the vodka. "Mona O'Neill changed her story."

"What?"

He held up a hand. "Last Monday, Mona called and wanted to see Jim—Jim Drake, the partner who's overseeing the case, I'm consulting on it—and she said it was really important. I sat in on the interview." He licked his lips. "She was having a crisis of conscience, she said. It all had to do with her church being closed—St. Anselm's." He shook his head. "She was beginning to think that the church being closed was God's punishment on her for lying about the damage to Cypress Gardens, and Global Insurance was right—Luke Marino was trying to rob them, that the place was basically falling apart before Katrina, and he saw the hurricane as a chance to hold up the insurance company and get out of a bad deal."

"Last Monday?" I thought about the cashier's check from Morgan Barras, dated two weeks ago.

Loren nodded. "She claimed that all of the pictures she'd taken—which, I might add, she'd never allowed us to have the originals, only copies—were faked, and she was changing her testimony, she was going to tell the truth, and she was sorry to have to do this to Mr. Marino, but she just couldn't get up in court and lie for him anymore." He swallowed. "She also was going to claim that Luke had offered her several hundred thousand dollars in exchange for her testimony." He sighed. "Obviously, this would all blow our case out of the water."

"Did you believe her?"

"Of course I didn't believe her." Loren stared at me like I'd completely lost my mind. "They got to her, somehow. And now she's disappeared—and if she doesn't turn up before the trial starts, we can get her depositions entered in as evidence, of course."

"Did she give a deposition recanting her original story?"

He shook his head. "No."

And it suddenly made sense—why Loren McKeithen, whose specialty was criminal law, was sitting in my living room, wanting to pay me to find Mona O'Neill.

"So, who benefits from Mona's disappearance?" I said slowly, leaning forward in my chair. "That would be Luke Marino, wouldn't it?"

"We just want Mona found, Chanse," Loren replied, draining his glass of vodka yet again. He pulled a file folder out of his briefcase and set it down on the coffee table next to the vodka bottle. "This folder has a copy of Mona's original deposition, along with copies of the photographs she took. There's also a witness list—for both sides of the case." He smiled at me, but it wasn't a smile I felt I could trust. "Talk to whomever you wish—but you need to find Mona. We need you to find her."

"Why should I trust you? How do I know you aren't setting me up—again?"

Loren sighed. "Chanse, you're looking for her anyway, right? Why not make some real money for doing what you're doing anyway?" He reached into his briefcase and pulled out another folder. "Here's the contract of agreement. Have your own lawyer look over it, if you want." He shook his head. "Obviously, the goal is to find Mona O'Neill. Let's put our cards on the table, okay? I don't think she's dead. I think she's in hiding, and I think Global Insurance is behind it. That's why there's been no new deposition filed. They don't want her communicating with us before we go to court—which, I might add, can be viewed as contempt of court." His eyes glinted. "You see the position Global and their lawyers have put us in? She's technically *our* witness. Yes, she notified us that she is changing her testimony, and then two days later she disappears. We can't find her, can't question her."

"You don't want me to just find her," I replied slowly. "You want me to prove there's a link between her changing her testimony and Global Insurance. You want me to find proof they got to her." *And maybe they paid her fifty thousand dollars through an intermediary—like Morgan Barras. For all I know, he could be a majority stockholder in the damned company.*

"Just think about it, Chanse." Loren closed his briefcase. He poured some more vodka into his glass. "I can assure you, we want her found. If she insists on this ridiculous story, we'll deal with that when we find her." He smiled nastily. "Believe me, Jim and I can completely discredit her on the stand. But it also wouldn't hurt if you found some dirt on her."

"Like her son being murdered?"

If Loren was faking his surprise, he was a much better actor than I would have given him credit for. "I doubt Robby O'Neill's murder has anything to do with this," he said smoothly. "Although"—he scratched the side of his head—"if he'd fallen in with a bad crowd, you know, owed money to the wrong people, that could explain why Mona would accept a bribe from Global." His smile widened. "Far be it for me to tell you how to do your job, but I think Robby O'Neill's murder would be a good place for you to start—you know, looking for dirt, reasons why Mona would accept a bribe."

I looked at the check he'd given me and looked back over at him.

At least this time I knew he couldn't be trusted.

It was a decent amount of money.

"All right," I replied, standing up. "I'll have my lawyer look over the contract, see what he has to say. If it all checks out, I'll take the case."

"Great." Loren shook my hand, clasping his free hand onto my forearm as he gripped my right hand. "Chanse, I swear to you, you aren't going to regret this." His smiled broadened. "I've missed doing business with you—and hope this is the first step in our getting things back to the way they used to be with us. You are the best private eye in New Orleans."

"I bet you say that to all the dicks," I said, gently steering him toward my front door.

He laughed. "I'm hosting a fund-raiser this weekend at my place in the Marigny, for Danitra Adams. You should come." Danitra Adams was running for the state legislature—a young, well-educated black woman; one of the planks of her candidacy was gay equality.

"I might do that."

He paused at the door. "I hear you're seeing young Rory Delesdernier." His eyes narrowed. "I was actually kind of hoping he'd go to law school. He's bright, good-looking, and of course he's a Delesdernier. He could have a major career in state politics."

"Well, right now he's more concerned with changing the world."

"What better place to start doing that than Baton Rouge?" He shook my hand again. "Thanks again, Chanse."

I closed the door behind him.

CHAPTER SEVEN

I faxed the contract over to my lawyer for his review and made out a deposit slip for the check to take to the bank once he said it was okay for me to sign the contract. I locked the check up in my top desk drawer and headed for my back door.

As I walked out to my car, I couldn't help but wonder if I was making a mistake. I'm not big on trusting people who've fucked me over in the past. After all, it's been my experience people don't change all that much. I could only trust Loren as long as our objectives stayed the same. If somehow that changed, and it was in Luke Marino's best interests, he would push me right under the bus tires again with a big smile on his face even as an apology left his lips. I got in my car and started it, waiting for the air conditioner to start blowing cold. I sent Abby a text, asking her to see if there was a connection between Global Insurance and Morgan Barras. I put the car in reverse and backed out of my spot, using the clicker to open the electric gate.

I hated the idea of working with Loren again.

On the other hand, part of the problem the last time was I hadn't seen it coming. This time, I could watch my back and hopefully stop the knife before it went in too far.

It wasn't a particularly reassuring thought.

I pulled out onto Camp Street and looped around Coliseum Square to Race Street. It might not have been smart to have not told Loren about the cashier's check I'd found in Mona's desk—but there was also no proof it was a payoff originating with Global Insurance, either. Besides, once I knew if there was a connection, *then* I could tell him.

I turned left onto Race and headed for Tchoupitoulas. Mona's lover's bar was on Tchoupitoulas, close to the intersection at Napoleon, in the same area as Tipitina's. But as I turned onto Tchoupitoulas and drove past the Wal-Mart, I started thinking about taking on Luke Marino as an additional client and decided the best thing to do was come clean with Jonny, let him know what was going on. Even though Loren was going to pay me a hell of a lot more money than Jonny was going to, he'd hired me first, and until I signed the contract and deposited Loren's check, he was my only client.

So I made the detour over to Constance Street.

Jonny himself answered my knock. His eyes were red and swollen, and he looked like hell. The black eye wasn't quite as swollen and was now a sickly shade of yellowish green. He hadn't shaved and looked like he hadn't really slept in days. Instead of letting me in, he came outside and motioned for me to sit on the edge of the porch. He plopped himself down. "Sorry, I know it's hot out here," he said, wiping at his eyes and snuffling a little. "Heather's not been sleeping too good because of the baby, she has trouble sleeping on her back and you know, since we found out, you know, about Robby"—he paused for a moment, to get a hold of himself before continuing—"she wasn't able to sleep at all last night, and she's just now managed to go to sleep, she can't take sleeping pills, you know, because of the baby, and I don't want to risk waking her up and her not sleeping can't be good for the baby either, and sometimes..." He sighed. "She's only got a month or so left, you know, before her due date and she's had some issues already, and so I don't want her getting any more upset than she needs to be, you know?"

I nodded, feeling sorry for him.

"I got the phone off the hook and got our cells turned to

vibrate." He gave me a sheepish grin. "Man, I'm so sorry you had to find Robby, that had to have sucked." He shivered. "I can't even imagine."

"Better me than his wife, or someone who's not used to dead bodies," I replied, choosing not to tell him it's something you shouldn't ever have to get used to. "Before I went out on my own, I was a cop, so…"

"Celia would have fucking lost her mind." Jonny shook his head with a wry laugh. "She's supposed to be back today, you know, and is gonna call me—I told her she and the kids could stay at Ma's—" He broke off again, taking a deep breath. "I mean, I assumed she wouldn't want to stay in the house where—you know."

"That's probably a good idea."

"Those police detectives—they gave me the name of a service that'll clean up the—" He swallowed. "The mess. Celia probably will want to have that done before she goes over there."

"Well, she's going to have to check with the cops before she goes in the house—it's a crime scene now." I took a deep breath. "Something's come up, Jonny, something that I need to talk to you about." I watched his face. "Did you know about the Cypress Gardens lawsuit?"

"Oh, that." He rolled his eyes. "I guess maybe I should have mentioned that to you? But it didn't seem like that big of a deal, you know? I mean, no big, right? Ma just worked there and she was going to have to testify. She didn't talk about it too much, though—when she did she just made it all seem like a big pain in the ass. She was just glad she could help out Mr. Marino." He shook his head. "I still can't believe Ma rode out the hurricane over there. Lorelle thought she was nuts, but she said she had to—it was her job. But Mr. Marino was always real good to her—to us."

"So, she liked him, then?"

"Oh, yeah." He grinned at me. "She thought the sun rose and shined out that man's ass, she did. He always treated us like we were family, you know? He kept telling me I needed to get good grades so

I could go to LSU. He'd let us have his football tickets whenever he wasn't going to use them." He rolled his eyes. "I wasn't ever much of a student."

"Can you think of any reason she'd change her mind?" I watched his face.

He looked at me like I'd lost my mind. "Change her mind? What do you mean?"

"About two weeks ago, she apparently met with Mr. Marino's lawyers and told them she was changing her testimony, was disavowing her deposition about the hurricane damage to the complex, and that the pictures she took of the damage were faked."

"Are you fucking kidding me?" His jaw dropped. "That don't make no sense. Ma was real pissed off about what that insurance company was pulling on Mr. Marino. She talked about it all the time, said they was nothing more than con artists or criminals, the way they were trying to screw him." He scratched his head. "And you're saying Ma was changing her story?" He shook his head. "I don't believe that for a minute. Not for one minute. Ma would never do that. Ever."

"I know this is hard to hear, Jonny, but do you think your mother would have taken a bribe to change her story?"

He just stared at me, his eyes wide and his mouth open, for a good minute before he shook his head. "Ma would *never* lie— especially if it was going to hurt Mr. Marino." He swallowed. "Ma always said the worst thing anyone could ever do was lie—you always get found out and then your word's worthless, and then what are you gonna do? Nothing pissed her off more than being lied to. She wouldn't lie, ever—and especially not to hurt Mr. Marino."

"Jonny—she wouldn't lie, even if your brother was in trouble?"

"What do you mean, in trouble?" He looked confused. "What kind of trouble could Robby be in? I mean, he's kind of an asshole, but what kind of trouble could he be in?"

I took a deep breath. "Your brother's house—it looked pretty expensive, and so did the furniture." *Nothing in that house came from Wal-Mart, that's for sure.* "He was an investment counselor?"

"Don't they make lots of money?" Jonny nodded. "Yeah, and Celia had money. Her dad was society or something. He always bragged about how he'd married a Queen of Rex." He rolled his eyes. "That kind of shit meant a lot to him."

"So, you don't know if your brother was having money problems?"

"He wouldn't talk about that with me if he was." Jonny's tone made it clear it was a ludicrous idea. "And he sure wouldn't talk to Lorelle about it either—they don't hardly talk to each other anymore, I don't know why and Lorelle won't say. But he's always been kind of a dick to me, so." He shrugged. "I just figured she got tired of him being a dick to her. You think he was having money troubles?"

"Just looking at possibilities." I thought for a moment. "Can you think of anyone who'd want your brother dead?"

"Like I told the cops, Chanse, no." He hung his head. "Robby and me, we weren't close—we never were, we were too far apart in age." His voice broke. "He was my brother and I loved him, but you know, he never wanted to have a whole lot to do with me, you know? I always thought it was because he was so much older than me—his oldest isn't that much younger than I am, you know, but I always thought…" His voice trailed off. He added in a heartbroken whisper, "we'd have time. I mean, he *was* my brother."

I patted his shoulder. I'm generally not very good in these kinds of situations. There's nothing you can say that's going to make the person's pain go away, so I generally just don't say anything until the silence gets awkward and I wind up saying something lame. I genuinely felt bad for the kid—with a baby of his own on the way, his brother murdered, and his mother missing and most likely dead. I waited for him to get hold of his emotions again, and said, "Marino's lawyer wants me to find your mother, too, and wants to pay me a hell of a lot of money…but I won't take their money if you aren't comfortable with it—you hired me first."

"Why would I mind?" he asked, seeming honestly confused. "We both want the same thing, so I don't see what the problem is. The most important thing is finding Ma. As long as you find her, I don't care how many people are paying you to do it." He shook his head again. "I can't believe Ma was going to change her testimony. Chanse, it doesn't make any sense. You really need to find her, man."

I didn't have the heart to tell him she was probably dead. I didn't get into any of the issues, the possible conflicts of interest in having two clients with the same goal. There wasn't any point, really.

"I know you'll do the right thing." He smiled at me as I stood up to go. "So I don't have anything to worry about, right?"

He was still sitting on the steps when I drove away. I called Abby to get her take on the situation, but she didn't pick up. I left a voicemail and tossed my phone into the passenger seat.

The Riverside Bar and Grill wasn't very far from Jonny's and Mona's houses, actually. It was on a stretch of Tchoupitoulas Street where one side was a long brick warehouse that extended almost from the stoplight at Louisiana to the one at Napoleon. Tipitina's sat on the corner at Napoleon, and the Rouse's was kitty-corner from there. I could see the Tipitina's sign about a half block farther uptown from the big neon sign for the Riverside. I pulled into the gravel parking lot and sat there for a moment. There were only two other cars in the lot besides mine—one a battered-looking navy blue Chevrolet Malibu, and the other a gray Nissan SUV.

The Riverside itself was only one story, made of brick, and wasn't raised, sitting flat on the ground. It wasn't that big, maybe could hold a hundred or so people at most from the looks of it. There was another sign on the slanted roof that matched the one mounted on the pole alongside the street. The slanted roof was slate and was missing a few tiles. The windows were all blacked out, and there was a big commercial-sized Dumpster on the far side of the building. I could smell its contents when I opened the car door. The front door was glass and had the traditional warning sign about gaming machines and minors taped on the inside, facing out. I got out of my car and pushed the door open, entering the dark inside.

When my eyes adjusted to the gloom, I could see the place was set up in a very simple fashion, nothing fancy. To the right were three tired-looking pool tables, with lights directly over them hanging from the ceiling on chains. An old-fashioned bubble jukebox sat in the corner next to a cigarette machine and row of video poker machines. The jukebox was blaring an old Patsy Cline song, "Walking After Midnight." Some scarred tables were set up throughout the main area of the bar, with 1970s-style orange plastic chairs placed around them. Cracked black plastic ashtrays sat in the center of every table. The bar ran about two-thirds the length of the room, directly opposite the front door. The cement floor slanted toward the occasional drain. The overwhelming smell of Pine-Sol barely masked the reek of stale beer, urine, and old cigarette smoke.

A man with an enormous beer gut in a black T-shirt reading *Riverside* in white letters was wiping down the bar counter with a white rag, and I could see another man of indeterminate age through the window to the kitchen. The man in the kitchen was wearing a hairnet and a white T-shirt, and sweat glistened on his forehead. I walked over to the bar and sat down on a stool, which wobbled a bit before settling.

"What can I get you?" the bartender asked, still wiping the bar down.

"Abita Amber," I replied, putting a five down on the bar. He opened a cooler and popped the cap off the bottle, setting it down in front of me on top of a napkin that said *Riverside Bar and Grill* on it. He took the five and gave me a one and two quarters in change. I let it sit there. "Is Barney around?"

He crossed his arms, narrowed his eyes, and leaned back against the beer cooler. "Who's looking?"

I pulled out one of my business cards and put it on top of my change. "The name's Chanse MacLeod, and I'm a private eye. I'm looking for Mona O'Neill—her son Jonny's worried about her."

He stared at the card for a while, working the toothpick in his mouth. He put my card into his shirt pocket. "I'm Barney," he said, not offering me his hand. Instead, he filled a glass with the soda gun and took a drink. "I haven't seen Mona since Thursday night."

"What time did you see her?" I took out my notepad and pen.

"She came by here on her way to St. Anselm's." Barney thought for a moment or two. "Was around nine, I guess—yeah, that lesbian on MSNBC was on." He gestured to the silent big-screen TV mounted on the wall above the top-shelf liquor bottles. He grabbed a remote from under the bar and turned it on. Judge Judy was lecturing some penitent-looking man who was badly in need of a shower and some dental work. He muted the sound and put the remote back under the bar.

"How did she seem?"

"She was aggravated." Barney sipped his soda. "Donna Calhoun was supposed to sit up all night with her at the church, but she wasn't going to make it again, and Mona was fired up about it. Donna's not the most dependable person." He used his index finger to make a circle in front of his right temple. "I always told her not to get so worked up—Donna's not been right in the head in years, but Mona didn't like being there all night by herself. She came by here to see if I could sit with her." He shook his head. "She knew I was short-staffed—one of my regular bartenders wrecked her motorcycle and wasn't able to come in that night, so I had to fill in—like I'd been filling in ever since Serena wrecked the stupid bike." He made a face. "How many times did I warn that girl to not drive like a maniac?" He scratched his arm. "Donna was just a substitute in the first place, someone else had canceled out already. Mona was the only one who was dependable enough to sit vigil all night."

"Who was supposed to sit with her originally?"

He pondered this for a moment. "Don Sinclair, I think it was. Hold on for a minute." He knelt down and dug around underneath the bar, then stood up again with a stained manila folder. He flipped it open and looked at a computer printout of a June calendar. His finger traced along the page and tapped the previous Thursday. "Yeah, Don

Sinclair." He made a face. "He's not dependable, either—he drinks a bit. I think she really came by here looking to see if he was here, so she could put a bug in his ear. Mona did like to read people the riot act once she worked herself up to it." He snorted. "Besides, she knew I knew damned well Don was supposed to sit up all night in the church and had canceled on her. I wouldn't have served him if he'd come in here." He put both of his elbows on the bar and leaned forward. I could smell stale smoke on him. "I haven't heard from her since she left for the church. Jonny thinks something happened to her?"

"Is that unusual?"

He looked me square in the eye. "Mona and I have been seeing each other for about a year, mister. But we don't have no ties, we don't check up on each other—it's nice and casual, you know what I'm saying? Sometimes I don't talk to her for days, even weeks sometimes. I don't put no demands on her, and she don't put none on me. We like it like that."

"Apparently, no one's heard from her since Thursday night," I replied. "Her cell phone goes straight to voicemail, and no one's seen her car, either."

"Well, that ain't like her. She talks to her kids every day—especially Jonny. He's her baby, you know, and with that wife of his about to pop out a grandkid...no, that ain't like her at all." He rubbed his eyes and lit a Pall Mall with a book of Riverside matches. "We usually get together on Saturday afternoons, when we do, but I leave that to her. She didn't call me this weekend. I just assumed she was pissed I didn't go to the church with her, you know, or maybe something had come up, who knows? I figured she'd call when she was ready to see me, and that was just fine with me."

"How long have you and Mona been involved?"

"I've known Mona most of my life—as long as I can remember." He smiled faintly. "I went to de la Salle with Danny O'Neill, when she was at Sacred Heart. Her and Danny were always together, ever since they were kids, you know? We all grew up on the same block of St. Thomas Street in the Channel." His eyes got a faraway look

in them. "If it weren't for Danny, I might have married her myself."
His face twisted. "'Stead of some of them bitches I married—I'd
been better off not getting married at all." He refilled his soda. "I
started seeing Mona about a year ago, right around the time my last
wife Debbie ran off. It just kind of happened, you know? I never
thought Mona and me would have ever happened, but then Debbie
took off and…" He shrugged. "It's nothing serious, you know, just
companionship—we made that clear right from the start. Neither
one of us are wanting to get married again, you know? I've been
married four times and ain't about to put myself through that hell
ever again—and Mona, you know, she never wanted to get married
again after Danny died. What we have is real nice, you know? It's
comfortable, and at our age that's about all you can hope for."

"How often did you see her? Talk to her?"

"We talked pretty much every day—of course, I got more tied
up around here at the bar after Serena wrecked her stupid motorbike."
He gestured around the place. "I thought owning my own business
was the way to go after I retired, you know? But it's a hell of a lot
of headaches."

"Then sell the place and quit your bitching," the man in the
kitchen said, coming through the saloon doors with a steaming plate
of fried mushrooms. He set them down on the bar between us. There
was a little bowl of sauce in one corner. He wiped his hands on his
apron and held his right one out to me. "I'm Jermaine. What a nice
lady like Miz O'Neill ever saw in a jackass white man like this one
is a mystery to us all."

"Chanse." I shook his hand. "Were you here on Thursday
night?"

Jermaine nodded. "Yeah, the bar was busy but I didn't have
no food orders, so I was out here refilling ice and shit. She was real
agitated, not that this one ever noticed nothing unless it punched
him in the face." He grinned, and his bottom teeth were all gold.
"Something had been bothering Miz O'Neill for about a week or so,
I'd say—she hadn't been acting like herself for a while. Not that this
damned redneck ever noticed."

I dipped one of the mushrooms into the sauce and popped it into my mouth. It was hot, but the batter was delicious.

"Fuck you, Jermaine," Barney said pleasantly. "And get back to work. I'm not paying you to come out here and bother the customers. And who's paying for these mushrooms?"

"Ain't nothing to do in that damned kitchen right now except sweat, and you know it, so fuck you, and if I want to give the detective man a taste of what comes out of my kitchen I guess you can dock my pay for it if it means your sorry ass is gonna go broke." Jermaine smiled back at him. "Unless you got a problem with me talking to this detective man about what a shitty man you were to Miz O'Neill, who could have done better than your sorry ass if she just would put a little bit of effort into it." He turned back to me. "I never could figure it out, you know, unless it was just pure laziness on her part, you know?"

I gathered this was a regular sideshow act the two of them put on. Their words were insulting, but their tone was friendly. "You said something was bothering her—do you remember exactly when you noticed that?"

"Something was bothering her—he's right about that." Barney popped a mushroom in his mouth and chewed on it thoughtfully. "You need to put more beer in the batter, Jermaine. I'd say she started acting funny about a week or so ago." He scratched his forehead. "Let me think on it. Yeah, it was about a week ago last Thursday, right, Jermaine?"

Jermaine nodded. "Yeah, it was a Thursday night, because I'd been off the day before." He winked at me. "I generally have Tuesdays and Wednesdays off. She came in about seven, ordered a catfish po'boy and onion rings and a beer."

"Serena hadn't wrecked her damned bike yet, so I was in the office," Barney remembered. "I didn't even know she was here until I came out to get a Coke. Yeah, she was drinking a beer—which I thought was weird. That wasn't like Mona—she had to sit vigil that night and she never drank when she was going to the church." He ate another mushroom. "Not that Mona was a big drinker anyway—

she'd sometimes have a beer, or a glass of wine, but that was about it. She never was big on drinking—even when we were kids. Me and Danny tied on some good ones, but not Mona. I asked her about it, and she said she'd had a bad day—but that's all she would say about it. It was still bothering her when she came over that Saturday, you know, she always comes to my place, she was always afraid Jonny might catch us if we were at her place—but she didn't want to talk about it—and that was that. She's stubborn, you know—there was no point in pressing her about it—she'd tell me about it when she was ready to tell me about it, or she never would. That's just how she is." He looked at me. "I mean, we're casual, like I said. We don't press each other about stuff. If she wanted me to know, she'd tell me. Asking her would just piss her off, and I had other things on my mind, if you know what I mean."

I put that image out of my mind. "So, you had no idea what the problem was?"

"Well, I just assumed it was Jonny. I mean, it usually was." He made a face. "If it was something to do with the church, she would have told me, since I was part of Save Our Churches. It usually always was Jonny, anyway—and that piece of trash he married. Mona worries about the two of them all the time."

"You didn't think she was trash when she worked here," Jermaine observed.

"That was before she got knocked up by a kid five years younger than her," Barney snapped.

"Heather's five years older than Jonny?" I couldn't have heard that right.

Jermaine laughed. "Oh, yeah. They met here, you know."

"Jonny was always more trouble to Mona than he was worth," Barney added.

"Jonny was a problem for her?"

"Butter wouldn't melt in that kid's mouth, you know, but he's a real piece of work, that one is." Barney rolled his eyes. "Kicked out of de la Salle his senior year, never graduated—I don't think he even bothered to ever get his GED, either. He's always been a problem for Mona. He was a change-of-life baby for her, you know—and she always spoiled him. She wasn't that way with Robby and Lorelle, uh-uh, they toed the line and she disciplined those two. Jonny's always been wild and out of control—he's had some run-ins with the police, you know—and then he knocked up that trashy girl. Mona is always making excuses for him, not having a daddy, blah blah blah. And I told Mona buying him and Heather that house was a mistake, but she thought it might make him grow up." He shook his head again. "You see that place? What a fucking dump. It's a wonder the city ain't blighted it right out from under them. He can't be bothered to take care of it, doesn't mow the damned grass—Mona hired a neighborhood kid to do it, you know—and Jonny got mad because the kid tried mowing it in the morning before it gets too damned hot! Woke him up, and he needs his sleep, don't you know, because he's going to be a big champion fighter." He shook his head. "He needs to be spanked, is what he needs, the spoiled brat."

Jermaine exhaled. "The kid ain't that bad, Barney, and you know it. You're just mad because the girl—" He cut himself off.

"How long did she work here?" I looked from one to the other.

Barney shot daggers out his eyes at Jermaine before turning back to me. "She worked here about a year—behind the bar and sometimes waitressed. She was a good worker, I'll give her that." He said it grudgingly.

"How old is she, exactly?"

"Twenty-five." Barney laughed at the look on my face. "Yeah, that's right, she's at least five years older than Jonny. Now, what would a girl that age want with a boy his age? It ain't right—there's something wrong with that girl. And she's a thief."

"You don't know that," Jermaine cautioned.

"The hell I don't," Barney roared. "Every night that little bitch worked the registers came up short, didn't they? Only on the nights she worked. I never caught her with her hand in the till—but I was sure enough going to fire her thieving ass when she quit." He gave me a sour look. "She quit because she'd married Jonny, and she hasn't turned her hand to do a goddamned thing ever since." He blew out a long breath. "If something's happened to Mona—I'll bet you free drinks for the rest of your life, Mr. MacLeod, that little bitch had something to do with it."

CHAPTER EIGHT

I walked out of the bar into the heat of the early evening. The sun was setting in the west, and darkness was starting to fall over the city. Gravel and shells crunched under my feet as I walked across the parking lot to where I parked my car. I pulled the keys out of my pocket just as a couple of cars pulled into the lot and parked on the other side. My phone rang as I was unlocking my car. With a sigh I pulled it out of my pocket and glanced at the screen. Venus's face scowled at me, and I smothered a grin the way I always did when I saw the picture. I'd taken it one night when we were at the Avenue Pub, and her expression clearly was *take the picture and I'll cut you, asshole.*

I answered it as I slid my key into the ignition lock. "MacLeod. What's up?"

"Chanse, it's Venus." She sounded tired. "We found your missing person's car. You might want to get over here—I've got the lab working the car. No sign of your missing person, though—but like I said, you probably want to get over here."

"Where are you?"

"Annunciation and St. Andrew." She disconnected the call.

I had to wait for a few more cars to get situated in the parking lot before I could get out of there. I swung right on Napoleon and headed up to Magazine. The corner of Annunciation and St. Andrew was my neighborhood—the lower Garden District. St. Andrew and Magazine was the bizarre intersection that confused the hell out of tourists. If you were heading uptown on Magazine Street, that was the light where Magazine became a two-way street for the rest of the way through Uptown to where it ended at Leake Street in Riverbend. If you were heading downtown on Magazine, that corner was where you had to swing to the left to get onto Camp Street—because Magazine was a one-way going the other direction on the other side of St. Andrew. Annunciation was about a block or so on the river side of Magazine Street. That part of the neighborhood had been dangerous before the St. Thomas Projects had been torn down shortly after the turn of the century and a Wal-Mart erected in their place. Another mixed-housing complex, River Gardens, had been built over where the rest of the projects had been.

St. Thomas was probably best known as the place where Sister Helen Prejean had lived and worked—but the reality looked a lot worse than how it appeared in the movie *Dead Man Walking*.

I tried to remember the layout of the neighborhood, but wasn't familiar enough with it to say for sure. I turned right when I got to Jackson Avenue and tried to remember the direction of the one-way streets. Annunciation ran uptown, and St. Andrew ran to the river. I turned on Laurel and turned right again on St. Andrew—and saw the flashing lights at the next corner. There was a spot open halfway down the block, so I pulled over and turned off the car.

Several black women were standing on the sidewalk, and I nodded to them as I started walking toward the police lights.

"Oooh, you don't wanna go down there." One of them, her hair covered in a plastic bag, shook her head. There was a cigarette in one hand, and she had a gold tooth.

"What's going on?" I asked.

"Looks like they found someone's car who's been killed," another woman said. She was massive, wearing an incredibly tight pair of jeans and a baggy Saints football jersey. Her hair hung in long braids past her shoulders. "A nice car, too."

I nodded my thanks and kept walking. As I got closer to the corner, I could see the crime lab van was parked diagonally across

Annunciation Street. Down at the next corner, a cop was standing, prepared to direct traffic to turn up St. Mary Street at the next corner. There were three squad cars parked, their blue lights flashing. I saw Venus's SUV, parked on the other side of the lab van. Crime scene tape had been strung from streetlights, blocking off access to the green four-door Mercury Marquis. Crime scene technicians were swarming all over the car, searching, dusting for fingerprints, taking photographs, gathering whatever evidence there was in the car and placing it into bags, which they labeled for processing later. Blaine was on the other side of the Marquis from me, looking through the glove compartment.

Venus was standing just inside the crime scene tape, her arms folded, talking to two patrol officers. She was dressed in her standard gray slacks, red blouse, and gray jacket. Her stiletto heels added a few extra inches to her height, so she was actually looking down on the patrol officers.

Venus noticed me and gave me a barely perceptible nod, which meant *I'll be with you in a second, okay?*

I leaned against a streetlight and looked at the car.

It was a beauty, Jonny hadn't been kidding about that. The emerald green paint sparkled in the light from the street lamps, and the tires looked new. It didn't have a key lock on the driver's door, but buttons for a combination lock. The driver's side window had apparently been broken out—I could see a few shards of what was left of the glass sticking up in the frame of the door.

Not good, I thought, *not good at all.*

Venus patted one of the patrol officers on the arm, said something that made all three of them laugh, and ducked underneath the tape to walk over to me.

"Sorry to interrupt your evening," she said with a slight shake of her head. "Thought you'd want to know."

"It's her car?" I asked.

"Yeah, we ran the plate. Registered to Mona O'Neill. Pity—it's a nice car. Maybe I'll trade in the SUV for one of those." She nodded at it. "Driver's side window is broken out—as you can see, and there's glass all over the inside front seat and on the floorboards. The front seat's covered in blood." She shook her head. "That amount of blood—Mona O'Neill's not going to turn up alive." She qualified her statement, "If it's her blood."

"I never thought she would turn up alive, to be honest." I wished again that I hadn't quit smoking. "Any of the people who live around here see or hear anything?"

"The woman who lives in the corner house here," she gestured to a fuchsia double shotgun house, which had a crowd of people standing on the porch, "reported the car today, says she didn't notice it until Sunday morning—it could have been there longer and she didn't notice it. She didn't think anything about it, until one of her kids told her about the blood on the front seat. We canvassed the whole area, and nobody else in the neighborhood can say if it was parked here longer than that." She sighed. "How can you not notice a car like that?" She turned and looked back at the car.

"It does kind of stand out," I replied. I'd long ago lost my ability to be shocked at how unobservant my fellow citizens were—and I knew she was speaking rhetorically.

"The weird thing is, Chanse," she turned back to me, "the way the broken glass is—no one was sitting in that car when the window was broken."

"What?" I wanted to go take a look, but knew she wouldn't let me anywhere near the car. Then I got it. "There's glass all over the driver's seat."

"If someone was sitting there, sure, glass would have gotten on the seat—but a lot of it would have been on the person sitting there—and when they got out of the car, however they got out, most of the glass would have spilled out onto the street." She pointed at the ground around the driver's side door. "And there's very little glass there." She sighed. "I think the blood got there *before* the window was broken—I think someone just broke out the window to steal something from it, and it isn't related to the blood at all." She made a face.

I sympathized. If someone had broken into the car, the crime scene was contaminated.

"But at least now I can take over the investigation from Delvecchio—who, I might add, hasn't done a goddamned thing. He didn't even put out the APB on the car. Who knows how long it would have been before we found the car if Lucy Carter's kid hadn't checked out the damned thing?"

"What do you think happened?"

"My best guess right now—and it's a guess, mind you, don't be trying to hold me to it later—is whoever—and I'm not sure it was Mona O'Neill—left all that blood there, however that happened, it happened somewhere else, and the body was dumped somewhere we may never find, and then the killer dumped the car here." She tapped her pen against her chin. "We're far enough away from where she lives—and where her son lives—so the odds of someone seeing the car and recognizing it were pretty low. Not great news for the son and daughter—first the brother, now their mother." She made a tutting sound.

"Do you think—" I broke off.

"What?" she asked. "Don't be withholding evidence, Chanse. Friend or no friend, I'll run your ass in."

"I don't know, Venus. I don't have anything, but there was a lot going on in her life, and she was playing with some serious fire." I quickly filled her in on the check I'd found, and the issues with the Marino trial.

Her face was expressionless. "Sounds like quite a few people had some serious reasons for wanting to get rid of our Mona O'Neill. And you found the check in her desk?"

I nodded. "I made a copy and took the original. It's in my safe."

"All right. I'll have to get over there later, take a look around the house." She arched an eyebrow at me. "I'm not going to have to worry about you interfering with my investigation, am I?"

"Until a body's found, I have to operate on the assumption she's still alive—even though I think she's not." I gestured to the car. "That may or may not be her blood. And if it's not, well—some people definitely want to see her dead. She might just be hiding out somewhere."

"No activity on her credit cards since last week."

"Plenty of places in New Orleans that take cash."

"But no activity on her bank accounts, either."

"She could be hiding out at a friend's place."

She sighed. "Yeah, that occurred to me, too. I guess I better get back over there." She took a few steps away from me before stopping and turning back. "You're going over to the kid's, I take it?"

I nodded. She kept walking. I got back into my car and drove over to Jonny's house. My mind was racing. There was something trying to form in my mind, a theory, but it was just not coming together. I pulled up in front of Jonny's house. The lights were on, but there wasn't a car in front. I turned off the car and walked up to the front door. I knocked and heard someone shuffling across the living room.

"Oh, it's you," Heather said unpleasantly when she opened the door. "What now? Someone kill Lorelle?"

"Where's Jonny?"

"Training." She moved away from the door, her house shoes barely leaving the floor as she walked across the living room with both hands pressed to the small of her back. She plopped down on the couch and scowled at me. "I'd offer to get you something to drink but I'm a little bit pregnant. Sorry—I'm sure you're used to much better hostesses than me."

I sat down in the chair I'd used on Sunday morning, which fortunately hadn't been recovered in clothes since then. "The police found Mona's car."

"The green Mercury?" She made a face. "Was it in front of a motel out on Airline Drive?"

"Actually, over in the lower Garden District, at the corner of Annunciation and St. Andrew." I watched her face. Her expression remained bored. "The driver's seat is covered in blood, and the driver's side window is broken out. Doesn't look good for your mother-in-law, I'm afraid."

She shrugged. "What do you want me to say?"

"You don't seem too concerned."

"Mona's a bitch, and she's always treated me like shit." She flashed a brittle smile at me. "I'm supposed to be sorry something *might* have happened to her?" She gave a halfhearted shrug. "Okay, I'm sorry. I'm sorry for Jonny—he'll be crushed if something's happened to her. I'm sorry she's always been a bitch to me. I'm sorry she doesn't think I'm good enough for her precious son." Her face twisted. "Like he's some great fucking prize, which makes the whole thing crazier, you know." She rolled her eyes. "He doesn't even have a fucking high school diploma, you know. De la Salle kicked him out." She placed her hands on her swollen belly. "I at least graduated from fucking high school. And my kid's not going to end up like his father, or like me for that matter." Her eyes narrowed. "I won't allow it. My kid's going to work hard in school and go to college, or I will kill him myself."

"Why Jonny?" I asked. I was frankly curious. "Why a high school dropout so much younger than you?"

"You wouldn't ask that question if I was younger than him, would you?" She laughed bitterly. "Don't give me that shit. He's a charmer, isn't he? Don't pretend like little Jonny didn't sucker you in, too." She sneered at me. "He gave you a hundred bucks, you didn't even sign a contract with him, and you start looking for Mona? I looked up your website, you know—you always make your clients sign a contract and pay money up front. And I saw what your rates are. Why'd you make all those exceptions for Jonny?" Her eyes glittered. "He charmed you, didn't he? He turned on the big smile and his eyes lit up and you fell for his line of bull hook, line, and sinker, didn't you?"

I was jolted. "What?"

"Don't feel bad—everyone does." She waved her hand tiredly. "Jonny is a charmer—he could sell ice to Eskimos. He just gets that earnest face and opens his eyes wide and gets them to twinkle, and people will do whatever the fuck he wants them to. I've seen him work people, you know. It's a sight to see. If he had a brain he could be seriously dangerous." She patted her stomach again. "Me, I spread my legs for him, and look where it got me. You think I would have married him if I hadn't gotten pregnant?" She looked off in another direction. "Yeah, I would have—but he wouldn't have married me, you see what I mean? That's the difference. I fell for it, too. He only married me because he's Catholic and he was afraid I'd get an abortion." She barked out a laugh. "And don't think his pro-life Catholic mother wouldn't have hauled me down to Planned Parenthood and whipped out her own checkbook and paid for the whole thing herself, if I would have gone along with it."

"You were working at the Riverside? That's where you met him, right?"

"Yeah—you've talked to Barney, haven't you? That lecherous old fuck. Bet he talked some serious shit about me. I'll tell you a secret." She leaned toward me, and winced. "That asshole tried to get in my pants from day one—and I wouldn't let him. Why do you think Mona hates me so damned much? She knew Barney wanted me, and she didn't like that one damned bit." She laughed again. "I actually met Mona first—she was a regular there, you know, because she was fucking Barney—she'd come in there every damned night and have a sloe gin fizz." She rolled her eyes again. "She'd just sit there and sip her stupid drink until he was done for the night—waiting for Barney to get done in the office so they could go back to his place and fuck, you know. We all knew about it—Barney's not exactly one for keeping his trap shut, you know?" She shuddered. "And until she came in, he would brush up against me when he didn't need to, groping and copping a feel, the dirty old fuck."

"How long were they seeing each other?"

She shrugged. "I don't know—and I didn't really care much. I was just glad, you know, when she'd come in because then he'd be on his best behavior. But she knew what he was up to." She whistled. "But whatever they had, it was already going on when I started working there, and that was a year and a half ago—Serena, she tended bar, she was the one who told me about it and pointed Mona out to me." She sighed. "I thought she was nice at first, if you can believe that. She always tipped well, a couple of bucks for just the one damned drink, and she was friendly, you know? Never a problem, always wanted to chitchat if it was slow, you know, wanting to know all about me and everything. I really thought she was a nice lady. And then it all changed." Her face clouded. "Someone told her that Barney was trying to get it on with me. I think it was Jermaine, that damned cook, to tell you the truth. He was always a pain in my ass."

"Actually, when I was in there earlier, Jermaine took up for you when Barney was talking smack about you." I smiled at her.

She widened her eyes. "I'll send him a card."

"So, how did you meet Jonny?" I asked, ignoring the sarcastic tone.

"He came in one night—him and bunch of the other guys he trains with. After a fight, over at the Harrah's, when they used to have fights there." She shrugged. "They still might, for all I know. All I know is he has to drive over to Biloxi to fight at the Chateau Barras place. He fights for a different promoter now—it's better money. He keeps telling me they think he's going to make it big. Whatever. I'll believe it when I see it, you know?" She exhaled heavily. "I used to go over there with him, you know, before I got too big." She sighed. "You ever see that? It's weird, I don't know that I care for it too much. Brutal, you know. I don't know that I like watching people beating the shit out of each other too much." She made a face. "And for money." She shuddered. "It's barbaric, I think. And the crowd—those people, you should see them, how worked up they get—especially when someone starts bleeding. It gives me the creeps. I don't know why he wants to do it, but what else is he going to do? Wash dishes or work at McDonald's? He don't have no skills."

"So he came in one night?" I prompted, trying to get her back on the subject.

"Yeah." She smiled at the memory. "He had a black eye and a

swollen lip, and they all came in to celebrate. He wasn't old enough to drink—he still isn't, and Barney knew it, so he just would order Cokes, but he had those little airplane liquor bottles and would spike his own. I told Barney—you're not supposed to bring in your own, you know, but Barney said it was fine, as long as we didn't serve him we'd be okay." She shrugged. "That ain't the way it works, but it wasn't my bar, you know—and then when I figured out that Jonny was Mona's kid, then I understood better, you know? Barney was always trying to make up to Jonny, whenever he came in."

"But Jonny didn't know about Barney and Mona?"

"You heard him." She fixed her eyes on me. "The other day. He thinks Mona's the fucking Virgin Mary, doesn't he? He don't have a clue about Barney and Mona, not a damned clue. I guess Mona never brought Barney back to her place—Jonny was living with her, you know, right up till the day we got married and got this place." A faint smile played at the corner of her lips. "That first night he came in, he started flirting with me right off, you know. He was cute, and I went along with it even though I knew he was too young for me." She rolled her eyes. "Just goes to show, doesn't it. If I'd known then…but he wanted to come back when I got off work and…" Her voice trailed off. "You don't know how many times I've regretted saying yes."

"You're sorry you married him?"

"I—" She shook her head. "I sometimes think we'd both be better off, yeah." Her hands went to her stomach. "Jonny ain't old enough to be a father—he's just a kid himself." She sighed. "In a lot of ways, he's just a kid. If I didn't make him give me all his money and put it in the bank, he'd just blow it on crap—you know, video games, getting drunk with his friends, that kind of stuff. Kid shit. Or give it away. But I give him credit—he don't ever act like he's sorry we got married." She rubbed her stomach. "And he's crazy about this kid."

"So, why did you marry him?"

"Hello?" She looked at me like I'd lost my mind. "I'm pregnant, dumbass."

"That doesn't mean you have to get married anymore—it hasn't for a long time."

"My parents weren't married," she replied, looking away from me. "I was raised by a single mom, okay, with a dad who couldn't be bothered to make his support payments and sure as hell couldn't be bothered with the daughter he didn't want. I haven't seen my father since I was a baby. My mother's worked her ass off her whole life, and where did it get her? Nowhere, that's where. I didn't want that for me, and I didn't want my kid to go through what I had to, okay?" She looked around the dingy, dirty room. "Though I can't say this is a whole hell of a lot better, is it? Be careful what you wish for." She made a face. "But one day Jonny's gonna make it big in the octagon, and we'll be set for the rest of our lives." She rolled her eyes.

"And Mona was against it? You two getting married?" I remembered the photo of Mona and Jonny on her wall from his wedding day, and the conspicuous absence of any pictures of Heather.

"You could say that." She gave me a sour smile. "Can you believe it? A cocktail waitress wasn't good enough for her high school dropout son. She fucking hit the roof." Heather ran a hand through her hair. "You know, all that shit about us being too young and Jonny throwing his life away." She glared at me. "You know she tried to buy me off? Yeah, Miss Catholic offered to pay for me to get an abortion and give me another ten thousand dollars to blow town and never come back. I told her to stick it up her ass."

"Where did Mona get ten thousand dollars from?"

"There was a settlement when her husband got killed—she set up trusts for the kids." She waved her hand. "That's how we got this palace."

"What about your other in-laws? Did they agree with her?"

"We didn't see Robby much," she replied, covering her mouth to belch. "Him and that wife of his—Celia—thought they were way too good for us, don't you know? They didn't bother to come to the wedding—I guess it wasn't a posh enough affair for that bitch. Just a little ceremony at St. Anselm's, of course—although a justice of the peace would have been good enough for me." She laughed. "But it wasn't just me and Jonny, you know—Robby and Celia thought they were too good for Mona, which really chapped her ass, you know? You'd think the way Celia looked down her nose at Mona, she'd be a little nicer to me, but no, not Miss Christian Charity." She snorted. "All that business with her going to Mass all the time, and trying to save that stupid church? You'd think she'd be more of a Christian, but no." She gnawed on a finger for a moment or two. "Lorelle, though—she's a nice lady, she is—you'd never know she was Mona's kid, you know? She's always been real nice to me. She came to the wedding, with her husband and her kids, they call me Aunt Heather, and she gave me a real nice wedding gift—the nicest one we got—and she's always real nice, calls me once or twice a week to see how I'm doing. She gave me all kinds of baby stuff, so we wouldn't have to buy anything—a crib and a high chair and all that kind of stuff. I like her. I mean, I know I won't be going to lunch with her and her friends any time, but she's nice to me. She don't treat me like trash." Her chin went up. "I ain't trash, even if I didn't go to Sacred Heart."

"You don't know if Robby was having money trouble?"

"They don't confide in us—but I can't imagine they would. That Celia has money, you know—her dad left her a lot of money when he died a few years back. Jonny told me that was when they bought that big house on Napoleon." Her face grew sly. "Though the way they went through money, it wouldn't surprise me none if they were broke—you think maybe that's why someone killed Robby?"

I shrugged. "It's a possibility."

"I know he was arguing with Mona about money last week." Her pinkie finger went back into her mouth. "I walked over there, to see if Mona had some sugar—Jonny was at training and I wanted to make some cupcakes but I didn't have no sugar, so I walked down to Mona's. Robby's big SUV was parked out front, and I could hear them yelling at each other from the street." She chewed on a cuticle. "So I went up on the porch where I could hear better. Robby needed some money, bad—he kept saying he was going to be in deep shit if he didn't come up with the money and Mona kept saying she didn't have that kind of money laying around, and he said she could take it out of Jonny's trust and that made me pretty mad, you know, that money's for the baby, and I was about to go inside and give them both a piece of my mind—"

"Jonny's trust?" I prompted her.

She nodded. "His dad was killed on the docks, you know. Verlaine Shipping paid Mona a shitload of money, and she put some of it into trusts for the kids. Jonny's is the only trust left, Robby and Lorelle got theirs cashed out years ago. Anyway, Mona won't cash out Jonny's, because she don't trust us with the money." She made a face. "She's right about that. Jonny would spend every cent of that money if he got his hands on it. She's holding on to it for our kids. She probably doesn't want me getting my grubby hands on it, but I ain't stupid. Anyway, before I could go in there, Mona let him have it with both barrels, about how she wasn't going to steal from Jonny, and he should have thought about that before he blew through his money like it was on fire, and let me tell you, that woman could cuss up a blue streak when she put her mind to it. And then he said something, quiet so I couldn't hear what it was." She sighed. "And then out of the clear blue she said there might be another way to get the money, if he would let her have a couple of days. He said he didn't have much choice and he stormed out of there. He didn't even say hello when he went past me on the porch, you know—acted like I wasn't even there." Her jaw tightened. "Looks like he got what he deserved, doesn't it?"

"How did Mona seem?"

"She acted like nothing had happened, you know, but I could tell she was upset. She gave me the sugar and I got the hell out of there."

So, Robby was having money problems. "Did you talk to the police about this?"

She stared at me like I'd lost my mind. "Why would I? I haven't talked to the police at all."

"I'm going to have to tell them about the argument you overheard," I replied. "And they're probably going to want to talk to you."

"Whatever." She pushed herself to her feet, not without difficulty. "I'm kind of tired, you mind? I need to go lay down."

I stood up. "Thanks, Heather."

She waved her hand wearily. "Whatever."

CHAPTER NINE

Y ou've thought she was dead from the very beginning, haven't you?" Abby said matter-of-factly as she slathered cream cheese on her toasted bagel. She took a bite, washing it down with coffee.

We were sitting in Mojo's Coffee Shop the next morning. I'd already finished my first bagel and had moved on to my second by the time Abby showed up. She'd woken me from a deep, dreamless sleep at three in the morning, her voice bubbling over with excitement. The moment I somehow managed to gather myself enough to say "MacLeod," she'd started babbling a hundred miles per hour, the loud hip-hop music blaring in the background tipped me off that she was at the Catbox Club. Between the music and the rapid-fire staccato of words shooting out of her mouth into the phone—and to be fair, I wasn't even fifty percent awake and conscious—I couldn't understand a thing she was saying. Finally, I managed to cut her off, and asked—pleaded, actually—to let it keep until the next morning. Resentfully, she'd agreed it could wait until morning. It was nine now, and given the fact she'd been wide awake six hours earlier, I found her alertness more than a little annoying.

She was also taking her time telling me what she'd learned— punishing me for "harshing her buzz" at three in the morning.

She wasn't wearing any makeup and wasn't wearing a wig. She could have passed for a teenager in her baggy madras shorts and an enormous, shapeless Saints jersey that hid the size of her breasts. Her brown hair was pulled back into a perky ponytail mounted high on the back right side of her head.

"Well, yeah, I did." I popped the last bite of my second bagel into my mouth and watched her face. "That doesn't mean she is, though. But no activity on her credit cards? No bank withdrawals? Doesn't look good that she's hiding out somewhere. And why would she be hiding out in the first place?"

"Maybe she killed her son." Abby frowned at her bagel before smearing more cream cheese on it. She took a bite and melted cream cheese ran down her fingers. She licked it off expertly. "And she's on the run."

"Without her car and without any money." I shook my head. "And leaving behind a fifty-thousand-dollar check in her desk drawer. People don't go on the run and leave that kind of money behind—especially when all she had to do was cash it. Then she'd have a shitload of cash—she could hide for a long time with that kind of nest egg. So, no, it's not likely."

Abby nodded. "Most people wouldn't think about not using their cards, either." She sighed. "I mean, if she killed Robby, she probably wouldn't be thinking that clearly anyway—clearly enough to cover her tracks so thoroughly."

"I don't know—she doesn't strike me as the kind of mother who could kill her child, even if he was kind of an asshole—and he seems to have been a major asshole." I got up and walked back to the counter to get a refill. The guy behind the counter put down the book he was reading—*The Stranger* by Albert Camus—and refilled my cup. He was wearing a pair of what had once been dressy brown polyester dress pants, scuffed-up black shoes, and a white T-shirt that didn't cover the tattoos on his neck and arms. His black hair was gelled so it stood up in a faux Mohawk in the center of his head, and there was a blue streak on the left side. His left eyebrow and nose were pierced.

Apparently, he also wasn't a big fan of deodorant.

I put a dollar in the tip jar and sat back down at my table. Abby had finished devouring her bagel and was now using her index finger to scoop the rest of the cream cheese out of the little tin before licking her finger clean.

"I've just been trying to figure out how the blood got in the car," she said as she crumpled up the little tin and placed it on her plate. "Maybe she was shot or cut or whatever when the door was open. The killer took her body out and dumped the car on St. Andrew. But why the need to hide her body? That's what I don't get." Her eyebrows came together just over her nose.

"Well, we still don't even know for sure that it was Mona's blood," I replied, stifling a yawn and taking another swig of coffee. Even though I'd slept well, I was still sleepy. If given my preference, I would have gone back home, crawled into my bed, and slept the rest of the day away. Since that wasn't possible, I promised myself I'd give myself a day in the near future to just sleep. "Venus said there was a lot of it—she wouldn't let me go near the car, of course." I raised the cup to my lips again. The coffee wasn't helping me wake up, and I'd had so much that my stomach was starting to churn. I put the cup back down.

She shook her head, the ponytail swinging. "Do you think Robby O'Neill's money problems are at the bottom of this whole mess? Why Mona's disappeared and why he was killed?"

"Frankly, I can't think of anything else right now. Can you?" She shook her head again. "I wish I knew why Mona O'Neill suddenly changed her testimony in the Marino lawsuit—that's another piece that doesn't fit. It doesn't sound like her. She was close to the Marinos, from all accounts, and this change came from left field."

"Unless someone paid her to—if she was trying to come up with the money to help Robby out..."

"But there was a cashier's check in her desk drawer, courtesy of our carpetbagger billionaire." I watched her face. Her expression didn't change. "Why didn't she just cash it and give the money to Robby? Wouldn't that have solved their problems?"

"You're right, it doesn't make any sense. Nothing about this stupid case makes any goddamned sense—which means we just haven't dug deep enough, right?" Abby replied with a sigh. "And we don't even know why Robby needed money in the first place." She held up her hand. "I know, I'm going to work on that today, and see if there's a connection between Barras and Global Insurance. It's on my to-do list, okay?"

"I'm going to see if I can talk to the widow—she came back to town yesterday." I sighed. "I was going to try to talk to her yesterday, but got distracted."

"It's a puzzle wrapped in an enigma inside of a mystery." She scratched her forehead thoughtfully. "An interesting conundrum."

"Yes." I resisted the urge to pound my head against the wall. "Are you going to tell me what happened at the Catbox last night, or are we just going to talk around it all morning?"

"I didn't think you'd ever ask." She grinned at me, her eyes glinting. "For one thing, I made over five hundred bucks—and for another, Morgan Barras is one cheap-ass son of a bitch." She laughed. "That prick is worth how many billions? But he won't give a working girl more than a five-dollar bill. What a cheap douchebag. Of course, he tried to screw every one of his ex-wives when he divorced them. Every one of them had to take him to court and get a judge involved. What an asshole."

"That's interesting, but is any of it relevant to the case at hand?" It came out sharper than I'd intended, so I smiled to try to take the edge off.

It didn't work. Her eyes narrowed. "The character of a suspect is always relevant, isn't it? You always say so—or has something changed?"

"Sorry, didn't mean to be so harsh." I suppressed a grin and waved my hand. "Go on, then. Tell me everything."

"The girls said he generally comes in around ten, so I got there about nine and hung out backstage, watching to see when he got there." She grinned. I'd never seen her perform—but she had to be good at it. The manager of the Catbox Club pretty much let her do whatever she wanted. "Big Man Billionaire came in right on schedule, about quarter after ten, so I went to work." She smiled. "All of his wives were eastern Europeans, so I put on one of my best platinum blond wigs, and of course I can do an Eastern European accent in my sleep. I put on a pair of Daisy Dukes and a bikini top, and just walked around the club asking men to buy a poor immigrant girl a drink—and he couldn't take his eyes off me." She mimed patting herself on the back. "I have to say, I think Katinka is a good role for me, she might have to come back." She said it in a thick accent that sounded vaguely Eastern European. The way she held herself changed, as did her facial expression. In a blond wig, she *would* be convincing.

"Impressive," I replied. "Just don't become Wife Number Five or whatever number he's on."

Her face twisted. "Oh, as if." She shuddered. "I would never marry a pig like that, I don't care how much money he has. Blech."

"Okay, I was just kidding."

"I eventually made it around to his table. He came in with a group—a couple of them were obviously bodyguards. I didn't know who the other guys were—Merrily told me one of them is on the city council, some important muckety-muck who has a lot to do with zoning and stuff, I don't know. I wrote his name down." She started reaching into her purse.

"It can wait—just put it in the report when you write it up," I instructed her.

"Cool." She smiled at me. "So, of course he wanted me to sit with him, tell him all about myself, so I asked him to buy me a glass of that shitty champagne they make us hustle. He thought we should get to know each other better." She rolled her eyes. "The current Mrs. Barras is in Europe, shopping and doing some charity thing—I verified it online, so it didn't take a rocket scientist to see Mr. Billion Dollar Barras was looking for a little company, and he certainly was." She opened her eyes wide. "He definitely wanted more than just talk, but I told him I might work as a dancer but I wasn't a whore. He told me I misunderstood—he was looking for companionship, not sex."

"You didn't go back to his place?" I stared at her. "Abby, that wasn't—"

"I can take care of myself," she replied, but she gave me a smile and touched my hand to show she was grateful for my concern. "I'm pretty good with the self-defense, you know. And you know the club's too loud—the music and people talking and all that crap. He wasn't going to tell me anything useful there in the club, not with his bodyguards and that city council dude sitting there."

"Still, don't take chances like that. I don't want to have to explain to Jephtha—"

"It's so cute that you worry." She touched my hand again. "But I was working at the Catbox Club before we met, Chanse, and I know how to take care of myself. I'm not crazy, all evidence to the contrary. I don't ever let myself get into situations I can't get myself out of."

I started to lecture her, but bit my tongue and said nothing. Like everyone else her age, she believed she was invulnerable and nothing bad would ever happen to her.

I just hoped that when something bad did happen to her, I'd be around to help.

Which is all anyone can do for someone else, anyway.

"So, he waited for me until I was done working—and given how little his tips were, no one really cared that I took him out of there at midnight." She smeared more cream cheese on the other half of her bagel. "It's so weird—Merrily told me the city council guy is usually a big tipper, but whenever he comes in with Barras, it's like little tips is catching, you know? And yeah, he can't give anyone more than a five, right, but he swept me out of the Quarter in a limousine." She rolled her eyes. "Like that's supposed to impress me after I've watched him giving the other girls fives for two hours? All it did was show me what a cheap-ass he is. And of course, it's not like I don't know how much it costs to rent a limo—and it was definitely rented." One of her brothers worked as a limo driver, for one of the largest limo agencies in the city. She and Jephtha could rent a limo for next to nothing anytime they wanted. "But, of course,

I acted like I'd never been in one before, and oohed and aahed appropriately, when it was called for, you know, and you should have seen him preen!" She made a gagging noise. "He's awful damned proud of himself. But, I have to say, the penthouse at Poydras Tower is pretty fucking impressive."

I made a face at her. "I'm still not happy about you going over there."

She patted my hand. "Don't go all knight-in-shining-armor on me, Chanse. I can take care of myself—and I had my gun in my purse."

"Yeah, but what if he and his bodyguards decided to pull a gang-rape on you? What if *that's* the kind of kinky shit he was into?"

Her smile faded. "Oh."

"Just don't do that again, okay?"

She nodded, obviously rattled. "Well, his living room is one entire end of the apartment, with the most amazing view of the city—when the curtains are open there's this panoramic view, Chanse. It took my breath away. The city is so beautiful at night with the lights and all." Her eyes took on a dreamy look for moment before she continued, "But he was a perfect gentleman—even after I told him the real reason I was there."

"He took it well?"

"He really did only want companionship—'a pretty young woman to talk to,' were his exact words. We drank champagne—I just sipped, he drank a lot—and talked. And once I showed him my badge, he was really amused—and was open to talking." She shrugged. "Whether he was telling the truth or not, I don't know. But he says the check was a finder's fee, for getting Jonny to sign with his MMA promotion. Jonny's got a pretty good deal there. Barras Fight Corporation is going to pay his gym fees and his trainers, and he gets to keep all the money he earns from fights or any endorsement deals he might get. Some supplement company is already interested in signing him as spokesman, and so is a workout apparel company."

"But Jonny's just a nobody. And what does Barras get out of it?"

"Ah, there's the rub, you see." Her eyes glinted. "The purse—that's what they call the money you win in a fight—isn't very much in MMA, but that can change at any time. The fighter makes most of his money by being sponsored by someone like Barras, and by getting endorsement deals. Barras makes *his* money from ticket sales and selling the TV rights. Barras thinks Jonny has the ability to be a champion, and not just in the cage. He's apparently really photogenic, and has a very real, likable charisma that comes across on film."

I shook my head. "Barras is a billionaire. I don't see how this could possibly make enough money to make it worth his while to be involved."

"Oh, Chanse." She started laughing, to the point where she finally got hiccups. She took a drink of water, and wiped at her eyes. "Barras isn't *just* all about money—you said so yourself. Barras is also about his ego—he likes seeing his face in the papers and getting on TV." She leaned forward. "He wants to make this MMA stuff as big as boxing—and go down in sports history as the man who made MMA a big-time sport. Part of his legacy, like Poydras Tower, the casinos, and all the buildings and deals he's done—he wants to be remembered. Besides, all the MMA fights are held in casinos—which brings people in to gamble—and that's where the real money is."

"So, the check had nothing to do with the church? Or the Cypress Gardens lawsuit?"

"He claims he's not interested in buying St. Anselm's—that's just an Internet rumor. And he said the lawsuit doesn't involve him—he did buy Cypress Gardens, but the suit is between Marino and the insurance company." She shook her head. "I'm with you, though, Chanse. I don't like the coincidences. Everywhere we turn with Mona, it seems, there's Morgan Barras. But he says he only knows her through Jonny."

"Did you believe him?"

"I'm not a human lie detector, but he did seem genuinely surprised when I brought up St. Anselm's and Cypress Gardens." She reached into her purse and handed me a business card. "He said that if either of us had any further questions, he'd be more than happy to talk to either one of us. I gave him one of yours—he asked. Said he liked to be prepared, in case he ever need a private eye."

I turned his card over in my fingers. It was thick, a rich cream vellum, with embossed gold lettering. It simply read *Morgan Barras* with a phone number underneath.

"That's his personal cell number."

I slid it into my wallet. "Nice work."

"All right, then. I'm going to go see if I can connect him with Global Insurance, and see what I can dig up on Robby. Is there anything else you want me to do?" She closed her purse and slid it over her shoulder.

I thought for a minute. "No, not right now. I'll talk to Celia O'Neill, see what she knows about what was going on with Robby."

"So any thoughts on what Robby's money problems were?"

"Hard to say." I shook my head. "But it'll be interesting to see what we can dig up."

She stood up. "Jephtha is still watching Mona's credit cards. He's still running the financials on Robby O'Neill—but if he borrowed money from the wrong people, it's not going to show on his credit report."

"I'm aware."

She smiled and walked out of the coffee shop. I watched her get into the battered Oldsmobile and drive away.

I glanced at my watch. My next appointment wasn't going to show up for another ten minutes or so. I took a sip of my coffee and started flipping through my notebook, going over everything in my head yet again.

Something definitely stank here—there were way too many coincidences for my liking.

I looked up as the front door opened, and I smiled.

Father Dan Marshall waved at me with a grin and walked over to the counter, where he ordered something from the hipster at the counter.

No one looking at him would ever assume he was a priest. A few inches over six foot, he had thick white blond hair that he was letting grow long, so that it brushed his shoulders. He was fair-skinned, but was one of the Nordic types whose skin turned golden when tanned—and Father Dan was always tanned. He was striking, rather than handsome. He had a long, narrow face and even, perfectly white teeth. His deep blue eyes were a little too small for his face and placed a little too close together for him to be considered handsome, but he definitely stood out in a crowd. There was something about him, something indefinable that just caught people's attention. He didn't seem to be aware of the affect he had on people.

He carried his coffee over to the condiment stand, and I watched as he shook out a pack of Sweet'n Low and dumped it in his coffee. He was definitely not dressed particularly priestly today. His red tank top stretched tightly across his muscular chest, and the straps exposed his defined, thickly muscled arms. He was wearing khaki clamdigger shorts that hung loosely from his hips but clung tightly to his round, hard ass—he had one of the best asses in New Orleans. His flip-flops slapped against the floor as he walked over to my table. He flashed me a dazzling smile as he sat down in the chair Abby had abandoned. "Good to see you, Chanse. What's going on? What can I help you with?" He raised his blond eyebrows. "I feel so cloak-and-dagger, helping out with an investigation."

Father Dan and I had originally met at a fund-raiser for the NO/AIDS Task Force. He hadn't been in his collar that night, either, and I'd actually tried to pick him up. I was horrified to find out he was a priest—I'd seen him around in gay bars before, and walking around shirtless during Southern Decadence, showing off his magnificent chest and ripped abdominal muscles—but once that initial awkwardness passed, I'd enjoyed his company. He had a great personality, a wicked sense of humor, and I appreciated the fact that he ministered to the LGBT community. The archdiocese knew what he was doing, of course, but as long as he flew under the radar and didn't bring any unwanted—or embarrassing—attention to the archdiocese, they were okay with it. As he always said, "In a city with this many Catholics, there are bound to be a large number of gays and lesbians who are falling away from the church because of the Vatican's stance on sexuality. But just because you're gay doesn't mean God doesn't love you, and I like to think that in my little way I am keeping people's faith alive. And what more can a priest ask for in his life?" His little ministry of Catholic queers was called St. Sebastian's, and they held Mass in an abandoned Catholic church in the Bywater.

"I need to ask you a few things." I sighed. "I'm sorry, but the case I'm working on might involve the archdiocese, even if only peripherally, Dan. Abby has a contact inside the archdiocese, and she's already talked to him, but I'm hoping you might be able to help me."

"That doesn't sound very promising." Dan frowned. "What exactly are you investigating? What kind of help are you looking for?"

I took a deep breath. "I don't want to get you into trouble. So—"

"Well, you don't have to worry about that, Chanse. I won't do anything that would get me in trouble, no offense." He laughed and took another sip of coffee. "St. Sebastian's is too important to me, and I'm not doing anything that could potentially jeopardize my ministry. I can't do that to my parishioners. If it was just me—" His tanned shoulders raised a bit. "It would be one thing. But it's not just me."

"Understood." I smiled at him and filled him in on Mona O'Neill's disappearance.

When I finished, his eyebrows knit together. "That's terrible. I don't know Mona well, but I've met her a few times." He shook his head. "She's a good woman—maybe a little misguided when it comes to the situation with St. Anselm's, but her faith is strong." He frowned. "I don't see how I can help you. I'm not involved in those decisions—I am rarely at the archdiocese offices, and I don't know anything about it."

"Who was the parish priest at St. Anselm's? They don't have services there anymore, do they?"

"Well, Tom Shannon was, but since the archbishop shut it down, he's been moved." He scratched his head. "I think he was moved over to either Gulfport, or was it Mobile? I can find out—that's easy enough to do. He was really close to Alex Perrilloux at Good Shepherd. Alex was pretty upset about Tom moving away." His right eye closed in a wink. "Really close, if you catch my drift."

"They were a couple?" That was a surprise.

"I didn't say that—I said they were close." Dan laughed. "Read into that what you will. Remember, the church doesn't frown on love—but she does demand celibacy from her priests."

"What do you think about the closings?" I watched his face.

"Me?" He shrugged. "It makes sense to me, but it's not my parish, either. As you can imagine, it's not like young men are breaking down our doors to get into the priesthood. When older priests die or retire, there aren't young ones to replace them anymore, not like there used to be. Young people just aren't that interested in marrying themselves to God anymore. It wasn't really about money, you know—it was about the availability of priests. They needed Tom in Mobile—I'm pretty sure it was Mobile—and they didn't have anyone to replace him at St. Anselm's. Tom was already doing double duty at Our Lady of Prompt Succor—so the archbishop decided to merge those two parishes into others. Yes, it also meant a cost reduction, but I really do believe it was all about lack of personnel, like Archbishop Pugh said. I know that's not a popular position to hold, but Archbishop Pugh isn't the monster everyone makes him out to be." He spread his hands. "He knows all about St. Sebastian's, for example, and he supports me completely." He winked. "As long as I keep a low profile, of course. The pasting he's taking in the local media is kind of unfair. But he's an outsider—if he'd grown up in Holy Cross or anywhere else in New Orleans, for that matter, none of this would even be an issue."

"New Orleans doesn't warm quickly to outsiders."

He rolled his eyes. "I'm sure Archbishop Pugh was caught off guard by all of this." He grinned at me. "The church expects— no, demands—obedience. I'm surprised he hasn't threatened to excommunicate the protesters."

"Excommunicate?" I stared at him. "Do they still do that?"

He laughed. "Yes, they do. And he would be well within his rights to excommunicate them, for defying him as head of the church in New Orleans. So, the next time you hear someone bashing him as a heartless bastard who doesn't care about his parish, remember that, okay?"

"So, there's no priest gossip about anything unusual going on at St. Anselm's? I've heard rumors that Pugh is looking to sell the property to a developer."

"Been frequenting the online message boards?" Dan laughed. "Don't believe any of that crap, Chanse. There are no plans to demolish the building or sell the land. Pugh is looking into having the building declared a historic landmark. Have you been inside? It is a gorgeous building."

I nodded. "Yeah. I can see why the parishioners are so dedicated to it."

"You know, I do have some 'priestly gossip,' as you call it, now that I think about it." He leaned across the table and lowered his voice. "That Save Our Churches group supposedly isn't what it claims to be."

"Then what is it? This is the first time I've heard anything like that."

He gave me a strange look. "The story I heard is that Save Our Churches wasn't founded by members of St. Anselm's parish, or Our Lady of Prompt Succor's—the founders weren't even Catholic."

"That doesn't make any sense, Dan."

"I'm just telling you what I heard." He gave me an apologetic look. "You might want to check into the group. I don't know why, or what their endgame would be. It's just what I heard. Maybe if you talk to Tom Shannon, he might know something more about it—after all, it was his parish. And after all, this O'Neill woman who disappeared—"

"Yeah?"

"This Mona O'Neill woman, if she was *supposedly* the leader of the group, and she found out she was being manipulated in some way, and that the whole point of the group really had nothing to do with keeping the churches open…" He held up his hands. "I know what you're going to say—what nefarious purpose would this group have? Why would they be trying to keep the churches open? I can't help you there, because I have no idea. I don't know if it makes any sense to me, I don't know if it's even true. But you said you wanted to hear anything, even if it was just gossip—and I've heard that from several people inside the church. I don't know, Chanse, maybe they're just looking for some kind of answers themselves, something to take the heat off the archbishop, who knows?" He shrugged again. "You see why I don't listen to gossip? There've been a lot of rumors, on both sides, about St. Anselm's. And the truth is buried somewhere in there, but who knows what's true and what isn't anymore?"

I hadn't thought about looking into Save Our Churches, and berated myself for not thinking of it.

Even if there was nothing there, I should have covered all of my bases.

"But it can't hurt to find out if someone might have a reason for wanting to cause trouble for the archdiocese—or just the archbishop himself." He glanced at his watch. "All right, I've got to run." He grasped my forearm. "It's good to see you, Chanse. Maybe I can have you and Rory over for dinner sometime soon?"

"That would be great." I smiled at him as he stood up.

"I'll call you." He smiled and walked out of the coffee shop.

I watched him go, then whipped out my cell phone. I sent Abby a quick text: *Add Save Our Churches to your to-do list. Find out everything you can about them.*

Two seconds later her response came: *Will do!*

I put my phone away and walked out of the coffee shop into the bright morning sunlight.

CHAPTER TEN

I spent the rest of the morning trying to track down Tom Shannon. A quick web search turned him up in Biloxi, as Dan had said, but I wasn't able to reach him. I left messages for him at several different numbers and tried to get a hold of Celia O'Neill. Again, all I got was the voicemail at Mona's house, so I left a detailed message. I also left one with Jonny, asking him to have Celia give me a call. I puttered around, finished some paperwork and paid some bills—and looked up Luke Marino's address online.

As I sat there, staring at the Uptown address on my computer screen, memories I hadn't thought about in years came back to me.

I'd grown up in a dusty little east Texas town called Cottonwood Wells, living in a trailer on the wrong side of town. We never seemed to have much money, and knowing that most everyone I was in school with considered me trash didn't help matters much. My clothes were always ill-fitting and from Sears, and I knew the kids whose parents belonged to the country club and bought their clothes at big fancy stores in Houston laughed at me, mostly behind my back but sometimes right to my face. My mom drank and my dad was violent. We always had to walk on eggshells whenever Dad was home because you never knew what would set off his mercurial temper. When he got mad his brown eyes turned black and spittle would fly from his mouth as he screamed at us. He smashed things, punched walls, took his belt and beat me and my brother and sister.

Even something as innocuous as watching a football game on television could turn ugly with no warning.

That was the worst part of it. Something that would make him laugh one day could send him into one of the rages another day—and there was nothing to do but ride it out. He made no sense, and nothing anyone could say would make the situation better. Anything you said was wrong.

My goal growing up was to survive until I was eighteen and then get as far away from Cottonwood Wells as I could—and never look back.

Football was my ticket out—of everything. Once I displayed talent and ability on the football field, all the snotty things kids would say about me ceased, and I became one of the "popular" kids, the football star everyone wanted to be associated with. But rather than embracing this wonderful change in my life, from trash to popularity, by now I knew I was gay and had to hide that from everyone else.

I chose LSU because it was the college offering a full scholarship that was the farthest distance from Cottonwood Wells. The others—the University of Houston, the University of Texas, Texas Christian—were too close.

And so I came to Baton Rouge as a big eighteen-year-old virgin, my first time away from home, entering a world that might as well have been another planet.

And Luke Marino was King of the Planet.

As a freshman tight end on the Tiger football team, I'd had a major crush on him. What wasn't there to like? He had thick, curly bluish black hair and olive skin, and the five o'clock shadow he always had by late afternoon tinted his cheeks and chin. He'd been around six feet tall or so and carried 220 pounds of solid, defined muscle on his frame. He actually liked working out—for me, it was always an odious chore, part of the price I paid to play football. He had the most amazing legs I'd ever seen to that point—his quads were so thick and powerful they could have easily cracked coconuts. He was also one of those guys who had no shyness about his body. Most guys on the team walked around the locker room or the training room with a towel tied around their waists. Not Luke Marino—he walked around either in just a jock or stark naked with a big grin on his face with everything exposed for everyone to see. He'd had a thick patch of hair in the center of his broad chest and a treasure trail leading from his navel down to the pubic thatch, and his massive legs were also covered in curly black hair. I tried not to stare, but would always steal surreptitious glances whenever I could so I could replay them in my memory later, when I was alone in my room at the fraternity house. I dreamed about him for years after he graduated—and for a long time, I always judged every man I met by how their looks compared to his.

In addition to that amazing body, he was also impossibly handsome, with big, round brown eyes with heavy lids, an aristocratic nose, impossibly white teeth, and a deep cleft in his chin. His sister managed a tanning salon in Baton Rouge, so he had a deep all-over tan. His eyes had a sparkle to them and were incredibly expressive underneath the thick black eyebrows.

He was a big star on campus—everyone knew who Luke Marino was. He might not be the fastest running back, or the strongest—but when Luke got the ball, it was practically a guaranteed three yards. He just put his helmet down and ran over everyone. He made all SEC his junior year, and his senior year we managed to win the SEC despite our loss to Florida. We went into the Sugar Bowl ranked fourth in the country, and humiliated our Big Ten opponent 44–14, which jumped us up to Number 2 in the final polls. I remember after that win partying on Bourbon Street with my teammates—and wondering where in the Quarter the gay bars were.

I found those on a solo trip down a few weeks later.

But Luke Marino was friendly and nice—no one had a bad thing to say about him. He never yelled at anyone on the team, never criticized or made fun of anyone—he always knew the right thing to say to make someone who was down get back up. He was a natural leader—he could fire up the team even higher than the coaching staff could. When he talked, his eyes flashed and you could hear a pin drop in the locker room. He made you want to play harder than you ever had before because you didn't want to let him down.

He had a steady girlfriend, Mandy Welles, who was one of the Golden Girls in the marching band. She was beautiful and was always waiting for him outside the locker room after games. He would kiss her, and they would walk off together, his arm draped around her shoulder, her long blond hair bouncing. They got married right after the Sugar Bowl. He entered the pro draft and was taken in the second round by the San Diego Chargers. I followed his pro career, such as it was. It never really got off the ground. The Chargers had a lot of high hopes for him, but when he got in to play during his rookie season he didn't exactly cover himself with glory. His second year, he blew out his right knee against the 49ers, ending his career.

And then he dropped out of sight of the public eye.

I'd seen him once in the years since I myself graduated—Paige and I had dinner at Marino's, his family's restaurant on Magazine Street, shortly after I got on with the NOPD. He and Mandy had been there with another couple, and he'd started gaining weight. Obviously, since leaving professional sports he simply didn't see the need to keep himself up with the kind of physical conditioning he had before. Our eyes had met at one point, and I could tell he recognized my face, just didn't know where he knew me from. I'd just nodded and turned away.

I thought about calling him, but decided to just take a chance and drop by the house.

The address turned out to be a big yellow house on Jefferson Avenue, about a block on the river side of Newman High School. It was a big place, with a circular drive and a gallery that ran along the entire front of the house. Two gas lamps bracketed the front door, and the curtains were closed in the big windows. There was an emerald green Mercedes parked in the driveway with MARINO 2 on the license plate, an LSU plate. There was also an LSU plate frame and a sticker reading GEAUX TIGERS on the right back bumper.

I parked on the street and sat there for a moment before getting out. I took a couple of deep breaths, trying to steel my nerve and making fun of myself for being so nervous. *He isn't the big star on the team anymore,* I reminded myself. I got out of the car and headed up the walk. I rang the doorbell and a dog started barking. I could hear someone yelling at the dog, and then the front door opened.

The years had not been kind to Luke Marino.

He was balding, and trying to hide it by combing his hair over the bare spots. The bluish-black hair was not only thinner but was shot through with gray. A second chin was forming beneath the original one, and his eyes were bloodshot. His face was wider and rounder than I remembered, and there were heavy bags underneath both of his eyes. He was still a big man, but his stomach had expanded exponentially, straining the buttons on his white shirt. He was wearing a pair of jeans that he had to belt low underneath the bulge of his stomach. His legs were also thicker—but I rather doubted that was muscle. I could see red veins in his nose, and grayish black hairs jutted out from his nostrils. He was wearing a T-shirt underneath the white shirt, but black hairs were poking out through the neckline.

He was only three years older than me, but he looked fifty.

At least.

"Mr. Marino?" I said, hoping my shock didn't show on my face. "I'm Chanse MacLeod—"

"The detective!" He smiled, managing to look a little less harried, and shook my hand. His was warm, soft, and damp. "Yes, Loren told me you might be coming by at some point. Thank you so much for taking the case! Great having you on board. Come on in." He gave me an apologetic look as he stepped aside to let me in. "I'm really sorry, everything that could possibly go wrong today has, and the place is a mess, the maid quit—" He broke off and shut the door behind me. ""But you don't care about that." He showed me into a living room, through a door to the right of the front hallway. "Can I get you something to drink? Iced tea?"

"Iced tea would be great—it's kind of hot outside."

"I'll be right back. Have a seat—make yourself at home." He disappeared through a door on the other side of the room.

The living room had been turned into a shrine to Luke's football career. No, shrine wasn't the right word—it was a temple. The long wall directly opposite the door had an enormous, almost life-size portrait of Luke in his uniform, holding a football and posing on one knee at the fifty yard line, smiling carefree at the camera. I stepped closer and marveled at it. He'd been even more handsome than I remembered, which made the present-day version even sadder. The entire wall was covered with pictures and awards certificates. His LSU diploma had a place of honor next to the massive portrait, and four team photos were hung directly beneath the diploma. I stepped closer—the team I was on was the lowest one. It had been mounted, and in the lower right corner was an oval-shaped duplicate of the massive portrait. I smiled—I had four of those framed team pictures myself, in a box somewhere in one of my closets. I picked myself out in the picture from Luke's senior year and smiled at my innocent young face. I was shocked at how young I looked—and how thick my hair had been. I ran a hand through it.

Yes, it had definitely thinned since then.

There was a case beside the front window with game balls and trophies, and I walked over and glanced at them. Luke's letter jacket from LSU was folded on the bottom shelf, nestled between some game balls and Mandy's Golden Girl costume. I put my hand against the glass. College seemed like it had been a million years earlier, I thought, and shook my head, turning my back to Luke's past. *I don't even know where all my trophies and letter jacket are*, I reflected.

I hadn't thrown any of it away—so it was probably all in a box somewhere.

There was a massive plasma television mounted on the opposite wall, and all around it were more framed pictures of Luke—these were from high school and from his brief career with the Chargers.

"Here you go." Luke walked back into the room and passed me

a tall glass of iced tea. I took a drink—it was over-sweetened, but I drank it anyway. "You an LSU fan?"

I gestured to the team picture from my freshman year. "I was a freshman when you were a senior."

He grinned. "I thought you looked familiar—sorry I didn't recognize you." He made a face. "But man, the older you get, the memory just goes. Sit down, sit down, please." He gestured at the sofa. "Did you play in the pros?"

I shook my head. "I blew out my knee in the Sugar Bowl my senior year. I wasn't sure if I could make it in the pros—wasn't sure if I should try." I shrugged. "I probably wouldn't have been drafted anyway, and truth be told, I was kind of sick of playing football, so the injury made it all a moot point. Probably for the best."

"Damned knees—they're a bitch, aren't they?" He slapped his left one. "That's what finished me with the Chargers. Got hit in a game with the 49ers and I heard it go. I still hear that crack in my nightmares sometimes." He grimaced. "It hurt like a son of a bitch. But like you said, it's just as well—I wasn't having much of a pro career, and it probably wasn't going to get any better, but if I hadn't gotten hurt I would have kept working, plugging away at it hoping to turn it all around. Still, I was glad to come back home and get my life back together."

I nodded. "Sorry to hear about the lawsuit."

He whistled. "Those thieving sons of bitches. I know they got to Mona somehow—and now she's missing?" He shook his head sadly. "When Loren told me Mona was changing her testimony, it broke my heart. I don't know how they did it, you know? Mona was like family to me. She worked for me at Cypress Gardens almost right from the beginning."

"When was the last time you spoke to Mona?" I pulled out my pad.

"It's been a few weeks—maybe even months. I wasn't really keeping track, you know?" He crossed a leg. "Mona came by here—she wanted my advice about a contract for Jonny—he got a really good offer from the Barras Casino Group, and she knew that was who I sold Cypress Gardens to—"

"When exactly did you sell Cypress Gardens?"

He nodded. "Didn't Loren tell you? Yeah, a couple of years after Katrina, I was having trouble keeping the place going." He shook his head. "I had to take out loans, you know, to do repairs and get the place going again because the damned insurance was taking so long to work out everything—I was stretched to the max, you know? If I didn't make the bank payments, I would lose the place, and every day I was wondering if that would be the day I would go bankrupt—which is what those motherfuckers at the insurance company were hoping for, you know?" He sighed. "Morgan Barras made me a hell of an offer—enough money to pay off the loans with a little left over to live on. What else could I do?" He made a face. "And now the insurance company is trying to *use* the fact I sold the place to get out from under what they owe me, may the bastards fry in hell for all eternity."

Surely it wasn't a coincidence that Morgan Barras had turned up yet again? Aloud, I said, "So she wanted you to look over the contract?"

He nodded. "She also wanted to know what I thought of Barras. Like I said, Mona was like family, and I knew Jonny pretty well—she would bring him around, you know, in the summer when he wasn't in school. He was a handful." He smiled, remembering. "I know she was worried about him—even after I sold Cypress Gardens—and you know, I gave her six months' severance—we stayed in touch. We tried to have dinner or lunch together once a month or so over the last few years. My wife and I—Mona was our babysitter of choice, you know. I still can't believe she wants to change her testimony."

"What did you tell her about the contract?"

"I told her it looked fair, but she should have a lawyer look it over. I told her to have Loren look at it—told her not to worry about the fee, I'd just have him bill me. She was family." He shook his big head again. "She was really worried about Jonny, you know. She didn't like the girl he married, and that he'd dropped out of high school, and I guess they're going to have a baby? I also told her that he might be a bit of an asshole, but Morgan was pretty trustworthy. I mean, he offered me a really good price for Cypress Gardens—and to be honest, I would have let it go for a lot less—it had turned into such a fucking nightmare after the storm, you know." He ran a hand over his head. "I'd have been more than happy to let it go for just taking over the loans, to tell you the truth. I was seriously fucked and was going to have to try to borrow money from my family."

"If you don't mind my asking, how much did he pay for Cypress Gardens?"

He shrugged. "It's a matter of public record. I sold him Cypress Gardens for fifteen million. After paying off the loans, I cleared about 1.5 million." He sighed. "I am suing the insurance company for twenty million—the amount of the loans, loss of business revenues, and legal fees. If the insurance had paid out like it was supposed to, I wouldn't have had to sell the place or take out the loans. Now they're saying since I sold out, they shouldn't have to pay."

"So, when you saw Mona, she didn't say anything to you at all about changing her testimony?"

"No. Not a word. When the lawyers called me and told me, you could have knocked me down with a feather. I couldn't believe it—I still can't believe it. There had to be a reason. Mona wouldn't just do that, you know?"

"Do you think they might have bought her off?"

"No. Mona wasn't like that. How can I make you understand that?" He drummed his fingers on his knee. "I would have trusted Mona with my life. She is one of the most honest people I've ever known. She wouldn't even borrow money from petty cash to buy a soda from the vending machines. So the idea that she could be bought off? It's ludicrous."

"What if she needed the money?"

"Well, if she needed money, she could have just asked." He

gestured around the room. "I may not exactly be rolling in money, but I'd help her out if she needed help."

"Can you think of any reason Mona might have needed money?"

"Mona's great with money—which was why she was such a great property manager. That woman knows how to stretch a dollar—she could pinch a penny till Lincoln winced." He laughed. "I can't imagine Mona herself ever getting into financial trouble— every once in a while I'd try to talk her into investing money, and she would always say the only difference between the stock market and a casino was at least you knew ahead of time the casino was out to take your money. So, bad investments? No, she wouldn't have ever done anything like that."

"But what about one of the kids? Did you know her other kids well?"

"I met Lorelle a few times—I liked her." He frowned. "The older son—Robby? Him, I didn't care for. There was just something about him I didn't like, you know? He was—" He fumbled for the words, finally adding, "a phony. One of those guys who want to get rich quick but don't want to work for it? His wife had money, I think—I didn't much care for her, either—she was Queen of Rex and he brought it up every time I talked to him, like I give a shit about that? Marinos weren't good enough for the old-line krewes, we never were. He kept wanting me to invest in things that never seemed legitimate, you know what I mean? He worked in investments, you know, a broker or advisor or something. He was always coming over here, wanting my business, you know? When I'd press for details there never were any—like I'm just going to give him money without a prospectus or something?"

"You didn't trust him?"

"Not as far as I could throw him." The contempt in his voice was unmistakable. "He struck me as the kind of person who had big dreams, but never really had the mentality or perseverance to make them happen. One of the big deals he tried to pitch to me was an apartment complex to be built on Claiborne, near the hospitals." He sighed again. "Now, we all know after Katrina there was a housing shortage here, but there was also a shortage of construction workers. And what he wanted to do was buy out a lot of his neighbors in Broadmoor and build the new complex there—but he couldn't say for sure whether his neighbors would sell, and blah blah blah." He scratched his nose. "Like I said, a dreamer with his head in the clouds." He snapped his fingers. "With no business plan? I would always talk to him, as a courtesy to Mona, but it never amounted to anything. And then a few weeks ago—when was it exactly? Anyway, he came by and wanted to borrow some 'venture capital' from me."

"And how much was that?"

"Fifty thousand dollars." He shook his head. "He had a promissory note and everything ready for me to sign. But he couldn't really give me any details about the venture…I told him I needed more information than that. He kept telling me how I could trust him, and so on and so forth…"

Fifty thousand dollars? The amount of the cashier's check in Mona's desk drawer?

I cleared my throat and interrupted him. "When exactly was this?"

He nodded. "A couple of weeks ago?" He frowned and stood up. "Let me get my appointment book and I can tell you exactly when it was." He walked out of the room.

I heard the front door open and close, and got up myself.

Mandy Marino had aged far better than her husband. She was still slender—she could probably still fit into the uniform in the trophy case. She still wore her blond hair long, but she was able to pull the look off. Her face was remarkably free of wrinkles, and her makeup was perfect. She might have thickened a bit in the waist and her breasts might have been a little heavier, but she was still an incredibly beautiful woman.

She walked into the living room and gave a start. "I'm sorry."

She plastered the smile that she'd used as a Golden Girl on her face. She dropped her purse on the sideboard and held out a hand to me. "Mandy Marino, nice to meet you."

"Chanse MacLeod. I'm investigating the disappearance of Mona O'Neill."

"Has there been any word? I'm worried about her." The smile faltered a little bit as she sat down. "I still can't believe Mona would betray us the way she has. It's just not like her, you know."

"It does seem out of character," I agreed with her.

"I guess it just goes to show you never really know someone." Mandy got up and poured herself a glass of whiskey. "Do you mind? Would you like one?" I shook my head, and she tossed it back with a single movement. She smiled and sat back down. "It's been a rather trying day, Mr. MacLeod."

"Chanse, please."

"You must call me Mandy, then." She crossed her legs. "My mother is ill and doesn't want to stay in the hospital anymore. Which is fine, but she also doesn't want a full-time nurse—she wants me to take care of her, which just isn't practical. Does that seem cold and selfish to you?"

I shook my head. "No."

"Thank you—my mother seems to think I'm some kind of monster because I don't want to drop everything and take care of her." She closed her eyes, and pressed her fingers against her temples. "She doesn't seem to understand—or care—that I have four children that need their mother, and a household of my own, and I can't just abandon that to go stay with her and wait on her hand and foot. And wouldn't it better for her to have a nurse, someone who would know what to do in the case of an emergency? But oh, no, not my mother." She waved a hand tiredly and blew out a breath in a deeply tired sigh. "I'm sorry to bore you with this. What a horrible hostess you must think I am!" She gave me a wan, tired smile. "So, you're looking for Mona? Do you have any leads?"

"A few." I nodded. "Did you know her well?"

"Apparently not." She made a face. "I thought I did. I considered her a friend—and I know Luke certainly did. She was like a member of the family, Mr. Mac—Chanse. To have her stab us in the back the way she did—well, I certainly would have never thought her capable of it." She compressed her lips into a thin line. "I hope she's happy with the thirty pieces of silver Global Insurance gave her." She rubbed her forehead. "I'm sorry, I suppose I shouldn't be bitter. I'm sure she has her reasons for what she's doing. Although how she could do this…" She focused her eyes on me. "I'm sorry, please forgive me, my mind is all over the place, I can't just focus. So Mona's disappeared."

"She was last seen on Thursday night around nine p.m. No one has seen or heard from her since."

"But that was *days* ago." She looked horrified. "You don't think it has something to do with the lawsuit?"

"I'm exploring all possibilities, Mandy. It may, and it may not."

"It was two weeks ago," Luke said as he walked back into the room, his appointment book open in his hands. "Two weeks ago yesterday, in fact. Hello, dear." He kissed Mandy on the cheek. "I didn't hear you come in. Is everything okay with your mother?"

"We can talk about that later, dear." She gave him a brittle smile. "Did you know Mona is missing?"

"Loren called me this morning and filled me in—you'd already left for the hospital, and I didn't want to bother you with this while you were dealing with your mother," he replied. "Loren's engaged Mr. MacLeod here to look for her." He beamed at me. "Did Chanse tell you he played ball for LSU—he was a freshman when we were seniors."

"Two weeks ago yesterday?" I cut off Mandy's squeal of delight before she could say anything.

Luke nodded. "Yes. He stopped by here."

"And when did you find out she was changing her testimony?"

"That was last Monday, wasn't it?" He looked over at his wife for verification.

Mandy nodded. "Yes, because that was the day I had to take Mother to the hospital, and after dealing with that all day I came home and you told me about it." She looked at me. "Now, *that* was a shitty day—today was nothing in comparison."

"Okay, great. Thank you both—I'll get out of your hair now." I stood up and shook hands with them both. "I'll be in touch if I have any further questions."

"Certainly—any time, anything we can do to help, you just let us know." Luke walked me to the front door, with Mandy trailing along behind us. They walked out onto the porch with me.

"Once this lawsuit thing is taken care of, perhaps you could come join us for dinner sometime," Mandy said. "A Tiger is always welcome in our house."

I smiled and nodded. Once I got into my car, they waved again before they went back inside.

Robby O'Neill had tried to get Luke Marino to "invest" fifty thousand dollars with him two weeks ago.

Fifty thousand dollars—again.

Another coincidence?

My cell phone dinged to let me know I'd just gotten a text message.

I picked up the phone and looked at the screen.

It was from Abby.

Morgan Barras is a minority shareholder in Global Insurance.

I smiled and texted back, *Want to meet at Slice and compare notes?*

Not even ten seconds passed before this came back: *On my way!*

I put the car in gear and headed downtown.

CHAPTER ELEVEN

I ordered for you," Abby said when I sat down across from her at Slice. She was toying with an Italian salad. "You always get the same thing, so I figured why waste time? I'm starving." She shrugged.

She was wearing what we called "professional drag": a black shoulder-length wig, minor makeup application, and a business suit— navy blue skirt and jacket, white silk blouse, and a rope of costume- jewelry pearls. She'd gotten the entire outfit at a consignment shop on Magazine Street for seventy-five dollars.

"Cool," I replied as our waitress set a glass of Coke down in front of me. I smiled my thanks at her.

"Your food should be right out." She smiled back at me and walked away to another table.

"So what's with the professional lady outfit?" I asked, sipping Coke through my straw. Abby hated dressing up like a businesswoman and only did it when it was necessary.

She gave me a crooked smile. "I thought it might be a good idea to interview Robby O'Neill's boss—and his secretary." She gestured at her outfit with distaste written on her face. "And stuffed shirts respond better to this kind of drag."

"Learn anything?"

She paused while our waitress placed a medium combination pizza on a stand in the center of our table. "Anything else I can get you?" she asked. We both shook our heads and she wandered away.

"Robby O'Neill was going to be fired yesterday morning, and possibly have criminal charges filed against him," Abby said, using the spatula to put a large piece on her plate. She added parmesan cheese, and then liberally shook crushed red pepper all over it.

I waited for her to take a bite and swallow.

She smiled at me brightly. "About two weeks ago, the chief accountant at his company noticed some discrepancies in the accounts—and called for an outside audit."

"Around the time Robby started trying to come up with fifty thousand dollars," I added.

She nodded. "It didn't take long for them to discover that the discrepancies were all in Robby's client accounts. He was smart—he never took a huge amount from anyone at a time—a thousand here, a couple of hundred there." She took another bite. "Ordinarily, his boss certainly would have never told me anything about this internal problem, but with Robby being murdered and all—and he wants to cooperate in any way he can to make sure the killer is caught. Criminal or no, Robby was like family." She made a sour face. "Family he was going to send to jail, but family. But the total was between forty and fifty thousand dollars, yes. Apparently, when he was confronted, Robby confessed to everything—he was overextended, and he just borrowed here and there to stay ahead of the credit cards, the house payment, etc. He always intended to pay it back, of course. They fired him on the spot. But, and this is the important part—they gave him until Monday morning to pay the money back. If he didn't give them the money, they were filing embezzlement charges."

"Nice of them to give him an out."

"Yeah, well." She rolled her eyes. "That's the company line, of course, the big magnanimous 'we didn't want to prosecute him' line. His assistant told me the real story." She laughed. "Typical company bullshit—they didn't want to prosecute. Bad publicity for the firm, you see, and it wouldn't look too good to their clients—who might decide to move their business to another firm. And then, of course, on Monday they found out he was dead and there was no chance of getting the money back. But at least now we know he didn't owe a loan shark or drug dealers. He wasn't killed for the debt—nobody from the company would have killed him over it. They wanted to sweep it all under the rug as much as they could—and my guess is they still haven't let the clients know and are trying to figure out if they can keep covering up Robby's embezzlement."

"Maybe one of the clients found out?"

"He never took more than a thousand dollars from any one client—he spread it around. That's why it took so long for the accountants to catch on. He was pretty smart about it—but you know how that works, you take some here and get away with it, so you take some from someone else, and it just snowballs."

"I don't understand why he didn't just scale back."

"Yeah, well, he didn't. And so Robby O'Neill needed fifty thousand dollars by Monday morning. But his money problems don't solve the question of what happened to Mona—and his boss... I can't see him killing Robby over the embezzling, you know—and if none of the clients knew..."

"Was Jeph able to get into Mona's computer?" I took another slice from the tray. It was really good—but then Slice was one of my favorite pizza places.

She laughed. "Yes, and like most people, she'd saved all of her passwords." She speared a piece of pepperoni off her pizza and popped it into her mouth. "Mona O'Neill was one smart lady."

"What do you mean?"

"You'd never think someone in the Irish Channel would be worth so much," Abby replied with a shrug. "I mean, she wasn't Garden District or even State Street rich, but she wasn't worrying about how to pay the power bill or scrounging to buy milk, either." She sighed. "She has no debt. She paid for her car in cash. If she used her credit cards, she paid them off every month, never carried a balance. The house was paid for. She has several hundred thousand dollars in CDs and another hundred thousand or so invested in stocks—Entergy, Shell. Her basic savings account wasn't huge, but it was healthy."

"She got a settlement when her husband was killed on the job," I observed. "She was smart with the money, I guess."

Abby nodded. "The trusts she'd created for Robby and Lorelle each had less than a thousand dollars in them. The one for Jonny still carries a balance of about sixty thousand dollars." She whistled. "Jonny's house is completely paid for—he owns it free and clear. According to city records, she paid a little less than two hundred thousand for it—it was a fixer-upper. The insurance assessed its value at $350,000 a few months back, right around the time Jonny and Heather moved in, so Jonny must have done some really good work on the place."

"It still looks like a dump." I took a drink from my glass of sweet tea. "I can't imagine anyone being willing to pay that kind of money for it. But real estate prices in this city have been out of control since Katrina."

"They were out of control *before* Katrina," she pointed out. "It just got worse after."

"True." I nodded. I was lucky—my landlady, Barbara Castlemaine, could get a hell of a lot more money for my apartment than what I was paying. But I'd gotten her out of what could have proven to be an incredibly sticky and embarrassing situation, so she gave me a great deal on my rent. She also paid me a ridiculous amount of money annually to work as a security consultant for her company, Crown Oil.

"And you know damned well there's a big difference between insurance value and market value. You can claim a value at anything, but whether you can get that is a whole different story." She took a drink from her iced tea. "Jeph couldn't get back far enough into her online banking records to see how much money was in Jonny's trust before she paid for the house and so forth, or how much all the trusts had in them to begin with. The Verlaines had to have been awfully generous with her, though—she's got an awful lot of financial resources for a widow who worked as a property manager."

"The Verlaines have always been generous when buying someone off," I commented. It was something I knew from bitter firsthand experience. "What I really don't understand is why wouldn't she give Robby the money he needed?" I brooded over it for a moment. "You'd think she'd want to keep him out of jail."

"Well, we also don't know for sure what their relationship was like," Abby replied. "He wasn't close to either of his siblings, and he didn't have much to do with his mother—didn't Jonny say that?"

"Lorelle," I corrected her. "But no matter how bad the situation was, I can't believe she'd let her son go to jail—if for no other reason than her grandchildren."

"Well, he'd already been fired." Abby shrugged. "He was going to lose everything. It was just a matter of time before he defaulted on those credit cards and lost the house on Napoleon. What did it matter if he went to jail or not? I bet he was getting really desperate—and desperate people do desperate things. And if she bailed him out of the embezzlement—between the house and the credit cards, she'd have to come up with a couple of hundred thousand dollars to get him out from under."

"Maybe that was why she sold out Luke Marino," I wondered out loud. "Maybe Global Insurance was paying her enough to buy Robby out of debt?"

She shook her head. "Credit is such a fucking trap. I don't know why more people don't realize what a rip-off it is." She sighed. "What they needed to do was take the kids out of Catholic school and put them in public schools, and sell that house on Napoleon and move into something less expensive, is what they needed to do. But people never seem to want to scale back." She scowled. "Idiot. Why would he ever in a million years have thought it was okay to steal from his clients? As long as I live I'll never understand people."

"It's the American way," I observed casually. "See how much debt we can accrue before we die. Whoever dies with the most debt and the most toys wins."

Abby rolled her eyes. "That doesn't make it any less stupid.

So, what do you think? Robby tried to get the money out of Luke Marino and then turned to Mona, who got it from Morgan Barras?"

"That doesn't make sense to me." I scowled at my pizza. "Why didn't she just cash in some of her CDs—or she could have taken it out of Jonny's trust. She had a lot of options—why would she sell out Luke Marino?"

"There's no proof anywhere she *did* sell out Luke Marino," Abby pointed out. "You keep approaching this from the perspective that she was fucking him over. Isn't it just as likely the insurance company was right—that Luke was scamming them, and she was playing along with him? Didn't someone say she was changing her testimony because she thought God was punishing her for lying by shutting down St. Anselm's?" She raised her eyebrows. "Seriously, you're not being objective. You—and everyone else in this city—hate insurance companies, and Luke's a local hero. You've never even considered the possibility it was all a scam to begin with. And insurance companies—may they all rot in hell—do get scammed. That's primarily why they act like such assholes in the first place."

I could feel my face coloring. She was right. Maybe Mona's conscience *had* gotten the better of her. Was it so hard for me to believe that Luke Marino might be a con artist?

Well, if I was going to be completely honest, I didn't *want* to believe he might be a con artist—which didn't mean he wasn't one.

Our waitress asked us if we wanted anything else, and I asked for the check.

"You know, I never really bought the story that Mona was so dedicated to her job that she rode the storm out at Cypress Gardens and sent Jonny out of town with Lorelle." Abby stretched. "And it's not very likely Lorelle or Jonny would get up on the stand and call their mother a liar, is it?"

She was right again. "I'll talk to Jonny about it." I kicked myself mentally.

Abby smiled at me. "You going to go interview the widow? Or would you rather I do it? She might be more likely to open up to another woman—you know, the whole 'we're sisters, men are such idiots' approach."

I thought about it for a moment and shook my head. "No, I think it's best if I go. I wonder what she told Venus and Blaine."

"Who knows?" she replied. "Want me to ask them?"

I shook my head and slipped a twenty into the leather case containing our bill. I stood up. "I'll cruise by Mona's, see if she's there. If she isn't, well, I do have some other questions for Jonny."

"Anything for me to do?"

"Just keep going over the financials. Something's got to be there."

Dark clouds were moving in from over the West Bank as I started my car, and as I turned onto Magazine Street, fat drops of rain were starting to hit my windshield. By the time I pulled up in front of Mona O'Neill's house, it was a full-fledged downpour. Constance Street was already under a couple of inches of water, and the drainage ditch alongside the road was filling up. I opened my umbrella and got out of the car. There was a big black Lexus SUV parked in Mona's driveway; I assumed it belonged to her daughter-in-law.

The rain pounded down on top of my umbrella, and a blast of wind almost ripped it out of my hands. I almost lost it again as I struggled to get the gate open with one hand. By the time I made it to the porch I was soaked from the knees down.

The front door opened as I climbed onto the porch and shut the umbrella, shaking it free of the beads of water. "You must be Jonny's detective," a woman said from inside the screen door. The dark clouds had made the day as dark as night, and I couldn't get a good look at her. She was simply a backlit silhouette. "He said you might come by at some point, and he said you were a big man. He wasn't exaggerating." Her voice sounded slightly amused.

"Yes, ma'am, I'm Chanse MacLeod," I replied, giving her my most reassuring smile. "I'm sorry to bother you, but—"

She interrupted me with a sigh. "You just missed the police detectives, a black woman and a white man." She opened the screen door. "Come on in out of the storm. Might as well get it all over with—putting this off isn't going to make it any easier, and I'm already raw from the cops. You want some coffee? I've got a fresh pot brewing."

"That would be nice, thank you. Cream and Sweet'n Low, if it's not too much trouble, ma'am." I stepped inside and got a good look at her in the light from the chandelier in the living room.

"Please don't ma'am me—my name is Celia." She was of average height, maybe about five-six or so. She was wider in the hips than she was in the shoulders, but she kept herself fit. She was wearing a pair of black fleece sweatpants and a black T-shirt. Her breasts were small and sat high on her chest. She wasn't wearing makeup, and her dark hair was cut short. There were some telltale strands of gray scattered throughout it. There were lines around her eyes and at the corners of her mouth, but she was still a handsome woman. She had oval-shaped dark eyes, framed with long lashes, and a pert little nose. They were a little swollen, and red from crying. She'd been a knockout when she was a young woman.

She padded off to the kitchen to get the coffee, and I looked around the living room. It wasn't nearly as neat as it had been on Sunday, when Jonny showed me around. The magazines on the coffee table had been moved, and one lay open. The television was on—some court show with a black female judge, but the sound was muted. The table next to one of the reclining chairs had a McDonald's bag sitting on it, and a burger wrapper was sticking out of the top. There was also a stack of mail on the coffee table, and an open purse on the floor.

She gave me a weak smile as she handed me the cup, gesturing for me to have a seat. I sat down on the couch, and she took a seat in the reclining chair, folding her legs underneath her. She grimaced at the McDonald's bag, crumpling it up and putting it on the floor next to her purse. "I really can't help you with Mona—I really don't know anything about that." She shifted awkwardly in the chair. "We were never really close, and I haven't spoken to her for over a month." She shrugged halfheartedly. "Robby didn't encourage it. He never encouraged me to get close to anyone in his family. Lorelle and Jonny have been absolutely lovely since—" Her voice broke, and she took a moment to gather herself. "Since this all started. Lorelle's watching my kids now—said I probably needed some time to gather myself. She's very kind."

"Did Robby ever give you a reason why he avoided his family?"

She sighed. "Robby never really appreciated his mother, you know. I used to tell him he should be grateful at the very least that she was still alive—mine died when I was a little girl—but all they ever did was argue and fight. He was ashamed of her, and she knew it."

"Ashamed?"

She gestured around the room. "He didn't like having blue-collar roots—he thought growing up in the Irish Channel was some kind of disgrace, if you can believe that." She rolled her eyes. "Like that really matters to anyone anymore? Better to have honest parents who work hard and love you, isn't it?"

"I suppose," I replied, remembering my own roots in the Cottonwood Wells trailer park. I'd done a pretty good job of distancing myself from there, and from my family.

"I always wondered if he married me because he loved me or because of who I am—who I was." She put her coffee cup down on the table.

"I don't know your maiden name, ma'am, but Lorelle mentioned you'd been Queen of Rex."

She started laughing. "Good Lord, not that idiocy again!" She put her coffee cup down on the table. "Mr. MacLeod, I was *never* Queen of Rex. I was a maid the one year my parents could afford it—just the one year, and I thought it was a terrible waste of money. I certainly was never Queen—not of Rex, not of any krewe." She rolled her eyes again. "Robby liked to tell people that, which I always told him was really stupid—what if someone checked? Then he'd just look stupid, and like a liar, to boot. But he always said the only people who would check wouldn't have to check." She sighed.

"It's all so stupid, isn't it? But he cared about things like that—like he thought people cared. But he said it helped him get clients, and keep them. He said people like to invest money with people who had connections to society."

"He was an investment counselor?"

She nodded. "Yes, and he was a good one, too. But it was never enough for him. He always wanted to make it big, you know? Make a lot of money." Her face twisted. "He had this crazy idea that it mattered to me. But it didn't." She got a faraway look on her face. "I come from an old-line New Orleans society family, Mr. MacLeod. I grew up in the Garden District, I went to McGehee, all of that idiocy that really doesn't matter anymore. But we didn't have any money—we were name rich, money poor. My father had to scrimp and save to send my sisters and me to the right schools so we could marry money." She shook her head. "I always thought it was a waste, you know? The house—" She laughed. "The first floor of our house was a showplace, and we never let anyone upstairs— because the upstairs was a wreck. All the money went into the first floor, so we could keep up appearances. Stupid, really. But Robby never understood I didn't care about that stuff. I'd rather have had a smaller house and sent my kids to public school than for him to steal."

"So you knew about the embezzlement?"

"I found out." She sighed. "That's why I took the kids and went to Sandestin for the summer—one of my sisters has a beach house there. I needed some space, some distance from him. I didn't know if I could stay married to a thief." She bit her lip. "Guess I don't have to worry about that anymore, do I?"

"I thought Robby drove over on the weekends?"

She shook her head. "I haven't seen him since I left him—we just talked on the phone." She ran a hand through her hair. "That sounds like something Robby would have told someone who asked where me and the kids were. He was all about the appearances, you know."

"Can you think of anyone who might have wanted him dead?"

She sighed. "I'll tell you what I told the cops—I have no idea, none at all." She crossed her legs. "Robby didn't talk to me about his work—every once in a while, when he'd come up with one of his great ideas—what he called his 'million-dollar ideas'—he would tell me about it."

"Do you know what his latest idea was?"

"No, I'm afraid I don't." She thought about it for a moment, looking away from me. "He had a big argument with Mona—that was how I found out about the embezzlement, you know? I heard them, in his office, where his body was—found." She swallowed, closed her eyes, and took a moment before continuing. "I heard enough to know he needed money, and quite a bit of it, and fast. After Mona left, I confronted him." She sighed. "I was horrified, absolutely horrified—especially at the thought he'd stolen money *because he thought he needed to maintain a lifestyle I wanted.*" She shook her head and looked away from me. "It was like he had no idea of who I was—after being married for almost fifteen years, he knew nothing about me, who I was as a person—and even if I cared about that stuff, Mr. MacLeod, I never in a million years would have condoned *stealing* to maintain it. My sister had always offered to let us stay at her place over there, and so I took her up on it. I took the kids and left. Maybe if I hadn't—"

"Then you and your kids might have been in danger, too, Mrs. O'Neill. Leaving here was the smartest thing you could have done."

"Celia, please, and thank you for saying that. Hopefully someday I can believe it."

"Were you aware of the money problems before you overheard him arguing with his mother?"

She nodded. "Robby handled our money, and I knew we were having trouble. The economy, you know—people lost a lot of money in the markets, and I know we did, too. Robby wouldn't tell me how much we lost, but I know it was a lot. I noticed—" She bit her lip. "He took my debit card a couple of months ago and told me to use a credit card to pay for things—groceries and so on. I know he closed the household account. I also knew that wasn't a good sign, you know. He was having trouble sleeping, and I think…oh, hell, he's dead, right?" She gave me a crooked smile. "I still can't believe he was stealing from his clients. They trusted him."

"But none of them knew?"

"Oh, no, the company certainly kept that all on the hush-hush—his boss called to offer his condolences—but he sounded like he was more concerned about finding out what I knew about what Robby'd been doing. I suppose that's only fair, but I'm afraid I was a little rude to him." Her eyes filled with tears. "It breaks my heart that Robby thought he had to embezzle to keep me happy…" She shook her head. "My family—yeah, we were old New Orleans society. But our money ran out a long time ago, Mr. MacLeod. A long time ago. Like I said, I know what it's like going to the best schools and then going home and eating macaroni and cheese because you can't afford anything else. My father so desperately wanted to keep up appearances, so I know firsthand how pointless and stupid that is. Both of my sisters married money, you know— they didn't want to have to worry about paying their bills and putting food on the table. Me? I loved Robby." She sighed. "I didn't need that big house. I didn't care if my daughter went to McGehee or if my son went to Jesuit. None of that matters. I told Robby that over and over, but he never listened. I would have been just as happy in a small house in River Ridge." She wiped at her eyes. "And where did it get him? Dead. And his mother's missing." Her voice shook. "The cops were pretty open about it. Do you think she's dead, too?"

"I—"

"You can be honest with me. I have no use for platitudes."

"When people disappear, Mrs. O'Neill, they usually disappear because they don't want to be found. From everything I've found out about your mother-in-law, there was no reason for her to walk away from her life and her family. So it stands to reason that she's dead. And all the blood in her car—"

"But it wasn't *her* blood."

I paused. "I beg your pardon?"

"Those cops—they said the blood in her car wasn't hers. It was the wrong blood type."

I didn't know what to say. I stared at her for a few moments while scenarios ran through my head—none of which made a lot of sense.

"So it's possible she's still alive." Celia O'Neill went on like I wasn't goggling at her like a simple-minded fool. "But I can't think why she'd just disappear."

"You said Robby had an argument with her?"

She nodded. "They used to fight all the time. Every once in a while he'd find some great investment opportunity and would try to convince her to invest. Mona controlled Jonny's trust fund, and she had her own investments. She always said no, and Robby would always get mad. He felt like she babied Jonny too much." She shook her head. "He really didn't like Jonny. He never told me what he had against his brother, but he literally hated him." She shuddered. "I never could understand how someone could feel that way about a family member. I mean, my oldest sister's a bitch from hell, but I don't hate her. Not the way Robby hated Jonny."

"Could it have just been sibling rivalry?"

"Maybe, I don't know." She covered her face with her hands. "I know it sounds like my marriage was a complete failure—but it wasn't. We were really happy. I loved him. I didn't care if we lost the house, filed bankruptcy, had to put the kids in public school. But he wouldn't—" Her voice choked off in a sob. "I guess that's all in my future now, isn't it? But we'll be fine."

"I'm sorry, I didn't mean to upset you."

She got control of herself and gave me a weak smile. "It's okay. I have to get used to the idea that he's gone."

"What are you going to do?"

She shrugged. "There's a life insurance policy—we both had one. And I know he had another one through the office." She looked away from me. "I probably should apologize to Ross—that's his boss."

"Can I ask you one last question, and then I'll get out of your hair?"

She bit her lower lip and nodded.

"I'd been told that Robby was really interested in Jonny's fighting career?" I made it a question, and raised my eyebrows.

She nodded. "Yeah, that's true. He didn't like Jonny, but when he thought his brother had a chance to make it big…" She shook her head. "He thought Jonny should sign with the casino where he fought, and that Mona was holding him back."

I stood up. "Thank you for talking to me, Mrs. O'Neill. I'm really sorry for your loss."

She walked me to the door, and opened it. "You sure you don't want to have some more coffee, wait out this storm?"

"Thanks, but I need to get going." I shook her hand. "A little rain never hurt anyone."

Constance Street was now under about a foot of water. I opened the umbrella and splashed down the walk. The water in the drainage ditch was washing over the walk, and my feet were soaked as I sloshed through the fast-moving dirty water to the driver's side of my car. I unlocked the car and closed the umbrella, getting drenched again before getting my door closed. I drove down a block.

Jonny's car was sitting out in front of the ramshackle shotgun house.

Jonny himself opened the door. He wasn't wearing a shirt, and his basketball shorts hung from his narrow waist. "Dude, get in out of the rain." He flicked on the light switch and I stepped into the house, shivering.

"How you doing?" I asked as Heather gave me a look. She pushed herself to her feet.

"I'll leave you two to your business." She shuffled out of the room, both hands pressed against the small of her back.

"I'm sorry about your brother," I said.

Jonny nodded. "Thanks, man." His eyes were red. "I can't get over it, you know? Thanks for helping me out the other night." He closed his eyes and his lower lip trembled. "I hope I don't ever have to identify another body, man. I can't get the image of his face out of my head."

"I just talked to your sister-in-law. She mentioned you and Robby didn't get along?"

"I wouldn't go that far." He didn't look at me, just kept staring at his hands. "I mean, we were like sixteen years apart in age. We just didn't have a lot in common."

"Celia seemed to think that he really didn't like you."

A tear rolled down his cheek. "He did."

"Jonny." I softened my voice. "He's dead now, and your mom is still missing. You need to be completely honest with me, okay, or I can't do my job."

He nodded. "Robby was always mean to me." He wiped at his face. "Always. He called Heather a whore when I called him to see if they'd come to the wedding. And the last time I talked to him—" His voice broke. "He told me I wasn't Dad's." He looked at me, pain written all over his face. "That Mom had cheated on Dad, that I wasn't really his full brother. Why would he say something like that to me?"

Whatever I'd been expecting to hear, it wasn't that. I stared at him. "Did he say who your father really was?"

Jonny shook his head. "When I asked him, he just laughed and told me to ask Mom."

"Did you ask her?"

"I called her, but just her voicemail. So I left a message." He gnawed his lip.

"When was this?"

He chewed his lower lip, and wouldn't meet my eyes. "Thursday afternoon. He came by and wanted me to talk to Mom, get her to let him borrow some money from my trust fund. I said no, and he went off on me." He wouldn't look me in the eye. "I punched him and threw him out." His voice cracked. "The last time I saw my brother I punched him."

I wanted to shake him, but resisted the urge. "Did you say anything about it in the voicemail?"

He nodded. "I'm sorry I didn't tell you about it. But I didn't ever want to talk about that. Ever. To anyone." He looked at me. "You don't think that's why Mom ran away, do you?"

"It just might be," I said and slammed the door behind me.

CHAPTER TWELVE

That must have been annoying," Paige said, taking a drink from her bottle of Abita Amber and sighing in delight. I'd just finished ranting about Jonny—a rant that started the moment I opened my front door to let her in.

"That's putting it mildly," I replied as I unwrapped my shrimp po'boy. I popped an errant shrimp into my mouth.

The last thing I'd seen as I'd stormed my way out of the dumpy little shotgun house was Heather, standing in the hallway with a self-satisfied smirk on her face. *I told you so.*

I'd been more than a little furious with Jonny—it was pretty much all I could do not to strangle him. My phone had begun ringing the very moment I got in my car—it was Jonny. He left a long, rambling, apologetic voicemail, which just made my blood boil even hotter as I listened to it. He kept apologizing over and over for not telling me about the argument with Robby, insisting that he hadn't thought it was all that important, and no, he wasn't keeping anything else from me, he swore, please don't stop looking for his mom.

I deleted it without bothering to answer.

Paige made a face. "Well, he's what? Twenty? It's possible he really didn't think it mattered. Remember what we were like at that age? It's embarrassing to remember some of the stupid shit we used to do—and besides, cut him a little slack, his mom's missing and his brother's been murdered." Paige took another long drink of her beer and belched rather loudly.

"Always the lady," I commented as I took a bite of my sandwich and sighed with satisfaction. Paige had called me just as I was pulling into my parking space, still shaking with anger. She'd invited herself over and offered to bring food. I hadn't realized until she mentioned it how hungry I was, so I agreed and hung up before running through the rain to my back door. When I got inside, toweled off, and changed into dry clothes, I'd called Abby and filled her in.

"You think this changes anything?" Abby had asked.

"We need to find out—see what you can find out about Mona's distant past." I hung up and tossed the phone on my bed. I stalked into my office area, turned on the computer, and updated my file on the case as my mind tossed around any number of possibilities while I calmed down.

But I couldn't help coming back to the possibility that now Mona herself had an even stronger motive for killing her son and disappearing.

Maybe the blood in her car was Robby's.

"This is nice," Paige went on, dragging a steak fry through a puddle of ketchup. "It's been a while." She sighed as she chewed the fry. "And that's my bad, I'm sorry. This job—" She shook her head. "Had I known how time-consuming it would be running a magazine, I would have stayed with the paper. But then, I'd probably no longer be with the paper, given the buy-outs and so forth. At least there's money behind *Crescent City*, and I don't have to worry about job security there. For a few more years, any way—until the Internet finishes killing the print industry."

Paige and I had been close friends ever since I was a freshman in college. We'd met during little sister rush at my fraternity, Beta Kappa. I'd gone back to my room to get away from the drunken debauchery and found her sitting on my bed, smoking a joint. We'd hit it off from the first—it turned out she was doing an undercover report on little sister rush for the student paper, but she kind of liked Beta Kappa and took a bid, ditching the story. She was the first person I'd come out to and had been my beard all the way through college. We'd both moved to New Orleans after graduating—me going to work for the NOPD and she getting a job with the *Times-Picayune*. She'd witnessed a convenience store shooting, written a powerful editorial about it that got her nominated for a Pulitzer prize, and her career had taken off from there.

She'd always wanted to be a novelist and for years had been working on a historical romance called *The Belle of New Orleans*. After Katrina, she put it aside and wrote a memoir about her experiences in the city after the levee failure. She'd offered to let me read it, but I declined—that first year afterward had been rough enough to experience firsthand, let alone relive through someone else's words. A major New York agent had taken it on, but no publisher had wanted it. She'd sworn she was going to finish *Belle*, but she never talked about it anymore. I assumed that between her job and the guy she was seeing—Blaine's older brother Ryan—she didn't have the time to work on it anymore.

"Do you ever miss being a reporter?" I took another bite of the po'boy. I was curious—when she'd been working the crime beat for the paper she'd always bitched about what she saw every day, and every night she'd come home to drown herself in wine and smoke pot.

"We-ell." She munched while she thought for a moment. "Yeah, I do sometimes. I miss having my finger on the city's pulse the way I used to—I mean, I still kind of do, but the magazine is more about the arts, politics, and culture—I don't really know what's going on with the working class and the poor the way I used to, you know? I know, I used to always feel like I'd never get clean when I got home every night, and I remember having to drink a lot of wine and smoke a lot of pot to anaesthetize myself, and I don't miss that. And I don't miss having a city editor breathing down my neck, telling me what I can and can't write, blah blah blah, telling me I dressed like a gypsy and making fun of me all the time." She'd had a great relationship with her original city editor, but then he retired. She always called his replacement "that bitch Coralie." Coralie didn't appreciate Paige's unique style of dressing. Right now she was wearing a flowing black silk skirt and a red peasant blouse with full sleeves. She went on, "I do like having some control over what we put in the magazine—and Rachel is so great to work with." In one of those "New Orleans is a small town" twists, the magazine's publisher was Rory's older sister. "Would I like us to focus on some of the social issues in the city, the poverty, the quality of public education? Sure I would. But compared to all the other headaches that came with working at the paper? Nah, I don't miss any of that shit at all." She beamed at me. "But I do miss having the time to hang out like I used to." She ran a hand through her mop of red curls. "And I miss helping you with your cases—that was always a lot of fun."

I laughed. "You used to always act like it was a huge ordeal."

"Yeah, well." She winked at me. "Didn't want you to take me for granted."

"I miss having someone who can dig through the archives of the paper for me."

"Meh." She shrugged. "Jeph can hack into just about anything, can't he?" Paige was the one who'd found Jephtha for me. She'd done a story on him—he'd been sent to juvie when he was caught committing credit card fraud online—he'd also hacked into his school's computer system and changed grades for cash. He was what she considered a classic example of the failure of the New Orleans public school system—this incredibly bright kid with an almost supernatural talent for computer work who'd fallen through the cracks and wound up breaking the law. And of course, with his background, he couldn't get a decent job as an adult. He was washing dishes in an Uptown restaurant when she profiled him for the paper, and in his free time he was designing computer games, trying to make it big. I'd given him a test assignment—and he's worked for me ever since. He was still working on developing the games, but he didn't have to wash dishes in a hellishly hot kitchen anymore.

"I don't know what you're talking about." I winked. I preferred not to know how Jeph and Abby got the information I asked them for. "I'm sure Jeph would never risk doing anything that would put him behind bars again." I finished my po'boy and crumpled up the butcher paper as I chewed. I tossed it into the garbage can next to my desk and washed the last bite down with another swig of Abita. I leaned back in my chair and sighed. I was full, and it felt great.

Paige carefully wrapped up the second half of her sandwich and placed it in her enormous Louis Vuitton knock-off purse. "Which brings me to why I'm here," she said carefully, not meeting my eyes.

"And here I thought you missed me." I faked an injured tone. "I'm wounded. You mean you only come see me when you want something from me?"

"Fuck you." She gave me a look that could sterilize a lizard. "Last time I checked, the phone works two ways, asshole. You haven't exactly been ringing my phone off the hook since you started seeing Rory." She sniffed. "You get a cute boy in your bed on a regular basis and your friends cease to exist. I see how you are."

"Just yanking your chain." I laughed. "It is good to see you, you know. And what can I do for you?"

"Yeah, well, I *do* feel bad about it, but the damned magazine takes up so much time, and then Ryan on top of that…" She conceded with a nod, leaning back on the couch and putting her sandal-clad feet up on my coffee table. "But we're working on a story about the Luke Marino lawsuit, and oddly enough, your name came up when I was meeting with Martin—the reporter I've got chasing the story." She smiled at me. "And I figured you'd be much more likely to talk to me than to some reporter you don't know."

I frowned, shaking my head. "I really don't know a lot about the suit itself, Paige. You'd have to talk to Luke, or Loren McKeithen— he's not the lead attorney on the case, but he does love to see his name in print."

"Loren was the one who gave my reporter your name," Paige replied. "As soon as Martin filled me in, I told him to let me handle talking to you. He wasn't too happy about it." She grinned. "Like I'm going to horn in on his story. I've never once stolen a story in all my years in journalism."

"Don't bullshit me, Paige." I crossed my arms. "You know damned well all you had to do was call and ask me to talk to this Martin guy, and I would have. So?"

"We-ell, okay, the thought of leaving the office early was kind of appealing, and I haven't seen you in weeks, and it's been years since we've sat around brainstorming about one of your cases," she admitted, pulling a joint out of her purse. "And Ryan got some killer stuff last week." She passed it to me. "Take a whiff."

I held it to my nose and inhaled, and whistled. It was good pot, very strong and green smelling. And we did used to get stoned and talk about my cases—several times, it had helped break the case.

I passed it back to her with a frown, looking over at the clock on my desk. "I don't know if I should get stoned," I said slowly. "There's a lot of work I can still do on the case today—" I broke off and thought about it for a moment. Rory was doing bar testing that night and wasn't coming by because he wouldn't be off work until after eleven.

A night off wouldn't kill me—and was there anything I could do tonight that would make a difference? No, there wasn't—and Abby was still on the case.

I lit the joint and inhaled, passing it back to her.

"What do you want to know about Luke Marino?" I asked after blowing the smoke out in a massive plume toward the ceiling fan. "I can't say much about the suit because I really only know the bare bones—why he's suing and what it's about."

"Why do you think Mona O'Neill decided to change her testimony?"

"Therein lies the rub." I grinned. My mind was getting softer around the edges, and I could feel my muscles relaxing. It was very good pot. "Maybe Mona's testimony was a lie to begin with."

"Oh?" Her eyebrows went up.

I explained what Abby and I had been theorizing at Slice. "I mean, you remember what it was like those last few days before Katrina came ashore, right? The panic and terror? Do you believe she would have sent her teenage son off with her daughter and driven across the bridge to keep an eye on Cypress Gardens—when the *owners* left town?" I shook my head. "That story always bothered me."

"And after all these years, she gets a guilty conscience because her church is closing?" Paige rolled her eyes. "But you said Jonny confirmed that he left town with Lorelle and her family."

"That doesn't mean Mona didn't leave herself. Maybe she sent Jonny off with Lorelle, drove over to check out the place, and left herself later."

"And Luke got her to go along with a plan to scam the insurance?"

"The only person who can really answer that is Mona, and I don't think anyone's ever going to be able to ask her again."

"You're pretty sure she's dead." Paige passed the joint back to me. I took another hit and handed it back. She stared at it. "What if you're wrong?" She put it to her lips and inhaled. "What if she's in hiding somewhere?"

I shook my head. Even though I was getting stoned, I wasn't about to tell Paige the theory that Mona might have killed Robby and gone into hiding. I didn't have any proof—and while I knew I could trust her, it didn't feel right. "I'm not wrong," I replied. "She hasn't touched her debit card or any of her credit cards. Her bank accounts haven't been touched. Unless she was carrying a big wad of cash around with her—which I rather doubt—she's just vanished. People don't vanish without money—you know that as well as I do—and she left behind a check for fifty grand, which she could have just cashed."

"Maybe she's in protective custody." Paige tried to pass the joint back to me but I waved her off. She pinched it out and placed it in the ashtray on the coffee table. "The Feds aren't exactly going to give two shits about letting you know where she is—or Loren or the cops, for that matter."

"Protective custody?" I stared at her. How stoned was I? I wondered. "Where on earth did you get that idea?"

"Ah, sit back and let me tell you some things *you* don't know."

She gave me a sly glance. "After the storm—Luke Marino was approached by Social Justice—do you remember them?"

I did, vaguely.

After the levees failed and eighty percent of the city had been left homeless, a group called Social Justice had come to the city in late September and set up a campground in a park on the West Bank. They had a medical clinic, a food tent, and supplies—providing a place for people to stay when they came back to check on their houses, or to stay while they waited for FEMA trailers to be delivered while they worked on their homes. I had considered volunteering there myself when I heard about it—I saw a piece on CNN about it while I was evacuated in Dallas. The guy in charge was a large African American man with dreadlocks named Hakim Ali, and he spouted a lot of anti-government, anti-Republican rhetoric during the course of the interview.

"Did you know that in the early spring of 2006, when Luke Marino was struggling to rebuild with no help whatsoever from his insurance company, he contracted Social Justice to run Cypress Garden?"

I shook my head. "I still don't see the connection."

Paige rolled her eyes. "Some things never change. You really need to start reading the newspaper." She opened her massive purse and pulled out a folder, which she put on the coffee table. "Hakim Ali didn't found Social Justice on his own, or run it. He was the face of the group, but he was partnered up with a white guy—Alex Davis. Is any of this ringing a bell?"

Paige always lectured me on my refusal to be up on the news. "Not a bit."

"Alex Davis turned out to be an FBI agent, working undercover to get evidence on Hakim Ali for the federal prosecutor." She laughed. "I can't believe you didn't hear about any of this. Seriously, Chanse. Anyway, Alex disappeared without a trace in late 2006. Still nothing?"

There was something there in the dustiest corners of my memory. "I remember vaguely hearing about a Fed snitch vanishing."

She nodded. "That's when the story broke—when Alex Davis disappeared. About a week later, when he hadn't checked in, the FBI came looking for him and the story broke. It was a big deal—Hakim claimed it was all a government conspiracy because he criticized Bush and FEMA publicly, and because he was black, it was all racist, blah blah blah."

"They never found Alex Davis, did they?" It was starting to come back to me slowly. "And they never were able to prove Hakim or Social Justice had anything to do with him disappearing."

"Sound familiar?" She winked at me. "Hakim is a witness in the Marino case, you might be interested to know—a witness for Global Insurance."

"Seriously?" I couldn't help myself—I started laughing. "Mr. Power-to-the-people-corporations-are-evil-and-destroying-the-planet is siding with an insurance company? What a fucking hypocrite."

"I know, it made me laugh my ass off when I first found out about it."

"You think there's a connection between the Alex Davis disappearance and Mona's?"

She shrugged. "Who knows? Mona was involved with Cypress Gardens and was a star witness for Luke Marino. Hakim Ali was on the other side, under investigation from the FBI, and now she's gone. Maybe she knew something—we don't know what she knew."

I shook my head. "It doesn't make sense, Paige."

"So the dots aren't all connected." She lit a cigarette. "But something about all of this stinks to high heaven. Maybe Mona somehow found out something about Hakim Ali, and the Feds put her into protective custody—"

"Doesn't explain Robby's murder." I closed my eyes and leaned back. "This case! It's driving me crazy, nothing makes any sense." I thought for a moment. "I think the key to all of this is Mona changing her testimony. That's the one thing that doesn't fit with everything else I know about her." I started ticking things off on my fingers. "She was loyal, she was honest, she was deeply religious, she was like family to the Marinos. So why would she stab them in the back, at the last minute?"

"Her son needed money." Paige shrugged.

"But even that doesn't make sense." I shook my head. "I mean, I'm not her, but if my son needed fifty grand, she had ways of getting it besides selling out to Global Insurance. Jonny's trust still has about sixty grand in it. She had certificates of deposit she could have cashed in. She could have taken out a mortgage on her house. *And* she had a cashier's check for fifty grand from Morgan Barras, made out to her, that she could have turned into cash any time she wanted to." I shook my head. "All she had to do walk into a bank, and voilà. Problem solved."

"Maybe that money was the payoff for changing her testimony. You do know Morgan Barras is a shareholder in Global Insurance? And he bought Cypress Gardens from Luke a few years back."

"The check was dated two weeks earlier," I pointed out. "Why would she have held on to it for so long if she took it to help out Robby?"

"That doesn't mean it was given to her two weeks ago," Paige blew a few smoke rings toward the ceiling fan. "She may not have gotten it until it was too late. Maybe she went over to Robby's to give it to him, found the body, and got the hell out of town."

"Without her car and with no money?" I blew out a breath. "I wonder whose blood that was in her car."

"Maybe she killed Robby. Or maybe she got his blood on her when she found his body. And that's how it got in the car."

"I can't believe she would have killed her own son." I shook my head. "No matter how much he might have pissed her off, it just doesn't play with everything else I know about her. I mean, even if he exposed that she had an affair and Jonny was her lover's child, who cares? It was twenty years ago."

"Well, someone killed him—and Robby sounds like he needed killing." She stubbed the cigarette out. "I mean, why would he tell Jonny they didn't have the same father? And you said they looked alike, right? That's just a shitty thing to do."

"They looked like their mother," I replied absently. There was something there, and I cursed myself for getting stoned. My mind was too foggy to grab hold of the idea that was trying to form in the back of my mind. Someone had said something—but the more I tried, the more it slipped out of my grasp.

"If she did have an affair, she wouldn't be happy to have it all come out, even if it was twenty years ago, but you're right, she wouldn't have killed her son over it." Paige glanced at her watch. "Damn, when did it get so late?" She tapped the file she'd placed on the coffee table. "This is some of what we've dug up on Social Justice. Take a look—you might find something useful." She stood up and picked up her bag.

I kissed her on the cheek at the door. "This was fun—and thanks."

"Yeah." She gave me a hug. "I miss you, you know. But with everything—"

"No worries." I kissed the top of her head again. "We all get busy."

I watched her walk to her car and waited for her to drive off before going back inside and bolting the door.

My mind was still a little muddled, so I microwaved a cup of coffee and carried it back into the living room. I picked up the file and started reading.

Hakim Ali had quite a checkered past indeed, I thought when I closed the file an hour later and put it back down. He'd been born here, in the St. Thomas housing projects—and was a product of the New Orleans public school system. But he was the kind of success story people could get behind—no father, his mother had been a drug-addicted prostitute, and he'd grown up in the projects. He'd worked hard in public school, not joined a gang or gotten involved in drugs, and had gotten into LSU—he was actually there at the same time as Luke and I. He'd worked his way through college, eventually getting a double degree in political science and African American studies. While at LSU, he'd gotten involved in several organizations that would have most likely set off some alarms at the FBI—he'd converted to Islam and changed his name, joined the college Communist Party and a black power group reputed to have ties with some anti-American Islamic groups in Africa.

After finishing his degrees, he'd gone to Africa and worked there with relief missions in war-torn countries for a few years before returning to the United States, where he'd become highly active in a group called Mindpower—whose focus was encouraging young African Americans in the inner cities to give up gangs and drugs and focus on education. He'd been arrested several times at protests and returned to New Orleans shortly after the turn of the century. He'd led the opposition to the demolition of the St. Thomas Projects and had formed Social Justice as an organization to help the evicted tenants of St. Thomas find other places to live in the city.

Social Justice had barely subsisted until Katrina roared ashore and the federally built and maintained levee system failed so spectacularly and was witnessed by the entire world. The entire country—and world, for that matter—had been riveted to their television screens as news crews broadcast the daily horrors going on in a once-proud American city. The natural human instinct when witnessing horror is frustration at one's helplessness—and the next instinct is to open your wallet and give money. With so much attention focused on the displaced New Orleanians, it was a very ripe time for a group like Social Justice to get some cash. Their donations rose exponentially, and apparently Hakim had approached Luke Marino about taking over management of Cypress Gardens in the spring of 2006. The complexes were sitting there empty, there was a need for low-income housing, and the contracts were signed. Social Justice took over in the late summer 2006.

Luke and Hakim—they'd both been at LSU at the same time. Was it possible they'd known each other from then? The football star and the radical black activist?

Stranger things, I reflected, had happened on college campuses before.

Luke Marino turned around and sold the complex to Morgan

Barras in spring of 2007, and Barras evicted everyone—including Social Justice.

Which would explain why Ali is testifying for Global Insurance—it's payback, I mused as I stared at the ceiling. And it was around that same time that Alex Davis disappeared.

Paige's reporter had compiled a lot of interesting information about Alex Davis. He'd been in his mid-thirties when he disappeared, leaving behind a wife and two young daughters. He'd been sent to New Orleans to infiltrate Social Justice in 2004, and the Feds had put up the investment money to get him into the group. But there was nothing in the file about *why* the Feds were willing to spend the money and go to the trouble to infiltrate Social Justice.

Unless they thought Hakim Ali was a terrorist—since 9/11 no expense was spared to investigate possible terrorist cells.

I picked up the file again and turned back to the countries where he'd worked.

I smiled. How could I have missed it? Somalia, Yemen, and Ethiopia.

So, the Feds thought Hakim Ali was a terrorist and Social Justice was a terrorist front.

Because of course a terrorist front would try to find housing for displaced poor people in New Orleans after a natural disaster.

I walked over to the computer and signed in. I scanned my e-mails—nothing from Abby or Jephtha.

I sent Jeph a quick e-mail, asking him to find out whatever he could about Hakim Ali and Alex Davis.

I doubted there was anything there, but I always found it better to rule things out.

That way they couldn't come back to bite you in the ass.

CHAPTER THIRTEEN

Abby woke me up shortly after seven, waking me out of an incredibly deep and restful sleep, insisting that I meet her at the Please You for breakfast. I could tell by her tone she was excited about something—I could practically see her bouncing up and down on the balls of her feet. Reluctantly, I agreed to meet her in about half an hour—which would give me enough time to shower, gulp down some coffee, and try to wake up. I got the coffee going while I brushed my teeth and got in the shower. The hot water splashing over my body somehow managed to wash the sleep out of my eyes and soak the tired out of my muscles. The coffee was ready once I toweled off, and I poured a big steaming mug of it. It looked gray outside—which meant we were due for more rain. I put on a light T-shirt and pulled on a pair of loose-fitting khaki shorts, finished the coffee, and walked out the front door. The air felt close and heavy—which meant it was definitely going to rain at some point in the day. I kicked my way through the cluster of stinging caterpillars undulating on the front porch and headed down the walk to the gate. By the time I got to the sidewalk, my underarms and forehead were damp with sweat. The humidity was lying on my skin like a hot wet towel. I could also feel pressure starting to build in my sinuses.

Abby was already seated at our usual booth drinking coffee when I walked through the front door. The Please You was crowded—every stool at the counter was taken, and there wasn't an open booth or table to be had. I'd never been in the café that early—it was like a completely different place. The air-conditioning was blasting—which was why the windows had been covered in condensation—and the staff was moving at a remarkably fast clip. I could smell coffee brewing and could hear bacon sizzling on the grill. The mixed odors of eggs, toast, pancakes, and bacon made my stomach growl and my eyes water just a little bit.

Abby grinned as I slid into my seat. There was a cup of coffee sitting beside the place mat on my side of the table. Gratefully I dumped some cream and a packet of Sweet'n Low into it and took a big drink.

"Damn, boss, you look like you're still asleep," she teased me. Her hair was all pulled up and shoved into a black Who Dat baseball cap, and she was wearing a baggy navy blue T-shirt.

The coffee was strong, and I took another big gulp of it before growling, "And what was so goddamned important that I had to get out of bed this early?"

She made a face at me. I ordered scrambled eggs, bacon, toast, and grits from our waitress, and resisted the urge to tell her to leave the coffeepot. I raised my eyebrows at Abby. "You're not eating?"

"I'm not hungry—I'll just have coffee." Once the waitress moved away to check on another table, Abby pulled her battered navy blue backpack up from the floor and placed in on the table. She unzipped the main compartment and removed a green file folder, which she shoved across the table at me. Her eyes danced. "I can't wait for you to read that," she said in a low voice, leaning across the table.

"What is it?" I didn't bother to open the folder. I could tell she was dying to tell me what was inside, so I just picked up my coffee cup again and took another drink. The caffeine was starting to clear my brain—but I still wanted to go back to bed. "Just tell me—I can read it more thoroughly later. My brain's not quite working at a hundred percent yet. Too early."

"It's the paperwork for the trust the Verlaines' lawyer set up for Mona and her kids—I was able to find it on one of the city's court websites. The settlement and the trust were set up through the courts. It makes it more official that way." Her voice rose in excitement. "They could have just done the whole thing privately, but my guess is the Verlaine lawyer wanted it done this way so Mona couldn't ever come back and sue again later—I don't know that it was absolutely necessary, but from what you've told me about the Verlaines—"

"Oh, yes, that's exactly the kind of thing the Verlaines would do," I commented sourly. "Protect their family at all costs, that's their motto."

She glanced at me. "I'll take your word for it. Anyway, the primary thing that really caught my attention was the way this was set up to really take away options from Mona—like the Verlaines almost didn't trust her to do right by her kids."

I narrowed my eyes. "What do you mean?"

"If the Verlaines had just settled the money on Mona, she could have set up the trusts herself and done with them as she pleased," Abby went on. "But they didn't. All of this was done by the Verlaine Shipping Company attorneys under the supervision of a civil judge. So the trusts were set up by the court. Mona was the trustee—she could put money in or take money out, but she couldn't dissolve the trusts. She would have to go to court to do that. Remember how there's like a thousand dollars each left in Robby's and Lorelle's? She can't simply close the trusts without going back in front of a judge, and she's just never bothered, she just left the trusts alone. But you want to know the best part?"

I smiled at our waitress as she slid my plate of food in front of me and topped off my coffee again. Once she was out of earshot, I said, "Well?"

"The Verlaines' lawyer—Matthew Pennycuff, who I am still trying to track down, by the way, he retired just before Katrina and apparently never came back to New Orleans, it's so weird, it's like he just vanished off the face of the earth—took care of everything. But the settlement *wording* is the most important thing." She took a deep breath. "Are you awake enough, or do you need more coffee?"

"Yes," I growled back at her. "Get to the point."

"The Verlaine settlement was worded this way." She cleared her throat. "It settled the sum of 1.3 million dollars to be equally divided into separate trusts for the widow of Danny O'Neill and his children." She paused expectantly, a grin playing at the corners of her mouth.

"So?" Maybe the coffee wasn't working, because I didn't see what that mattered.

"You are so not a lawyer." She blew out a breath in exasperation. "Chanse, don't you get it? I mean, it was pretty sloppy of Pennycuff, but the wording—the way it was worded—in the law, wording is everything." She licked her lips. "The children weren't *specifically* named; the settlement, approved by a judge, I might add, simply said 'the children of Danny O'Neill.' Now do you get it?"

A light went on in my head. "So, if Jonny wasn't Danny's son..."

"He wasn't entitled to any of the money, according to the settlement paperwork filed. Again, this isn't a big deal, because Mona was the trustee and she could do whatever she wanted— except that the trusts were also set up so *the money could only be used for the needs of the person the money was in trust for.*" She sat back in the booth, a self-satisfied smirk on her face. "So, if Jonny isn't really Danny O'Neill's biological son, a case could be made that he's not entitled to any of the money in the trust, and if Mona knew he wasn't Danny's son, she committed fraud."

My head was spinning a bit, so I took another drink of the coffee. "She was also defrauding herself, though, wasn't she? If Jonny wasn't really an O'Neill, and the money should have only been split three ways—between Mona, Lorelle, and Robby, she was cheating herself."

"She was also cheating the Verlaines." She tilted her head

to one side. "A case could be made that the amount the Verlaines settled upon Danny's heirs was based on there being four of them, not three." She shrugged. "I doubt the Verlaines gave a shit. But Robby was desperate for money."

"And he was claiming Jonny wasn't really Danny's son." I finished my grits. "So, if he got the fifty grand from Mona to pay back the money he embezzled—"

"He's still pretty heavily in debt, and unemployed. But if he goes to court and proves Jonny didn't deserve to have a share of the money—"

"Then the money would be split between the three of them, Mona, Lorelle, and Robby. And the house Mona bought for Jonny and Heather—"

"Also belonged to them; Mona had no right to take the money and use it for Jonny. In fact, both he and Lorelle would have a case against *her* for cheating them." Her eyes danced with excitement.

"And it gives Mona herself a much stronger motive for killing Robby than I'd thought," I mused. "But did Robby know for a fact Jonny wasn't Danny's son? And who could Jonny's father have been?"

Robby had been sixteen or seventeen when his brother was born. If his mother had been cheating on his father, would he have known? And could he prove it, twenty years later?

I took out my phone and made a note to myself to call Celia later in the morning.

"It makes sense, doesn't it?" Abby went on. "This would take care of all of his problems. He could pay back the money he stole from his clients and get another infusion of cash to help keep him going. And so what if his mother gets humiliated in the process? He couldn't stand his mother, right? If he knew she'd cheated on his dad, and his dad was killed...no wonder he couldn't stand her." She laughed. "I mean, think about it. She was cheating on his dad, his dad dies, and she's set for life. Humiliating her would just be an added plus for him."

"It could also explain why Robby always resented his little brother," I said. "If he'd always known his little brother wasn't really an O'Neill, all of this makes the family dynamic a little more understandable." I felt myself liking the theory more and more. "I wonder—" I broke off.

"What?"

"But why did he wait so long?" That was the fly in the ointment, the thing that didn't make sense. *Why* would he have waited this long to expose his mother and disrupt the trusts? Granted, now that he was about to go to jail—and his mother refused to help him…

Abby leaned closer to me across the table. "Okay, I have to confess something—but you have to promise you won't yell or get mad at me."

"I don't like the sound of that."

"I didn't really download this from a city website," she confessed, lowering her voice. "Jeph found it."

I could feel a sick feeling forming in the pit of my stomach. "And just where exactly did Jeph find it?"

She had the decency to blush. "He hacked into Robby's e-mail account."

"What?"

It came out much louder than I intended; any number of other patrons stopped talking and turned to stare at us. I felt my face turning red, and made an apologetic gesture. After a few moments, they turned back to what they were doing.

"Sorry, boss, I know you don't like us to do that, but what was the harm, really?" She whispered in a rush, "You know the cops are going to go through his computer, and they're going to find it just the way we did. And you know what date this e-mail was sent?" She leaned back triumphantly. "Last Thursday. It was sent to him in the morning, and he opened it, downloaded the file, and read it Thursday afternoon. And it came from a lawyer." She slid a Post-it Note across the table to me. "That's his name and office number." She looked at my plate. "Are you going to eat those eggs?"

I slid the plate across the table. "I should put you over my knee and spank you."

"That's just gross." She stuck her tongue out at me. "And that would give Mona a reason to kill him. If Jonny wasn't entitled to any of the money from the settlement—because of the wording—and she could be legally liable for defrauding Robby and Lorelle—I mean, I doubt it ever occurred to her that the way this settlement was worded would ever come back to bite her in the ass, you know? This is the kind of quibbling about wording and legalities that a lawyer would jump on, but your average housewife wouldn't." Her eyes glinted. "I had to explain it to you, for example, and you know more about the law than the average citizen."

"Thanks for that," I replied sourly. "So, you're saying she killed Robby and has disappeared so the cops can't find her." I shook my head again. "I don't know, Abby." I scratched my head. "None of it makes any sense in the first place. She could have taken care of Jonny with the money *she* had in trust. She didn't need to share the settlement with him—and why the big need to keep it from him?" I drummed my fingers on the table. "Then again, if she didn't have a trust set up for Jonny, Robby and Lorelle would want to know why not—and eventually he'd want to know, too. So, maybe it was all just easier for her? I don't know if I buy that."

She nodded. "Chanse, her husband *died.* After he was dead there wasn't any need to keep anything quiet anymore—and she never remarried. What does that tell you?"

"It tells me you're speculating without any evidence."

She rolled her eyes. "Which tells me *you* aren't a woman. Women aren't like men, in case you've never noticed. Women, as a rule, don't have sex just for sex's sake—we take it a little more seriously than that. Women generally only have sex with men they love—"

"Which totally explains singles bars."

She made a face at me. "That's different. Mona O'Neill was married, quite happily from all accounts, and was a devout Catholic.

She wouldn't have an affair because she needed to get laid, Chanse, or just for some good sex. She would fall in love with another man, that's the only way she'd do it. And if she kept this all quiet for twenty years, there had to be a reason."

"He's married?"

"I don't know." She put a forkful of eggs into her mouth and moaned in ecstasy. "How the hell do they manage to make the food here so damned good? The married man thing seems so 1950s to me, you know? People get divorced left and right these days, so I can't imagine all the need for secrecy." She shrugged. "Sure, there might be a scandal, but does anyone really give two shits about that anymore? And I can't imagine things were that much different twenty years ago."

"Twenty years ago a sex scandal would kill a politician's career," I pointed out. "Now you can pay hookers to dress you in diapers and you don't have to resign."

"True." She spread grape jelly on her toast.

"We also don't know for sure that Mona had an affair," I pointed out. "No evidence—we're just making assumptions. We don't know Jonny wasn't Danny's child."

She made a face at me. "Okay, Mr. Expert Private Eye—have you gotten any other facts besides Mona's missing and her son was murdered?"

I was about to make a snide remark when my cell phone started ringing. I glanced down at it.

Morgan Barras Calling.

"MacLeod," I answered.

"Mr. MacLeod, this is Morgan Barras. I was wondering if you were free around eleven this morning?"

"Yes." I glanced over at Abby, whose eyebrows had gone up. "Where shall we meet?"

"Come to Poydras Tower. The security guard will let you in." He hung up.

I put my phone down. "I've been summoned to go see Morgan Barras. I wonder what this is about?"

"Who knows?" She pushed the plate away, and I signaled for the check. It was almost nine—I had time to do some more follow-up before heading to Poydras Tower. I paid the check and said good-bye to Abby on the sidewalk in front of the café. She offered to give me a lift home, but I decided to walk. The sky was gray and the air felt even heavier than before, but I was pretty certain I could get back to the apartment before the rain started.

I called Lorelle as I crossed St. Charles, watching for errant drivers on their cell phones and not paying attention to the road. "Hello, Mr. MacLeod," she said, picking up on the third ring.

I got to the point. "Lorelle, I'm sorry to have ask you this, but is there any possibility that Jonny wasn't your father's child?"

I could hear her sharp intake of breath on the other end, followed by a deep sigh. "I suppose it was inevitable you'd hear about that," she said. "No, Jonny was most definitely Dad's kid. I was hoping to never hear about that again." She went on to explain that her parents had separated briefly when she and Robby were teenagers. "Robby always thought it was because Mom cheated on Dad, and he never forgave her for it. But it wasn't true—Dad cheated on *Mom*. And she was already pregnant with Jonny when she threw him out."

"Well, where did Robby get the idea that—"

"He overheard them arguing and got the wrong impression. Mom never knew—she never knew. I didn't know Robby thought that myself. If I'd known back then, I would have corrected him." She barked out a harsh laugh. "I *caught* Dad with his girlfriend. I was the one who told Mom. By the time Robby finally dropped his little bombshell on me, we were in college and he wouldn't believe me when I tried to tell him the truth. That's why we weren't close anymore." She paused. "How did you find out?"

"Jonny told me. The last time he spoke with Robby, Robby told *him*."

"Oh, that bastard!" Her voice rose. "If he wasn't dead, I could just kill him! Poor Jonny—like there's not enough for him to deal with right now—and thank you for telling me. Is there anything else?"

"Not at the moment—"

She hung up the phone before I could finish the sentence.

Well, I thought as I walked across Coliseum Square, I never really thought Mona killed Robby and went on the run.

One possibility down, a few more to go.

An hour later, I opened my umbrella as I stepped down off the St. Charles streetcar at the corner of Carondelet and Poydras. The rain had started to fall when the streetcar made it around the loop at Lee Circle and was coming down in earnest now. The gutters were already filling, discarded cups and leaves swirling around in the dirty water. Sheets of water washed down the slanted sidewalk down to the gutter. I shivered and crossed the street when the light changed.

As I headed up Poydras to keep my appointment with a billionaire, I wondered what Morgan Barras was really like.

I haven't had a lot of luck with rich people, if you take my landlady and primary client, Barbara Castlemaine, out of the equation. She's the exception that proves the rule. It's been my experience—and I freely admit to being biased—that rich people tend to think the law doesn't apply to them and they can use their money, and the power it gives them, to pretty much buy their way out of everything. It's like where their conscience and soul are supposed to be, they have money.

Poydras Tower rose at the corner of Poydras and Rampart Street. An enormous modern tower of glass and steel, a lot of people in the city hated it, called it an ugly eyesore. It didn't bother me. I think most people hated what it *represented* more than what it actually looked like—a carpetbagger who'd swept into town after a man-made disaster to exploit suffering and make a few bucks. Given the fact that there'd been nothing on the site for years other than some abandoned buildings and a hideously ugly parking lot, I kind of thought the Poydras Tower was an improvement. It wasn't as tall as One Shell Square, the Entergy Building, or the Benson Tower, and seriously, there's only so much one can do with steel and glass. It looked modern and new—and that never plays particularly well in New Orleans, either. About three floors up, the building extended out over the sidewalk on every side.

And I had to admit that while the overhang over the sidewalk might be ugly, it sure came in handy during a downpour.

I walked into the lobby and signed into a visitor's log at the security desk. The guard, an overweight white man in his late fifties whose blue uniform shirt's buttons were straining not to pop, didn't smile. "You're expected," he said, standing up and gesturing at me. "Follow me." He walked over to the glass doors and punched in a code. There was a buzzing sound, and he walked through.

I walked behind him to an elevator. He put a key in a lock pad and turned it. The elevator doors opened silently. "Thanks." I smiled at him as I stepped inside. He ignored me and walked away as the elevator doors shut. There were three buttons: PH, L, and P. I pressed PH—which I assumed stood for penthouse—and the elevator started rising.

The doors opened and I walked out into an overdone foyer that was astonishing in its tackiness.

Another security guard was sitting at a desk and he picked up a phone, motioning me to stay where I was. He mumbled something I couldn't understand into the phone before walking over with an electronic wand in his hand. "Raise your hands," he instructed. I obliged, and he moved the wand rapidly over my body. Once he was finished, he said nothing—just went back and sat down behind his desk again.

The door opposite the elevator opened, and a slender woman in her mid-thirties appeared. She was much shorter than she appeared, given the height of the stiletto heels she was wearing. Her cream-colored silk blouse hung shapelessly on her. Her light brown hair was cut short, she was wearing practically no makeup on her pale face, and the crease in her black trousers easily could slice through skin. She didn't look like she had much of a shape to her, or that could have just been the illusion her clothes created. "Chanse MacLeod?" she said, forcing the corners of her mouth up into what was supposed to pass for a smile. But her eyes remained cold.

"Yes." I smiled back at her.

She held out a hand. "I'm Nancy Shelby, Mr. Barras's personal assistant."

I shook it. "A pleasure, Ms. Shelby."

She nodded. "If you'll follow me, please?"

I followed her through the door into the apartment. There was a long hallway with a really thick white plush carpet with gold threads woven through it. The ceiling was really high, and ornate gold chandeliers hung from it at varying intervals. There was no furniture of any kind in the hallway—no tables or chairs. Art was hanging on the walls, and the occasional large gilt mirror, with no rhyme or reason to the art. There was no theme to it—it was like someone had just bought a lot of expensive paintings and hung them without putting any thought into it. I followed her down the hallway to the door at the far end, and she opened it. I followed her into an enormous room that was as wide as the apartment itself. Three of the walls were glass. To the right, I could see through the rain-streaked glass to the Superdome and Benson Tower, and the river in the far distance. To the left, the bridge to the West Bank was clearly visible. Uptown stretched out in front of me, and there was a door that led out to a large deck area with a swimming pool and a hot tub. The wind and rain was creating whitecaps in the pool, and the hot tub was covered.

A man was standing with his back to me, wearing a suit that looked like it cost more than I made in a year, looking out the window. In his hand, he held a glass with what looked like Scotch on the rocks. He was shorter than I would have thought he would be, and his shoulder-length reddish blond hair looked just as greasy in person as it did on television. His shoulders were narrow, and the suit hung on him like it was a size or two too big.

Nancy cleared her throat. "Mr. Barras, Mr. MacLeod is here."

He turned and dismissed her with just a wave of his hand.

Without a word she went back out, shutting the door silently behind her.

He walked toward me. His face was reddish, with a thin long

nose over thin lips that barely seemed to cover his enormous white teeth. Despite the thinness of his features, he had a round moon face that looked even rounder due to how slender the nose was. I wondered idly if he'd had it fixed. His face seemed rather rigid— and I realized there were no wrinkles and his skin seemed almost plastic.

He was even less attractive in person than he was on television.

He didn't offer me his hand, his beady little eyes narrowing as he got closer. "Have a seat, Mr. MacLeod." He gestured to the couch.

I sat down and crossed my right leg over my left knee. The couch was as uncomfortable as it was ugly. The whole room was full of ugly furniture and art—like it had been decorated by someone with more money than taste. He sat down in a chair on the other side of the coffee table from me. There were several magazines on the coffee table—*Fortune*, *GQ*, *Time*, and *People*.

Each cover featured his smiling face.

"You're digging around in my business." He watched my face as he spoke.

I shrugged. "Your name has come up several times in the course of my investigation. But only peripherally, which is odd, yes."

He sipped his Scotch. "And just what are those circumstances?"

"I really am not at liberty to discuss my investigation." I pulled a photocopy of the cashier's check out of my pocket and put it down on the coffee table. "This was the first time your name came up. What can you tell me about this check?"

He pulled a pair of reading glasses out of an inner jacket pocket and slid them on. He reached down and picked up the photocopy. He pursed his lips as he looked at it for a few minutes before setting it back down on the coffee table. "That was a bonus I paid Mona O'Neill," he said slowly, his face unreadable. "She manages her son, Jonny. He's got quite a future. She signed him to my MMA promotion, and that was her reward, a signing bonus."

"Isn't it usual for the athlete to get the signing bonus rather than the manager?"

The left corner of his mouth rose for just a moment. "Jonny received a check for the same amount."

"Isn't this a little generous?" I folded the photocopy back up and slid it back into my pocket. "That's a hundred grand, just for signing a contract. From what research I've done, I don't see how such a contract could be worth it to you."

"Mr. MacLeod, I plan on making MMA the next WWE," he replied, taking off the glasses and replacing them. "If Vince McMahon can make millions with his live-action cartoon, it stands to reason actual fighting can make more. I have several multi-million-dollar contracts being negotiated with cable channels to air the fights. We're going to do a reality show." He waved his hand dismissively, as though I were just one of those moronic little people who couldn't possibly understand how big business worked. "If you have some money lying around, you might want to invest. I guarantee you, this is going to explode."

"Even so, this seems like small potatoes for someone of your stature." I managed to change my tone on the word *stature*, turning it into a mildly veiled insult.

"Maybe." His eyes narrowed briefly. "It interests me."

"Is it true that you want to buy St. Anselm's from the archdiocese, turn it into a home?"

This time he did smile. His forehead and cheeks didn't move. "You really shouldn't take comments on Internet message boards seriously, Mr. MacLeod."

"When was the last time you spoke to Mona O'Neill?"

"When I gave her that check. It was on Wednesday afternoon, last week." He scratched his forehead. "Yes, it was Wednesday."

Abby was right, the check's date wasn't the same as the day she got it. Aloud, I asked, "How did she seem to you?"

He gave me a startled look. "The same as she always did— like a middle-aged woman who dyed her hair and wore too much makeup. I'm really not in the habit of having personal conversations with people like that, if that's what you're asking."

I bit my lip and clenched my hands into fists. It was taking a lot of my self-control to not launch myself across the table and punch the self-satisfied smirk off his face. Of course he didn't pay any attention to Mona O'Neill—she wasn't a twenty-year-old blonde with enormous breasts and a Slavic accent. "She was last seen the next evening—you haven't heard from her, have you?"

He suppressed a yawn. "Why would I? You're beginning to bore me, Mr. MacLeod."

"I didn't ask for this meeting," I retorted before I could stop myself—and then it struck me. *Why* had he asked me to come?

He wanted to know what I knew, and if it was a threat to him.

"I'd heard that you were asking questions about me, Mr. MacLeod, and I usually find it much easier to answer those questions myself." Again, the ghost of a smile appeared at the corners of his mouth. "But I now find that this is a colossal waste of my time." He waved his hand in dismissal. "You remember the way to the elevator, don't you?"

I rose, and walked to the door. I paused, and looked back. "You know, would you mind answering one more question for me, Mr. Barras?"

He gave me a bored look. "Yes, what is it?"

"The one thing I don't understand is, why did you buy Cypress Gardens from Luke Marino?"

A muscle in his jaw twitched. "I thought it was an excellent investment opportunity."

"A storm-damaged apartment complex being run by a non-profit organization providing housing to low-income families." I tilted my head to one side. "Somehow I doubt that. And you're a stockholder in Global Insurance."

"I own a lot of stock in a lot of different companies."

"Maybe you instructed Global not to pay out on Luke's claim so you could get a better price on the place?"

He took another drink of his Scotch, and was it my imagination, or was his hand trembling just a little bit? "I won't deny that Cypress Gardens came to my attention because of the Global Insurance connection, and maybe I got a better deal on the place than I would have if Global had paid out the claim, but I am not involved in the day-to-day business of the company, Mr. MacLeod. That wouldn't exactly be legal, now would it?" He sipped the Scotch again. "One thing that I thought was rather odd, though—it might be of interest to you."

"And what might that be?"

He licked his thin lips. "I have been trying to get Jonny O'Neill in my promotion for months now, Mr. MacLeod. He's been doing fights at my casino in Mississippi, but his mother was resistant. She didn't think I had her son's best interests at heart."

"Did you?"

"I'm always interested in my investments, Mr. MacLeod." He waved his hand. "Jonny has star potential, but that foolish woman didn't see it. She thought I was going to exploit her son. I offered her the rather generous signing bonuses several weeks ago, and she practically spat in my face. You can imagine my shock last Wednesday when she called me and asked if the offer still stood. I said, of course, and she came by the next day to sign the contracts and pick up the checks." He shrugged. "Curious, don't you think?"

"Maybe she just changed her mind."

"Perhaps."

"She seemed to be doing that a lot last week," I replied. "She changed her mind about letting Jonny sign with you, she changed her mind about testifying for Luke Marino—"

"She changed her mind about testifying?" His face didn't change, but his tone had altered a little bit.

I nodded. "She notified his lawyer she was going to change her testimony. You wouldn't happen to know anything about that, would you?"

His face remained impassive. "Why would I?"

I stood up. "Well, thank you for your time, Mr. Barras."

He stopped me as I started out the door. "Mr. MacLeod?"

"Yes?"

"That check you showed me?" He licked his lips again. "As I mentioned earlier, there were two of them—one for Mona, and one for Jonny."

I frowned. Had Mona given Jonny his check? He hadn't said anything about getting a windfall.

Then I remembered him saying *I got money* and handing me the hundred-dollar bill out of his pocket.

He smiled again. "Mona insisted that both checks be made out to her."

I bowed my head and walked down the hallway back to the foyer, my heart racing.

What happened to the other check?

Chapter Fourteen

I stood inside the front lobby of Poydras Tower, watching the cars crawling by in the nonstop downpour.

Fifty thousand dollars was missing, and so was Mona O'Neill.

She'd cashed the check on Thursday—the same day her son was murdered and she disappeared.

"Do you need a cab, sir?" the security guard asked.

"That would be great, thank you," I replied without turning around.

My phone started ringing, and when I pulled it out of my pocket I could see *Loren McKeithen Calling* on the screen. "MacLeod," I said, touching the red Accept button.

"Great news, Chanse!" he blustered in my ear. "The best possible news! Global *settled*!"

"Cool."

"So it's over—send me an invoice for what we owe you—"

"I hadn't deposited your check yet," I cut him off. "I'll e-mail the invoice and drop the check off at your office."

"No need—just send the invoice, and I'll bring you a replacement check by," he enthused. "We'll definitely need to celebrate. I should be finished here at the office today around six. Will you be home then?"

"I can be."

"See you then," he replied and hung up.

I put my phone back in my pocket and went out the front doors to wait for my cab under the overhang. The wind was blowing rain under it, but it only could get about halfway up the sidewalk—the half closest to the building was dry as a bone. Cars were still driving at a snail's pace through the rain, and visibility was poor. The water in the gutters had risen up over the sidewalk, and there was at least three inches of water on Poydras Street. The wind had picked up as well. The trees on the neutral ground were bending and swaying. Leaves were being ripped away and outer edges of branches were snapping off, turning into dangerous projectiles. I watched as a woman on the other side of the street struggled to keep hold of her umbrella, which finally turned inside out, her hair getting soaked and ruined in a matter of seconds.

So, I reasoned, the check in Mona's desk had been for Jonny. The other check had been the one she'd intended to use for herself, and she'd cashed it rather than depositing it. The only explanation for that was she intended to give the money to Robby, so he could make good his embezzlements and stay out of jail. Maybe, I reflected, all of this simply had to do with a robbery, pure and simple. The money was gone—but Robby's body had been left behind, so where was Mona?

Robby had been desperate. His marriage was crumbling, he was about to go to jail, and he was about to lose everything. Desperate people do desperate things—and threatening to go to court to break Jonny's trust and access the money, a move that would humiliate his mother and crush his brother, could, horrible as it was, be understood in the context that he was drowning and desperately trying to grab onto a lifeline—any lifeline—to save himself and his own family.

Mona herself had been in a terrible predicament. No matter how badly things between her and Robby had deteriorated, he was still her son—and no mother would want to see her son go to jail, even if he deserved it. She couldn't steal from one son to help out the other, so perhaps her decision to change her testimony had been an attempt to get money out of either Global or Luke Marino. But she'd never asked Luke for the money—wouldn't she have just asked him for a loan?

And why didn't she just cash in some of her own CDs or sell some of her investments? Wouldn't that have been easier and avoided compromising her own ethics?

And ultimately, she had sold Jonny out to get money from Morgan Barras—at least in her own mind.

None of this made the least bit of a sense.

A United cab sloshed through the shallow creek that Poydras Street was turning into and came to a stop in front of where I was standing. I dashed through the rising water, opened the back door, and slid into the seat, slamming the door behind me.

I still got drenched.

I gave my address to the driver, who just shook his head. "Man, I don't know how close I can get to that, Camp Street's under water."

I sighed. "The corner of St. Charles and Martin Luther King is fine—I can walk from there."

When he dropped me off, I paid him, opened the door and the umbrella. St. Charles Avenue crests in the center—the neutral ground with the streetcar tracks is higher than the road, which slants down to the sidewalk in both directions. The water was halfway up my calves, and I fought against the fast-moving dirty water to cross the street. Lightning pierced the heavy gray darkness, followed by an immediate crack of thunder that set off car alarms in every direction—and the stoplights and street lights went dark. The neutral ground was also under shallow water, and my thighs began to ache from the effort of moving my legs through the rising water. The umbrella was becoming more and more useless as I walked, as the blasts of wind drove the heavy thick drops into me, soaking my clothes through and making them cling to my skin. And I knew the closer I got to Camp Street, the deeper the water would be.

If it isn't the lowest-lying street in my neighborhood, Camp Street has to be pretty damned close. As I waded across Prytania, I could see through the gloom that people were already pulling the cars up on the neutral ground and on the higher ground of Coliseum Square. I saw an eighteen-wheeler heading downtown throwing up huge waves of dirty water, complete with whitecaps, as it made its way through the flooding street.

I just put my head down and kept walking.

I cut across Martin Luther King at the light and paused to catch my breath. I was cold—the wind was getting stronger and colder, and the massive branches of the live oaks in the park were swaying. I could see deep water cascading down my driveway into the swirling mass of water at the foot of my driveway. The sidewalk in front of my house, and my front yard, were already underwater, and I could see the waves being thrown up by cars and trucks lapping against the bottom brick step leading up to my porch. The water was rising even as I watched. Coliseum Street was also under a rising tide, and the longer I waited the worse it was going to be. I splashed across to the park, and my feet sank into the soupy mud, making sucking noises as I strained to extract my feet, one at a time, on my way over to Camp Street.

By the time I was weaving my way through the cars that had pulled up onto the park to wait out the flooding, I could see that the water was already up to my third step and halfway up the slope of my driveway. It was over my knees as I crossed Camp Street, and holding on to the umbrella was an increasingly difficult struggle with every step I took. But finally I was climbing my front steps, and I could see that my living room lights were on—so at least I hadn't lost power. I unlocked the front door, pushing it open as I kicked off my shoes. The porch was soaked, and I pulled off my socks and tossed them to the side. I closed the umbrella, put it down, and stepped inside, stripping naked as soon as I closed the door and locked the deadbolt. I ran to the bathroom and grabbed a towel, drying myself off and wrapping it around me as I walked into the bedroom. I slipped on a hooded sweatshirt and sweatpants before going back into the kitchen and starting another pot of coffee.

My teeth were chattering as the coffee brewed—my apartment was freezing, and I slid my house shoes on my wet, cold feet. I poured a cup of coffee and took a drink, letting the warmth flow through me as I walked back into the living room. I grabbed my notebook, sat down on the couch, and pulled a comforter over me as I flipped it open and started reviewing my notes while the computer powered up.

I plugged my phone into its charger.

I gnawed on the end of my pen.

The case didn't make any sense, and it never had, from the very beginning. It hadn't ever felt right to me—but it was nothing I could prove, nothing I could put my finger on and say *this is it—what the hell.*

The thing to do was go back to the very start and review everything, everything I'd found, everything I'd been told.

Fact: Robby O'Neill had embezzled money, had committed a crime. His employers were willing to simply fire him and not press charges if he returned the money he'd taken. He needed about fifty thousand dollars. He'd threatened to go to court and expose his mother as an adulterer and his brother as a bastard to get the money in Jonny's trust fund—but Lorelle claimed it wasn't true, so Mona would *certainly* have known it wasn't true, that the threat was empty. DNA tests were expensive and took a while, but that's all it would have taken—and Robby didn't have the time to wait. So, why would Mona have cared?

The only plausible reason she would have is *if it were true.*

So, Lorelle had either lied or simply hadn't known the truth.

Why would Lorelle lie?

I looked at my phone and thought about calling her, but decided there was no point. If she'd lied, she was hardly going to admit to it over the phone.

But if she *had* knowingly lied about Jonny's parentage, well, maybe she had lied about other things as well.

I flipped through the notebook to my notes from Lorelle's interview.

And there it was. At the time, it had gone right past me—I had no reason to think anything was odd about it.

Lorelle had said: *Morgan Barras had sold Mom and Robby and Jonny a line of bullshit...Robby and Celia both thought—I don't know, maybe I shouldn't say.*

Yet Lorelle had said she and Robby weren't close, barely spoke. She and Jonny had also said that Robby wasn't close to their mother. I thought back—no, come to think of it, *Jonny* hadn't exactly said that—he said that Robby thought he was "better than us." At the time, I'd just assumed he'd meant all of them.

But what if he'd just meant himself and Heather, and *not* their mother?

I shook my head. But what reason did Lorelle have for killing her mother and her brother? Somehow, I couldn't see her committing either crime. She was a suburban soccer mom.

But I'd never checked her financials.

I got my phone and called Jephtha. "Chanse!" He answered. "Dude, I'm glad you called—sorry, I've been meaning to call you."

I bit my lower lip. "Did you find out something important?" I somehow managed to say in a calm and clear voice. I could clearly hear a computer game running in the background.

"I'm sorry," he replied, and I knew he was—he always was. "But you know, I was working on this new game I think is going to be huge and I forgot to call you and I was going to pass it on to Abby but she went out while I was working on the game and she hasn't come back yet—" He paused. "You know, that's kind of weird. She said she'd only be gone about an hour or so, and it's been a lot longer than that and she hasn't called."

"What?" I looked at the clock. It was almost one. I'd left Abby before nine. "What time was it when she left?"

I could almost see him thinking. "Well, she woke me up at a little after nine, asked me if I wanted breakfast. I got up, and when I got out of the shower, she was on her computer—I got some coffee, it said it was nine forty on the coffeemaker, but Abby has that set about twenty minutes fast, and then she jumped up and said she had to go check on something, and she'd be back in an hour—so she's been gone almost three hours and she hasn't called." His voice began to sound worried.

I sighed. "It's probably nothing—it's raining pretty hard and the city's flooding, she's probably just riding it out somewhere."

"You're probably right." He sighed. "But usually she calls, you know?"

"What was the information you had for me?" I interrupted him, trying to get him back on track.

"Oh, yeah, sorry." I could hear papers rustling around, and the computer game went silent. "Here it is. I would have e-mailed it to you but I know how you are about stuff—" He stopped talking.

Which meant he'd hacked into a website or a computer. "Who'd you hack into?"

I heard a sharp intake of breath.

"Jeph?"

"Chanse—I'm really worried about Abby."

I sighed, getting a little annoyed. "Jeph, we talked about that—like I said, she's probably just riding the flooding out somewhere." As though to emphasize my point, thunder roared loud enough to shake my house. I got up and walked over to my front door, peering through the blinds. It was even darker outside than it had been—and the water was now up to the top of the fourth step. I bit my lip.

The water never went higher than the fifth step, at least I'd never seen that happen in all my years in this apartment. The pumping stations were already at work, and even if the rain kept up, by that time the pumps would be working at full capacity and the water would start receding. Coliseum Square was full of parked cars—and there was an abandoned car at the corner of Melpomene, sitting in water halfway up its doors. I shook my head in sympathy. I'd gotten caught in a flash flood shortly after I moved to the city, and it had taken about six hundred bucks to get my car running again.

And the musty smell had never really gone away.

"This is what she was looking at before she left this morning." His voice was trembling.

"How could she have been looking at something on your computer? You said she was at hers."

"Our computers are networked." He launched into a long technical explanation that made absolutely no sense to me whatsoever, but the bottom line of it was the document he was looking at had been looked at since he'd originally downloaded it at three in the morning, and the IP address was Abby's computer.

I wanted to reach through the phone and throttle him. "What the hell is it, Jeph?"

"I didn't think it was all that important, just thought it was kind of curious," he said defensively. "But if she was looking at it—"

"Get to the fucking point!"

"You know Barney Hogan?"

"What about him?"

"I thought I'd check his financials, you know—Abby had mentioned he was like one of the last people to see Mrs. O'Neill alive, right?"

"Yes."

"Well, he was about to lose his bar—he was behind a couple of months to the bank—and now he's not anymore."

I felt a chill run down my spine. "How much did he owe the bank, Jeph?"

"About thirty grand. He paid it back in full on Friday." He swallowed. "And that was what Abby was looking at before she left the house."

Chapter Fifteen

I ran over to the front door and peered out through the blinds.

The rain hadn't let up. If anything, it seemed like it was coming down even harder. But the swirling, dirty floodwaters looked like they were finally receding; I could see the top two steps in front of the porch. "Damn it." I cursed myself for not buying an SUV instead of my fuel-efficient Ford Focus. I tried to think of someone—anyone—I knew who owned one, and couldn't. I was stuck until the flood waters went down and I could safely get the Focus out of the parking lot.

There's nothing more frustrating than having to wait when you need to get somewhere.

I replayed my interview with Barney and Jermaine again in my head: Jermaine saying Mona had been extremely agitated when she'd come in on Thursday night, and Barney smoothly saying she was upset because her vigil partner had canceled on her yet again and wanted him to sit vigil with her.

I hadn't paid any attention, hadn't thought to pursue that line of questioning any further, just let it drop.

I cursed myself out yet again as I paced around the living room. I tried Abby's cell phone but it went straight to voicemail.

With a heavy sigh, I called Venus.

"Casanova."

"Venus, it's Chanse." I tried to keep my voice calm, tried to keep myself calm. "Abby's missing, and I think it's bad. I'm trapped, can't get my car out because Camp Street's flooded."

"Tell me about it." Venus sounded irritated and tired. "You'd think it never floods here, the way people are. We're all buried—wrecks, stranded motorists—what do you want me to do? Come get you?"

"She's in danger." I heard my voice starting to shake, and struggled to get a grip on my adrenaline, tried to slow my heart rate. Getting worked up wasn't going to solve anything, wasn't going to get me to where I needed to be. I started explaining what I believed, and she listened.

"You got any evidence, hard evidence, to back any of this up?" she asked finally.

My heart sank. "No."

"Chanse, you know I would if I could, but I can't." She sighed. "There's no way I can go to my boss and get relieved out of flood duty to go off on what might be a wild goose chase because you *might* be right. He wouldn't even bother to tell me no. You remember what it's like for the department when the city floods. I'm sorry, man. But the pumping stations have all come on line, and you should be able to get out of there soon. I'll do what I can, but man, my hands are tied."

"Venus—"

"Hang on a second." She must have put her hand over the receiver, because I could hear the muffled sound of her talking to someone, and then Blaine came on the phone.

"Chanse, this is Blaine. Look, if you need my SUV, take it. Use the spare key to let yourself in the back door—the alarm code is 6069—and the keys are hanging on a hook just inside the back door—the hook's labeled."

Venus must have grabbed the phone back from him. "And you call us for backup as soon as you have something, you got it? Don't be playing hero, you understand me?"

I hung up the phone and raced back to the bedroom. I pulled on a pair of jean shorts, a black T-shirt, and socks and shoes. I grabbed my umbrella and went out the front door.

The water was now down to the first step, but I could see the curb on the park side of Camp Street was only under a couple of inches of brown, murky water. I grabbed my gun and put it in my waistband, locked the front door, and headed across Coliseum Square. I was soaked by the time I got to the big house Blaine and his partner shared on the other side of Coliseum Square, a few houses from the corner at Polymnia Street. I found the spare key, let myself in, turned off the alarm, and grabbed his keys. I went into the garage, used the remote to open the door, and started up his gray SUV.

Two minutes later I had backed out onto Coliseum Street, and I headed for Race Street, the wipers slapping back and forth as the tires threw up a huge wake of water as I took the turn a little too fast and drove toward Tchoupitoulas. Cars were still driving at a crawl, and I swore as I illegally swung out around them to pass them. The SUV threw up huge wakes of water, and I felt a little bad about possibly swamping some of the cars I was passing.

After what seemed like an eternity, I was turning into the parking lot of the Riverside. Abby's Oldsmobile was sitting in the far corner. I parked alongside it and looked through the rain-drenched windows. Nothing.

I tried the driver's side door, and it was unlocked. I yanked it open and swore.

Abby's cell phone was plugged into the cigarette lighter, charging.

Wherever she was, she didn't have her phone.

I unplugged it and put it all into my pocket and headed for the front door of the bar.

I pushed it, and it swung open. I stepped out of the rain and flipped on a light switch next to the door. The bar was empty. "Abby?" I called. "Barney? Is there anyone here?" I walked behind the bar. There was no one in the kitchen, no one in the walk-in refrigerator. The doors to both the office and the storeroom were locked. I pounded on them and listened for sound, but heard nothing.

"Damn it, Abby," I swore under my breath as I headed back for the front door. "Where the hell are you?"

I dashed back to the SUV and checked Abby's phone. It had about a fifty percent charge, so I touched the icon for recent calls.

Sure enough, she'd called Barney Hogan. Obviously, she'd had him meet her at the bar.

And now they were both missing.

I got back in the car and called Jeph, ordering him to do whatever he could to find out if Barney Hogan owned any property anywhere in the city besides the bar. "Will do," Jeph replied. He hesitated. "There's something else I found since I talked to you last—I wasn't sure if I should call you…"

"What is it?" I replied, irritated.

He told me, and another piece of the puzzle clicked into place.

"Find out if Hogan owns any more property anywhere, and hurry," I snapped, hanging up. I cursed at myself for not checking into Hogan more thoroughly as I pulled back onto Tchoupitoulas Street.

I drove as fast as I dared over to Constance Street.

I parked in front of Jonny's house, which was ablaze with light, and splashed my way up the walk to the front door. I started pounding, and within minutes the door was opened. Jonny gaped at me. "What the hell are you doing out in the middle of such a terrible storm? Are you crazy?"

I pushed past him. "Where's Heather?"

She was standing in the doorway to the rest of the house, her hugely pregnant stomach out in front of her, a smirk on her face.

"Where is she?" I snarled. I wanted nothing more than to smack the smirk right off her face, baby or no baby.

"Who?" she said, her voice mocking.

"Dude—" Jonny said, coming around and getting in between me and his wife.

"Jonny, what do you know about your wife?" I asked. "Like what do you know about her father?"

Her face remained impassive. "I never knew my dad."

"That was true, I think, for most of your life, but it hasn't been true for a while, has it?" I didn't wait for her answer—it would have just been a lie anyway—and went on, "You know your father now, don't you, Heather?"

"You think you're so damned smart, don't you?" she jeered.

Jonny looked at her and back at me, his face puzzled.

"Your father is Barney Hogan," I continued, watching her face. "Your mother left him before you were born, that was true, and you grew up with a different last name—your mother remarried when you were a child, and her second husband's name is the one you grew up under."

Her face twisted. "Barney Hogan was my sperm donor, not my father." She waddled into the living room, her hands pressed into her back. She winced as she sat down on the couch. "He owed me. I didn't have anything growing up—my mother and stepfather worked their fingers to the fucking bone trying to keep a roof over our heads. So, yeah, when my mother died and she told me who my father really was, I wanted some payback."

"So, was the scam your idea or his?"

"Hey—I didn't know he was going to kill people." She held up her hand. "That wasn't part of the plan." She looked over at Jonny. "Nor was falling in love with Jonny—that wasn't supposed to happen either."

"What are you talking about?" Jonny's face was confused, his voice tentative.

"The money, Jonny, it was all about the money." I shook my head. "Your mother has quite a bit stashed aside—and *so do you.* Even after buying this house, there's about another hundred thousand in your trust fund."

"You married me for the trust fund?" He stared at his wife, his face draining of color.

"You think I would have married you for money?"

"Barney was definitely working Mona for hers," I went on. What I believed were Heather's motivations were immaterial—the two of them could work that out for themselves. "But what I want to know—what I need to know right the fuck now—is where is he keeping Mona and Abby?"

"Abby?"

"My partner."

Heather took a deep breath. "He has a fishing cabin out near Manchac, on the edge of the swamp." She hesitated, but when she saw the look on my face, quickly gave me directions. "That's where he was keeping Mona. I don't know anything about no assistant."

I walked out of the house, and the last thing I heard before the door shut behind me was Jonny saying in a very small voice, "All this time you've known where my mom was and didn't say anything?"

There were a lot of issues to be worked out there.

I started the SUV and headed for the highway. I hesitated—it might be better to call Blaine and Venus, but they were out of their jurisdiction in Manchac—they'd have to call the state troopers and get them involved, the local sheriff, and all the while time would be wasted. I made the decision to call them once I was on I-10 and out of the city.

I headed over to Claiborne Avenue, swearing at slow-moving cars and passing them whenever I could—sometimes illegally. I took the Claiborne entrance on I-10 West, but even on the highway people were driving slowly. I hoped the railroad underpass out past the Citypark exit, which was low and always flooded, had been pumped out. There was a massive pumping station running along the highway out there, so I kept my fingers crossed. The fact that traffic was moving was a good sign—if the underpass was impassable, the traffic would have been backed up all the way to the West Bank.

There was some water, but nothing the cars couldn't handle—yet they still slowed down and passed through tentatively, like they were afraid the ground would somehow open up and swallow the cars whole if they went faster than ten miles per hour. I swore at all of them, trying to keep calm.

The only reason Mona was still alive was because the other check from Morgan Barras was still not cashed.

It didn't make sense to me—once Barney knew he couldn't get his hands on the other check, why not kill her and be done with it, dump her body in the swamp somewhere? Hell, he could have *forged* her name.

But he didn't know where the check was—and neither had Heather.

Mona had been smart to hide the check. I'd only found it by accident, and I had to admire her courage and resolve in not telling him where it was. It was the only reason he had to keep her alive, and the moment she told him where it was, she was a dead woman. She had to know, and somehow she kept from telling him. Of course, she couldn't know I'd found it and Jonny had given it to me for safekeeping.

I remembered Jonny's confusion when he took me to his mother's—the lights were too bright, the air conditioner too low, which his energy-conscious mother would have never done. Heather had gone over there, to look for the other check.

The check was in my hands, and undoubtedly Jonny had told Heather about it.

That's when Barney should have killed Mona, when he should have known the game was up. The check was locked up and neither he nor Heather had any way of getting a hold of it—unless he came to my house, held a gun on me, and forced me to turn the check over. He would have had to kill me—and even though he'd killed Robby O'Neill, he seemed to have a real problem with killing people.

So why exactly had he killed Robby O'Neill?

Mona must have told him all about Robby's money problems—and how she intended to get the money for him. She must have cashed the one check and given it to Robby. That was the part I didn't get—*why* had he taken Mona? He'd killed Robby and stolen the money—sure, he and Heather had wanted to get their hands on the other cash as well—but that money was for Jonny.

Killing Mona—Jonny would have gotten all the money in his trust and the fifty grand on top of it if she were dead—and Mona's money would be divided between her three children.

So, why take Mona?

It didn't make any sense.

I flew past the Loyola exit and drove onto the bridge that led over the Lake Pontchartrain marshes and the Bonne Carre spillway. I hit the speed dial on my phone and cursed when I went straight to Venus's voicemail. I left her a long and detailed message and told her I was heading out there before hanging up and tossing the phone into the passenger seat. It bounced off and went into the floorboard. I cursed, but couldn't look away from the road. It was a bumper-to-bumper crawl, and there was no way I could take my eyes away from the taillights in front of me for even a moment.

I eventually made it to the turn-off for I-55 North and breathed a sigh of relief as I left the heavy traffic behind. The Manchac exit I was looking for wasn't that much farther along, and the fishing camp, while a bit isolated, seemed rather easy to find.

Twenty minutes later I found the dirt road leading back. I parked, blocking the way in and out, and tucked my gun into the back of my pants. The rain was still coming down hard, and the little road had turned into a river of mud. I walked along the gravel on the side, the soft earth giving under my feet, and eventually made me way around to a small clearing with a graying dock out onto the water just beyond what was little more than a shack with a tin roof.

There was a light on, but there was no car in sight.

I crept up to the window and glanced in.

I could see Abby, tied to a chair, a gag tied around her mouth.

There was no one else in sight.

I kicked in the door and stood there, crouched, my gun raised and ready.

A door to my right opened, and I swiveled, ready to shoot.

Mona O'Neill gasped and raised her hands. "Don't shoot!"

Chapter Sixteen

This is all my fault." Mona sighed. "I've handled all of this so damned badly right from the very start, I deserve whatever comes to me. I'll go to jail."

She was sitting at the small table, and I had my gun trained on her. I'd forced her to untie Abby, and now I wanted some answers before we headed back into the city.

"You killed your son, didn't you?"

Shamefacedly, she nodded. "It was an accident, I swear. I know, I should have called the police, but I panicked. Really, I panicked. I didn't know what to do. So I called Barney."

"What happened?"

"She got the money for him, all right," Abby said, watching her closely as she flexed her arms and legs, trying to get her blood flowing again. It was cold inside the little cabin, and the wind was whipping around it, getting in through cracks in the flimsy walls. The rain kept up a steady drumbeat on the tin roof.

"We argued." Mona hung her head. "I told him I was done with him—he wasn't my son after this, and I never wanted to see him or speak to him again, even if it meant not seeing my grandchildren. He was so horrible to me—you have no idea the terrible things he said to me in order to get the money. I'd sold out my baby to Morgan Barras to keep him out of jail, and all he could talk about was that I owed him, that I was a whore, that Jonny was my bastard." She sighed. "He made me so angry, I couldn't help it. I just picked up something and whacked him with it. He went down, and just like that—I'd killed my son." She closed her eyes and hugged herself. "I don't know how long I stayed there, just thinking oh my God, and cradling him. I got blood all over me. And finally, I called Barney. He told me not to call the police, to stay there, he'd have to wait until the bar closed, but if I waited there, he'd come meet me and fix things."

"And?"

"When he arrived, we put Robby in his desk chair, and then I cleaned." Her voice was deadpan, free of any emotion as she remembered the details. "I used bleach—I know that messes up the DNA—and then Barney shot him and fixed it so that his body fell. He said it would look like he got the crack on his head when the chair went over, and that the police wouldn't really do a whole lot of looking at it—with the two shots, they'd just assume he was shot and that would be it."

I bit my lower lip. Venus and Blaine were good cops, but the city morgue was overburdened and underfunded. There was a very good chance the coroner would just go through the motions and not look for anything further than the gunshots wounds.

"Barney said the best thing for me to do was hide out here," she went on. "And I was so crazy I listened to him. I wasn't in my right mind, you have to understand." She ran a hand through her hair. "I'd just killed my son! He told me that all I had to do was be gone for a while, and he would fix things. If I just hid out here, we could take the money and disappear together."

I opened my mouth to say something, but Abby cut me off. "That's a nice little fairy tale," she said rather snidely, "but it's full of holes. But it was a really nice try." She turned to me. "I went to see Barney at the bar—he drugged me and brought me here. I've kept my mouth shut—but I really wanted to hear what lies she'd spin." Abby laughed. "You're going to have to do a lot better than that if you want to avoid the death penalty, you miserable old bitch."

Mona's eyes narrowed. "Watch your tongue, girl."

"Why do you think she wanted the overnight shift at St.

Anselm's?" Abby went on. "It wasn't because she was oh-so-worried about her church being closed—that was a good thing, as far as she was concerned. She was worried about it, but not for the reasons she gave everyone." Abby walked over to Mona. "She was afraid there were records there—records that might, someday, come to light and cause a whole lot of embarrassment for her and her family, and might just cut off her gravy train."

"Shut up!"

"No one ever questioned the age difference between Mona's kids," Abby went on. "No one but me, that is. People would remark on it, sure, but to me, it just seemed weird, you know? I mean, it happens, but it's not as commonplace as people think. And all that stuff about Robby telling Jonny he wasn't Danny's son—that was all true, wasn't it? But most people would assume *Mona* had an affair, rather than what was the *real* truth, right?"

And it hit me—right between the eyes.

Why would the Verlaines *themselves* pay out over Danny O'Neill's death rather than their insurance company?

They wouldn't.

Who else had lied, over and over, to me?

"Jonny is Lorelle's son, isn't he?" I said slowly. "She slept with one of the Verlaines, didn't she, and got pregnant, and as a good Catholic, she couldn't have an abortion, could she?"

Mona's face crumpled, and she buried her face in her hands.

"They sent her away, and Mona pretended to be pregnant, raised Jonny as her own son," Abby went on. "Then Lorelle came home, and everything went on as before except there was a new baby in the house. Everything would have been fine, wouldn't it, except what? Did Danny get greedy?"

"Danny." Mona's voice sounded broken. "He didn't want money. He just thought Percy Verlaine should know that he had a grandchild out there, what his son had done. He'd raped her, you know. It wasn't an affair. We kept it from Danny—we didn't want him to know, you know? I faked my pregnancy—I pretended that because of my age, I needed lots of bed rest, and no sex, everything.

I didn't think we could pull it off—and we probably couldn't have if not for the help of Father Shannon."

I bit my lower lip. *Of course they enlisted their priest.*

"Father Shannon arranged for her to go away to a home for Catholic girls—he took care of everything. We told Danny she was going to work at a summer camp."

"I don't understand how you got away with the birth—"

Mona closed her eyes. "After Lorelle had the baby, she came back home and stayed at St. Anselm's with Father Tom. When Danny went off to work, we faked me going into labor." She moistened her lips. "Our doctor was also a parishioner at St. Anselm's, and Father Tom had recruited him to help us. No one knew. Danny came home and thought Jonny was his child."

"So, how did Danny find out the truth? That Jonny was really his grandson, not his son?" I asked.

"Lorelle slipped." She stared out the window at the pouring rain. "They'd gotten into a huge fight, and she screamed the truth at him. That was how Robby found out the truth, too."

And Lorelle had lied, lied when she'd told me about Robby thinking their mother had an affair that produced Jonny. Why not? Robby was dead and couldn't contradict her. Mona was gone, and if she turned up, wasn't going to talk.

"Danny was furious." Mona's voice sounded distant, as though she were reliving the whole thing. "He was so angry. He wanted to know why we hadn't called the cops, pressed charges." She laughed bitterly. "Like the cops would take Lorelle's side? Like they would believe a teenaged girl over one of the high-and-mighty Verlaines? I knew damned well what would happen—Lorelle's reputation and life would be ruined and nothing would come of it. Nothing good, anyway. I was damned if she was going to spend the rest of her life being the girl who cried rape." She shook her head vehemently. "But Danny—Danny was out for blood. He stormed out of the house and went to talk to old man Percy."

I didn't say anything. I knew she was right. Percy Verlaine

would have never allowed a member of his family to go to jail—and what was more, he might have tried to take the child away.

"Danny died that night." Her voice broke. "They found him the next morning, you know, on the docks. How the hell did he get down there? *Why* did he go down there? But some fancy lawyer showed up while the police were talking to me…I never believed it was an accident, but the lawyer—oh, he was a smooth one."

I had no doubt about that.

"He told me there was no reason to push anything about Danny—Danny went down to the docks and was killed, and we'd never know the reason why he went down there, or how those crates crushed him. But I knew." Her eyes narrowed. "But the Verlaines' fancy lawyer, Mr. Pennycuff, he had it all worked out."

I'll just bet he did, I thought.

"They paid me all that money, arranged the trusts, and it was all contingent on my silence," she went on.

"That's why they worded the trust settlement that way—the children of Danny O'Neill—Jonny would lose any claim to any of the money if the truth came out," I said.

"Exactly. There wasn't a damned thing I could do. If anyone ever told, we'd lose everything." Mona nodded. "If the truth ever came out, if Lorelle and I ever said anything, we had to pay back every cent." Her eyes filled with tears. "And the money was gone, you know. Most of it. I would have to sell my house, give up everything."

"So, that was why you signed Jonny with Barras," I said. "You had to give Robby the money to shut him up."

"We would have been homeless, we would have lost everything," Mona sobbed. "Selling Jonny out to Barras was the lesser of two evils. I got him to give me the money in two different checks—one I'd give to Robby, and the other for Jonny. That way Jonny would get something."

"But Robby wanted more money, didn't he?"

She nodded. "I gave him the fifty thousand, and he wanted

more. He wanted all of it. I didn't know what to do—and then Jonny told me what he'd said. He'd already spilled part of it to Jonny." She shook her head. "And—"

"And you killed him to keep his mouth shut once and for all." Abby cut her off. "You didn't hit him over the head. You shot him, and you got blood all over yourself and all over your car." She turned to me. "This all happened in the early evening. She went home and cleaned herself up, hid the other check away."

"No, that isn't what happened." I smiled at Mona. "Mona's not a killer, are you, Mona?"

"She's kept me here against my will—" Abby started, but I cut her off.

"You got the money out of Barras, but he also made you change your testimony, didn't he, in the Cypress Gardens case, right?" I smiled at her. "And you planned all along to disappear, didn't you? So you wouldn't have to go into court and tell lies against Luke Marino."

She nodded. "Yes. I intended to disappear all along—at least until after the trial was over."

"But Robby wasn't just trying to get money out of you, was he?"

She hung her head and didn't say anything.

"He was also trying to get money out of *Lorelle*."

"He was desperate," she whispered, barely audible.

"You went there, to his house, that night to give him the money—but Lorelle was already there, wasn't she?" I went on. It was all falling into place. "She shot her brother. That's why when you went back to the Riverside, you were so shook up. You'd called Barney, right, and he told you to come down there."

She nodded. "He told me that it would all work, you know, with the disappearance and everything already set up. They wouldn't find Robby's body right away—God only knew when Celia would come back from Sandestin—and by then, we could fix things. I told Lorelle to leave, I would take care of everything."

"And Barney wanted the money, didn't he?"

"It was the least I could do," Mona replied sharply. "I went by the church, and then Barney came by after he closed the bar. We drove back over to Robby's and got some of his blood to smear all over the driver's seat—that way, you know, no one would even think about Lorelle. We left my car in the Irish Channel, in a bad neighborhood—and then Barney drove me out here."

"And you hid the other check, right?"

She nodded. "That check was for Jonny."

"Hiding that check was the smartest thing you ever did," I replied grimly. "That's why you're still alive."

"What?" Her face drained of color.

Abby laughed. "Yeah. Now I get it."

"Barney's been playing you for quite some time now, Mona." I sat down, still keeping my gun leveled at her. "Did you know that Heather was his daughter?"

Her mouth opened and closed.

"I don't know if Heather was part of his plan all along, but when Jonny got her pregnant and married her, it played into his hands, all right. He's been wanting to get his hands on Jonny's trust for quite a while now. He was way behind in his mortgage on the bar and on his other bills—Robby's turning to crime came at a very opportune time for him. He took the money you gave him and paid off everything." I grimaced. "And Heather's been looking for that other check, you know. If she'd found it—"

"Barney would have killed you and you would have never turned up again." Abby finished for me. "I'm sure the murder weapon would have turned up, so the police would think *you* killed your son. Jonny and Heather would move into your place and sell theirs, more money for Heather—and Barney would have kept the other fifty grand."

"He kept asking me where I put it," she whispered, her voice shaking. "I—"

"Shh," Abby whispered, cutting her off. "Did you hear that?"

I hadn't—but in the silence that followed her holding up her hand, I could hear it—over the rain drumming down on the tin roof.

Footsteps, sloshing down the muddy drive.

It had to be Barney.

I went over to the window and saw him, wearing a rain slicker, come out into the clearing.

He had a shotgun.

He raised it and fired at the window.

I leaped out of the way as the glass shattered.

I rolled across the floor to the other window, reaching over and grabbing the door. It swung open and another shotgun blast roared through it.

I held my gun up and fired.

AFTERWARD

I dropped Barney Hogan with that one shot, and that was the end of him.

Mona begged us to pin Robby's murder on him, and I couldn't think of any reason not to—except of course for that nagging sense that justice wasn't being served. But Lorelle came forward herself and confessed—taking the decision out of my hands.

Heather gave birth to a baby boy, whom they named Daniel Chanse O'Neill. With Barney dead, there was no proof that Heather had anything to do with any of his crimes, and she denied everything. The only thing she would confess to was not telling anyone she was Barney's daughter—and that wasn't a crime. Jonny apparently forgave her, and they stayed together.

Mona, however, told me she was keeping an eye on her daughter-in-law.

Lorelle was represented by none other than Loren McKeithen himself, and he managed to plea her out for manslaughter. The judge was compassionate—after all, Lorelle was a rape survivor, and rather than jail time he gave her probation with a requirement that she get therapy. Mona says she is doing well with it.

Mona also apologized to Luke Marino, who completely understood the pressures she was under, and forgave her—although I suspect had Global Insurance not finally given in and settled, forgiveness might not have come so easily.

Jonny's fight career continues to rise—I saw him fight on

ESPN the other day, and he just mauled a former world champion, knocking him out in the first round. He has a title shot scheduled and has signed some major endorsement deals. He recently moved his little family into a spacious apartment in Poydras Tower and sold the run-down place on Constance Street.

Archbishop Pugh also was reassigned, and we got a new archbishop in New Orleans, one who isn't quite so determined to close the two endangered parishes.

I had some trouble sleeping myself—it's not easy to kill someone, and I hope I never reach the point where I'm able to just go to sleep after shooting someone—but I'm doing well with it. It helps when you have a great support system, the way I do.

Rory and I are talking about moving in together—but we'll see how that turns out. I suspect we're both a little too stubborn as yet to make that work.

We'll see how it goes, right?

About the Author

Greg Herren is the award-winning author of two mystery series set in New Orleans featuring gay detectives Chanse MacLeod and Scotty Bradley. He has also published two young adult novels, *Sorceress* and *Sleeping Angel*, and co-edited the critically acclaimed anthologies *Men of the Mean Streets* and *Women of the Mean Streets* with the award-winning author of the Mickey Knight mystery series, J. M. Redmann. He has also published several novels and short stories under various pseudonyms, as well as over fifty short stories in markets as varied as *Ellery Queen's Mystery Magazine* and the acclaimed anthology *New Orleans Noir*. He works as an editor for Liberty Editions of Bold Strokes Books and lives in the lower Garden District of New Orleans.

Books Available From Bold Strokes Books

Franky Gets Real by Mel Bossa. A four-day getaway. Five childhood friends. Five shattering confessions…and a forgotten love unearthed. (978-1-60282-585-7)

Riding the Rails: Locomotive Lust and Carnal Cabooses, edited by Jerry Wheeler. Some of the hottest writers of gay erotica spin tales of *Riding the Rails*. (978-1-60282-586-4)

Rescue Me by Julie Cannon. Tyler Logan reluctantly agrees to pose as the girlfriend of her in-the-closet gay BFF at his company's annual retreat, but she didn't count on falling for Kristin, the boss's wife. (978-1-60282-582-6)

Snowbound by Cari Hunter. *"The policewoman got shot and she's bleeding everywhere. Get someone here in one hour or I'm going to put her out of her misery."* It's an ultimatum that will forever change the lives of police officer Sam Lucas and Dr. Kate Myles. (978-1-60282-581-9)

High Impact by Kim Baldwin. Thrill seeker Emery Lawson and Adventure Outfitter Pasha Dunn learn you can never truly appreciate what's important and what you're capable of until faced with a sudden and stark reminder of your own mortality. (978-1-60282-580-2)

Murder in the Irish Channel by Greg Herren. Chanse MacLeod investigates the disappearance of a female activist fighting the Archdiocese of New Orleans and a powerful real estate syndicate. (978-1-60282-584-0)

Sheltering Dunes by Radclyffe. The seventh in the award-winning Provincetown Tales. The pasts, presents, and futures of three women collide in a single moment that will alter all their lives forever. (978-1-60282-573-4)

Holy Rollers by Rob Byrnes. Partners in life and crime Grant Lambert and Chase LaMarca assemble a team of gay and lesbian criminals to steal millions from a right-wing mega-church, but the gang's plans are complicated by an "ex-gay" conference, the FBI, and a corrupt reverend with his own plans for the cash. (978-1-60282-578-9)

History's Passion: Stories of Sex Before Stonewall, edited by Richard Labonté. Four acclaimed erotic authors re-imagine the past…Welcome to the hidden queer history of men loving men not so very long—and centuries—ago. (978-1-60282-576-5)

Lucky Loser by Yolanda Wallace. Top tennis pros Sinjin Smythe and Laure Fortescue reach Wimbledon desperate to claim tennis's crown jewel, but will their feelings for each other get in the way? (978-1-60282-575-8)

Mystery of The Tempest: A Fisher Key Adventure by Sam Cameron. Twin brothers Denny and Steven Anderson love helping people and fighting crime alongside their sheriff dad on sun-drenched Fisher Key, Florida, but Denny doesn't dare tell anyone he's gay, and Steven has secrets of his own to keep. (978-1-60282-579-6)

Better Off Red: Vampire Sorority Sisters Book 1 by Rebekah Weatherspoon. Every sorority has its secrets, and college freshman Ginger Carmichael soon discovers that her pledge is more than a bond of sisterhood—it's a lifelong pact to serve six bloodthirsty demons with a lot more than nutritional needs. (978-1-60282-574-1)

Detours by Jeffrey Ricker. Joel Patterson is heading to Maine for his mother's funeral, and his high school friend Lincoln has invited himself along on the ride—and into Joel's bed—but when the ghost of Joel's mother joins the trip, the route is likely to be anything but straight. (978-1-60282-577-2)

Three Days by L.T. Marie. In a town like Vegas where anything can happen, Shawn and Dakota find that the stakes are love at all costs, and it's a gamble neither can afford to lose. (978-1-60282-569-7)

Swimming to Chicago by David-Matthew Barnes. As the lives of the adults around them unravel, high school students Alex and Robby form an unbreakable bond, vowing to do anything to stay together—even if it means leaving everything behind. (978-1-60282-572-7)

Hostage Moon by AJ Quinn. Hunter Roswell thought she had left her past behind, until a serial killer begins stalking her. Can FBI profiler Sara Wilder help her find her connection to the killer before he strikes on blood moon? (978-1-60282-568-0)

Erotica Exotica: Tales of Sex, Magic, and the Supernatural, edited by Richard Labonté. Today's top gay erotica authors offer sexual thrills and perverse arousal, spooky chills, and magical orgasms in these stories exploring arcane mystery, supernatural seduction, and sex that haunts in a manner both weird and wondrous. (978-1-60282-570-3)

Blue by Russ Gregory. Matt and Thatcher find themselves in the crosshairs of a psychotic killer stalking gay men in the streets of Austin, and only a 103-year-old nursing home resident holds the key to solving the murders—but can she give up her secrets in time to save them? (978-1-60282-571-0)

Balance of Forces: Toujours Ici by Ali Vali. Immortal Kendal Richoux's life began during the reign of Egypt's only female pharaoh, and history has taught her the dangers of getting too close to anyone who hasn't harnessed the power of time, but as she prepares for the most important battle of her long life, can she resist her attraction to Piper Marmande? (978-1-60282-567-3)

Wings: Subversive Gay Angel Erotica, edited by Todd Gregory. A collection of powerfully written tales of passion and desire centered on the aching beauty of angels. (978-1-60282-565-9)

Contemporary Gay Romances by Felice Picano. This collection of short fiction from legendary novelist and memoirist Felice Picano are as different from any standard "romances" as you can get, but they will linger in the mind and memory. (978-1-60282-639-7)

Sex and Skateboards by Ashley Bartlett. Sex and skateboards and surfing on the California coast. What more could anyone want? Alden McKenna thinks that's all she needs, until she meets Weston Duvall. (978-1-60282-562-8)

Waiting in the Wings by Melissa Brayden. Jenna has spent her whole life training for the stage, but the one thing she didn't prepare for was Adrienne. Is she ready to sacrifice what she's worked so hard for in exchange for a shot at something much deeper? (978-1-60282-561-1)